Praise for Walter Tevis and Mockingbird

"Set in a far future in which humans run a world with a small and declining population, this novel could be considered an unofficial sequel to *Fahrenheit 451.*"
—*San Francisco Chronicle*

"A compelling and provocative read by a sensitive and persuasive writer." —*The Globe and Mail* (Toronto)

"[Tevis is] a master manipulator of archetypes, an artist capable of delving into the zeitgeist while nevertheless remaining on his own pure search for himself."
—Jonathan Lethem

"[Tevis's] work is unique, with that element of infinite rereadability Nabokov held the hallmark of great literature. Like his characters ... Tevis's work will endure."
—*Fantasy & Science Fiction*

"Tevis wrote like a dream, and he told some wonderful stories." —*Los Angeles Times*

"Walter Tevis never thought of himself as a science fiction writer. And when he wrote of aliens among us, or of the end of civilization, he did so as though he were inventing the form." —*The Boston Globe*

"Tevis has a gift for vivid characterization and propulsive narrative.... His style is direct and efficient, never calling attention to itself; yet it grows in power through the course of a novel by its very naturalness."

—Tobias Wolff

"With intense grace, Tevis finds the art to describe art."

—*The Village Voice*

"Tevis's characters, no matter how fantastic or farfetched, whether they are gamblers or aliens, always feel true. At times, reality has even bent toward his fictions, rather than the other way around.... His fiction feels as true as ever."

—*The Ringer*

Walter Tevis

MOCKINGBIRD

Walter Tevis is the author of *The Hustler*, *The Man Who Fell to Earth*, *Mockingbird*, *The Steps of the Sun*, *The Queen's Gambit*, *The Color of Money*, and the short story collection *Far from Home*. *The Hustler*, *The Man Who Fell to Earth*, and *The Color of Money* were all adapted for film. *The Queen's Gambit* was the basis for the Emmy-nominated Netflix series and *The Man Who Fell to Earth* is the basis of the Showtime series. Tevis died in 1984.

MOCKINGBIRD

MOCKINGBIRD

Walter Tevis

Vintage Books
A Division of Penguin Random House LLC
New York

For Eleanora Walker

The inner life of a human being is a
vast and varied realm and does not concern
itself alone with stimulating arrangements
of color, form, and design.

EDWARD HOPPER

MOCKINGBIRD

SPOFFORTH

Walking up Fifth Avenue at midnight, Spofforth begins to whistle. He does not know the name of the tune nor does he care to know; it is a complicated tune, one he whistles often when alone. He is naked to the waist and barefoot, dressed only in khaki trousers; he can feel the worn old paving beneath his feet. Although he walks up the middle of the broad avenue he can see patches of grass and tall weeds on either side of him where the sidewalk has long before been cracked and broken away, awaiting repairs that will never be made. From these patches Spofforth hears a chorus of diverse clickings and wing rubbings of insects. The sounds make him uneasy, as they always do this time of year, in spring. He puts his big hands into his trouser pockets. Then, uncomfortable, he takes them out again and begins to jog, huge and light-footed, athletic, up toward the massive form of the Empire State Building.

The doorway to the building had eyes and a voice; its brain was the brain of a moron—single-minded and insensitive. "Closed for repairs," the voice said to Spofforth as he approached.

"Shut up and open," Spofforth said. And then, "I am Robert Spofforth. Make Nine."

"Sorry, sir," the door said. "Couldn't see . . ."

"Yes. Open up. And tell the express elevator to be down for me."

The door was silent for a moment. Then it said, "Elevator's not working, sir."

"Shit," Spofforth said. And then, "I'll walk up."

The door opened and Spofforth walked in and headed across the dark lobby toward the stairway. He muted the pain circuits in his legs and lungs, and began to climb. He was no longer whistling; his elaborate mind had become fixed narrowly now upon his annual intent.

When he reached the edge of the platform, as high above the city as one could stand, Spofforth sent the command to the nerves in his legs and the pain surged into them. He wobbled slightly from it, high and alone in the black night, with no moon above him and the stars dim. The surface underfoot was smooth, polished; once years before Spofforth had almost slipped. Immediately he had thought, in disappointment, *If only that would happen again, at the edge.* But it did not.

He walked to within two feet of the platform's limit, and with no mental signal, no volition, no wish for it to happen, his legs stopped moving and he found himself, as always, immobilized, facing Fifth Avenue uptown, over a thousand dark feet above its hard and welcome surface. Then he urged his body forward in sad and grim desperation, focusing his will upon the desire to fall forward, merely to lean his strong and heavy body, his factory-made body, out, away from the building, away from life. Inwardly he began to scream for movement, picturing himself tumbling in slow motion, gracefully and surely, to the street below. Yearning for that.

But his body was not—as he knew it would not be—his own. He had been designed by human beings; only a human being could make him die. Then he screamed aloud, throwing his arms out at his sides, bellowing in fury over the silent city. But he could not move forward.

Spofforth stood there, alone on top of the tallest building in the world, immobilized, for the rest of the June night. Occasionally the lights of a thought bus would be visible, slightly larger than stars, below him, moving slowly up and down the avenues of an empty city. There were no lights on in the buildings.

And then, as the sun began to illuminate the sky over the East River to his right and over Brooklyn, to which no bridges ran, his frustration began to ebb. Had he been given tear ducts he would, then, have found the release of tears; but he could not cry. The light became brighter; he could see the outlines of the empty buses below him. He could see a tiny Detection car moving up Third Avenue. And then the sun, pale in the June sky, burst up over an empty Brooklyn and sparkled on the water of the river as fresh as at the dawn of time. Spofforth took a step backward, away from the death he sought and had been seeking all his long life, and the anger that had possessed him began to ebb with the rising sun. He would go on living, and he could bear it.

He climbed down the dusty staircase slowly at first. But by the time he reached the lobby his footsteps were brisk, self-assured, full of artificial life.

As he left the building he told the speaker on the doorway, "Don't let the elevator be repaired. I prefer the climb."

"Yes, *sir*," the door said.

Outside, the sun was shining brightly and there were a few humans on the street. An old black woman in a faded blue dress happened to brush Spofforth's elbow, looked up dreamily at his face. When she saw his marking as a Make Nine robot she immediately averted her eyes and mumbled, "I'm sorry. I'm sorry, sir." She stood near him, at a loss. She had probably never seen a Make Nine before and only knew about them from her early training.

"Go on," he said gently. "It's all right."

"Yes, sir," she said. She fumbled in her dress pocket and pulled out a sopor and took it. Then she turned and shuffled off.

Spofforth walked briskly, in sunshine, back down toward Washington Square, toward New York University, where he worked. His body never tired. Only his mind—his elaborate, labyrinthine, and lucid mind—understood the meaning of fatigue. His mind was always, always tired.

Spofforth's metal brain had been constructed and his body grown from living tissue at a time, long before, when engineering was in decline but the making of robots was a high art. That art too would soon decline and wither; Spofforth himself had been its highest achievement. He was the last of a series of a hundred robots designated Make Nine, the strongest and most intelligent creatures ever made by man. He was also the only one programmed to stay alive despite his own wishes.

A technique existed for making a recording of every neural pathway, every learning pattern of an adult human brain and transferring that recording to the metal brain of a robot. This technique had been used only for the Make Nine series; all of the robots in that series had been equipped with altered copies of the living brain of a single man. That man was a brilliant and melancholy engineer named Paisley—although Spofforth was never to know that. The network of information bits and interconnections that made up Paisley's brain had been recorded on magnetic tapes and stored in a vault in Cleveland. What happened to Paisley after his mind was copied no one ever knew. His personality, his imagination, and his learning had all been recorded on tapes when he was forty-three, and afterward the man was forgotten.

The tapes were edited. The personality was removed from them as much as was possible without harming the "useful" functions. Just what was "useful" about a mind had been determined by engineers less imaginative than Paisley himself. The memory of the life was erased, and with it much of the learning, although the syntax and vocabulary of English remained on the tapes. They contained, even after editing, a near-perfect copy of an evolutionary miracle: a human brain. Some unwanted things from Paisley remained. The ability to play the piano was in the tapes, but needed a body with arms and hands to be manifest. But when the body was made there would be no piano for it to play.

Unwanted by the engineers who had made the recording, but unavoidable, were fragments of old dreams, yearnings, anxieties. There was no way to rid the tapes of these without damaging other functions.

The recording was transferred electronically to a silvery ball, nine inches in diameter, made up of thousands of layers of nickel-vanadium, spun and shaped by automatic equipment.

The ball was placed in the head of a body cloned especially
for it.

The body was grown carefully in a steel tank, at what had
once been an automobile plant in Cleveland. The result was
perfect—tall, powerful, athletic, beautiful. It was a black
man in the prime of life, with fine muscles, powerful lungs
and heart, kinky black hair, clear eyes, a beautiful, thick-lipped
mouth, and large, strong hands.

Some human things had been altered: the aging process
had been programmed to stop at the physical development
of a thirty-year-old—which was where the body had arrived
after four years in the steel tank. It was equipped to control its
own pain responses, and was, within limits, self-regenerating.
It could, for instance, continue to grow new teeth, or new fingers or toes, as needed. It would never go bald or develop faulty
vision or cataracts or thickened arteries or arthritis. It was, as
the genetic engineers were fond of saying, an improvement
upon the work of God. Since none of the engineers believed
there was a God, however, their self-praise was unsound.

Spofforth's body had no reproductive organs. "To avoid distractions," one of the engineers said. The earlobes on each side
of the magnificent head were jet black to signify to any human
being who might be awed by this imitation man that he was,
after all, only a robot.

Like the Frankenstein monster, he was given active life by
electrical shock; he emerged from his tank fully grown and
able to talk, a bit thickly at first. In the vast and cluttered factory room where he was brought into awareness his dark eyes
looked around him with excitement and life. He was on a
stretcher when he first experienced the power of consciousness
enveloping his nascent being like a wave, *becoming* his being.

His constricted throat gagged and then cried out at the force of it—at the force of being in the world.

He was named Spofforth by one of the few men who still knew how to read. The name came at random, from an ancient Cleveland telephone directory: Robert Spofforth. He was a Make Nine robot, the most sophisticated single piece of equipment ever to be fashioned by human ingenuity.

Part of his first year's training sent him to monitoring the hallways and doing minor chores at a dormitory school for human beings. It was a place where the young were taught the ways of their world: Inwardness, Privacy, Self-fulfillment, Pleasure. It was there that he saw the girl in the red coat and fell in love.

Through that winter and through the early spring the girl always wore a scarlet coat with a black velvet collar, as black as anthracite, as black as her hair against her white skin. Her red lipstick matched her coat. In those days almost no one wore lipstick anymore and it was a wonder that she owned some. She looked beautiful wearing it. When Spofforth first saw her, on his third day at the dormitory compound, she was almost seventeen. His mind photographed her instantly and for all time. This picture was to become a major part of the sadness that began, in springtime, in June, to settle deeply into his manufactured and potent being.

By the time he was a year old Spofforth understood quantum mechanics, robotic engineering, and the history of state-

owned corporations in North America—all taught to him by
audio-visuals and by robot tutors—but he did not know how
to read. Nor did he know anything about human sexuality, not
consciously; although there were dim yearnings in what once
would have been called his heart. Sometimes when he was
alone and in darkness, his stomach would flutter for a moment
disturbingly. He was beginning to know that in him somewhere was a buried life, a life of feelings. On the first warm
evenings of his first June he began to be seriously disquieted
by it. Walking from one dormitory building to another, late at
night, he would hear the sounds of katydids in the trees in the
warm Ohio evening and there would be a strange, uncomfortable pressure in his chest. He worked hard at the dormitories,
doing much menial work for what was called "training"; but
the work seldom really occupied his attention and melancholy
had begun to fall on his spirit.

Some of the Make Four workers would break down occasionally; there never seemed to be enough repair equipment
to keep up with minor malfunctions. A few old men were
kept around to fill in when that happened. One of these was
a derelict named Arthur, who usually smelled of synthetic gin
and who never wore socks. He always spoke to Spofforth,
in a partly friendly, partly mocking way, when they would
pass each other in the dormitory hallways or on one of the
gravel paths outside the buildings. Once, while Spofforth was
emptying ashtrays in the cafeteria and Arthur was sweeping
up, Arthur stopped working, leaned on his broom, and said,
"Bob," and Spofforth looked up from his work. "Bob," Arthur
said, "you're a moody one. Didn't know they *made* moody
robots."

Spofforth was unsure whether he was being teased or not.

He continued carrying a stack of plastic ashtrays, filled with the morning's array of marijuana butts, to the garbage can in the corner of the big room. The students had left a short time before for a televised lecture on yoga.

"Never saw a sad robot before," Arthur said. "Is that because of those black ears?"

"I'm a Make Nine robot," Spofforth said defensively. He was still very young, and conversations with humans could make him uneasy.

"Nine!" Arthur said. "That's pretty high, isn't it? Hell the Andy that runs this school is only a Seven."

"Andy?" Spofforth said, holding the pile of ashtrays.

"Yeah, android. Andys is what we called you things—you guys—when I was a kid. Weren't so many of you then. Weren't so smart either."

"Do you mind that? That I'm smart?"

"No," Arthur said. "Shit no. People are so fucking dumb these days it makes you want to cry." He looked away, and then gave a little push to his broom. "Smart is smart. I'm glad there's some around somewhere." He stopped sweeping and made a loose gesture around the big empty room as though the students were still there. "I wouldn't want any of those dumb illiterates to be running the show when they get out of here." His wrinkled face was filled with contempt. "Hypnotized freaks. Jack-offs. They ought to put 'em in a coma and feed 'em pills."

Spofforth said nothing. Something in him was drawn toward the old man—some tiny hint of kinship. But he had no feelings about the young humans who were being trained and acculturated in this place.

He had no conscious feelings about them, of the usually vacant-eyed, slow-moving and silent groups of them, going quietly from class to class or sitting alone in the Privacy rooms smoking dope and watching abstract patterns on their wall-sized television sets and listening to mindless, hypnotic music from speakers. But in his mind there was almost always the image of one; the girl in the red coat. She had worn that ancient coat all winter and still wore it on spring nights. It was not the only thing different about her. There was sometimes a look on her face, flirtatious, narcissistic, vain, that was different from the rest of them. They were all told to develop them-selves "individually" but they all looked the same and acted the same, with their quiet voices and their expressionless faces. She swung her hips when she walked, and sometimes she laughed, loudly, when everyone else was quiet, absorbed in herself. Her skin was as white as milk and her hair coal black.

Spofforth thought of her often. At times, seeing her on her way to a class, surrounded by others but alone, he wanted to walk over to her and touch her gently, just place his big hand on her shoulder and hold it there for a while, feeling the warmth of it. Sometimes it seemed to him that she was watch-ing him from beneath lowered eyes, amused, laughing at him. But they never spoke.

"Hell," Arthur was saying. "You robots'll be running every-thing in another thirty years: People can't do shit for them-selves anymore."

"I am being trained to run corporations," Spofforth said.

Arthur looked at him sharply, and then he began to laugh. "By emptying ashtrays?" he said. "*Shit!*" He began sweeping again, pushing the big broom vigorously down the Permoplas-tic floor. "Didn't know you could fool a goddamn robot. And a Make Nine at that."

Spofforth stood there holding the ashtrays for a minute,

looking at him. *No one is fooling me*, he thought. *I have my life to live.*

It was a June night about a week after the conversation with Arthur that Spofforth was walking by the Audio-Visual Building under the moonlight and heard a rustling noise from behind the dense bushes that grew untended by the building. There was the groan of a male voice, and then more rustling.

Spofforth stopped and listened. Something was moving, more quietly now. He turned, walked a few steps until he was standing up against a tall bush and then pushed it quietly aside. And when, suddenly, he saw what was happening on the other side, he froze and just stood there, staring.

On her back, behind the bush, lay the girl, with her dress pulled up beyond her navel. A pinkish, naked, chubby young man was kneeling astride her; Spofforth could see a cluster of brown moles on the pink skin between his shoulder blades. He could see the girl's pubic hair under the man's thigh—curly hair, jet black against her pure white legs and white buttocks, as black as the hair on her head, as black as the little collar of the red coat on which she lay.

She saw him, and her face went grim with disgust. She spoke to him, for the first and last time ever. "Get out of here, robot," she said. "Fucking robot. Leave us alone."

Spofforth, a hand clamped on his cloned heart, turned and walked away. It was there he learned a thing he was to know for the rest of his long life; he did not really want to live. He had been cheated—horribly cheated—of a real, human life; something in him rebelled against living the life that had been thrust upon him.

He saw the girl again a few times. She avoided his eyes completely. Not out of shame, he knew, since there was no shame
for them in sex. "Quick sex is best" was what they were taught,
and they believed it and practiced it.

He was relieved to be transferred from the dormitory to a
more responsible job deciding the distribution patterns of synthetic dairy products, in Akron. From there he was moved to
the production of small automobiles, presiding over the making of the last few thousand private cars ever to be driven by a
once car-infatuated population. When that ended he became
Director of the Corporation that manufactured thought buses,
the sturdy eight-passenger vehicles made for an ever-dwindling
human population. Then he became Director of Population
Control, being transferred to New York for this, working in an
office on top of a thirty-two-story building, watching over the
aging computers that kept a daily census and adjusted human
fertility rates accordingly. It was a tiresome job, presiding over
equipment that was forever breaking down, trying to find ways
of repairing computers that no human any longer knew how to
repair and that no robots had been programmed to understand.
Eventually he was given another job: Dean of Faculties at New
York University. The computer that had served to direct that
institution had ceased functioning; it became Spofforth's job,
as a Make Nine, to replace it and to make the mostly minor
choices that running a university required.

There had been, he came to find out, a hundred Make Nines
cloned, and animated with copies of the same original human
mind. He was the last, and special adjustments were made in

the synapses of his own particular metallic brain to prevent what had happened to the others of his series: they had been committing suicide. Some had fused their brains into black shapelessness with high-voltage welding equipment; some had swallowed corrosives. A few had gone completely insane before being destroyed by humans, freaking out madly, destructively, rampaging down city streets at midnight screaming obscenities. Using a real human brain as a model for a sophisticated robot had been an experiment. The experiment had been judged a failure, and no more were made. The factories still turned out moron robots, and a few Make Sevens and Make Eights, to take over from the humans more and more of the functions of government and education and medicine and law and planning and manufacturing; but all these had synthetic, nonhuman brains, without a flicker of emotion, of inwardness, of self-consciousness in them. They were merely machines— clever, human-looking, well-made machines—and they did what they were supposed to do.

Spofforth had been designed to live forever, and he had been designed to forget nothing. Those who made the design had not paused to consider what a life like that might be like.

The girl in the red coat grew old and fat and had sex with ten dozen men and had a few babies and drank too much beer and led a trivial, purposeless life and lost her beauty. And at the end of it she died and was buried and forgotten. And Spofforth went on, youthful, superbly healthy, beautiful, seeing her at seventeen long after she had forgotten, as a middle-aged woman, the sexy, flirtatious girl she had once been. He saw her and loved her and he wanted to die. And some heedless human engineer had even made that impossible for him.

The University Provost and the Dean of Studies were waiting for him when he returned from his June night alone.

The duller of the two was the provost. His name was Carpenter and he wore a brown Synlon suit and nearly worn-out sandals and his belly and flanks trembled visibly in the tight suit as he walked. He was standing near Spofforth's big teakwood desk, smoking a joint, when the robot came in and walked briskly toward him. Carpenter stood nervously aside while Spofforth seated himself.

After a moment Spofforth looked at him—not just a bit to the right of him in the way that Mandatory Politeness required, but directly at him. "Good morning," Spofforth said, in his strong, controlled voice. "Is something wrong?"

"Well..." Carpenter said, "I'm not sure." He seemed disturbed by the question. "What do you think, Perry?"

Perry, the Dean of Studies, rubbed his nose with his forefinger. "Somebody called, Dean Spofforth. On the University Line. Called twice."

"Oh?" Spofforth said. "What did he want?"

"He wants to talk to you," Perry said. "About a job. A summer teaching..."

Spofforth looked at him. "Yes?"

Perry went on nervously, his eyes avoiding Spofforth's. "What he wants to do is something that I couldn't understand on the telephone. It's a new thing—something he said he had discovered a yellow or two ago." He looked around him until his gaze found that of the fat man in the brown suit. "What was it he said, Carpenter?"

"Reading?" Carpenter said.

"Yes," Perry said. "*Reading.* He said he could do *reading.* Something about words. He wants to teach it."

Spofforth sat up at the word. "Someone has learned to *read*?"

The men looked away, embarrassed at the surprise in Spofforth's voice.

"Did you record the conversation?" Spofforth asked.

They looked at one another. Finally, Perry spoke. "We forgot," he said.

Spofforth suppressed his annoyance. "Did he say he would call back?"

Perry looked relieved. "Yes, he did, Dean Spofforth. He said he would try to establish a connection with you."

"All right," Spofforth said. "Is there anything else?"

"Yes," Perry said, rubbing his nose again. "The usual curriculum BB's. Three suicides among the student body. And there are plans recorded somewhere for the closing down of the East Wing of Mental Hygiene; but none of the robots could find them." Perry seemed pleased to be able to report a failure among the staff robots. "None of the Make Sixes knew anything about them, sir."

"That's because *I* have them, Dean Perry," Spofforth said. He opened his desk drawer and took out one of the little steel balls—the BB's, they were called—that were used to make voice recordings. He held it out to Perry. "Play this into a Make Seven. He'll know what to do about the Mental Hygiene classrooms."

Perry, somewhat shamefaced, took the recording and left. Carpenter followed him out of the room. When they were gone Spofforth sat at his desk for a while, wondering about the news of the man who said he could read. He had heard of reading often enough when he was young, and knew that it had died out long before. He had seen books—very ancient things. There were still a few of them left undestroyed in the University Library.

Spofforth's office was big and very pleasant. He had decorated it himself, with prints of shore birds and with a carved oak sideboard he had taken from a demolished museum. On the sideboard was a row of small models of Robotic Engineering, roughly showing the history of anthropoid forms that had been used in the development of the art. The earliest, on the far left, was of a wheeled creature with a cylindrical body and four arms—very early, and somewhere between a servomechanism and an autonomous mechanical being. The model was made of Permoplastic and was about six inches tall. The robot had been, during its brief span of usefulness, called a Wheelie; none had been made for centuries.

To the right of the Wheelie was a more manlike shape, somewhat close to that of a contemporary moron robot. The statuettes became more detailed, more human, as they proceeded from left to right, until they concluded with a miniature of Spofforth himself—sleek, entirely human in appearance, poised on the balls of his feet and with his eyes, even in the model, seeming alive.

A red light began to blink on Spofforth's desk. He pressed a button and said, "Spofforth here."

"My name is Bentley, Dean Spofforth," the voice on the other end said. "Paul Bentley. I'm calling from Ohio."

"Are you the one who can read?" Spofforth said.

"Yes," the voice said. "I taught myself how. I can read."

————

The great ape sat wearily on the overturned side of a bus. The city was deserted.

At the center of the screen a white vortex appeared and began to enlarge and whirl. When it stopped it had filled more than half the screen. It became clear that it was the front page of a newspaper, with a huge headline.

Spofforth stopped the projector with the headline on the screen. "Read that," he said.

Bentley cleared his throat nervously. "Monster Ape Terrifies City," he read.

"Good," Spofforth said. He started the projector again.

The rest of the film had no written words on it. They watched it in silence, through the ape's final destructive rampage, his pathetic failure to be able to express his love, on through to his death as he fell, as though floating, from the impossibly tall building to the wide and empty street below.

Spofforth threw the switch that brought the lights back on in his office and made the bay window transparent again. The office was now no longer dark, no longer a projection room. Outside, amid the bright flowers of Washington Square, a circle of elderly graduate students sat on the unkempt grass in their denim robes. Their faces were vacant. The sun was high, distant, in the June sky. Spofforth looked at Bentley.

"Dean Spofforth," Bentley said, "will I be able to teach the course?"

Spofforth watched him thoughtfully for a moment, and then said, "No. I'm sorry. But we should not teach reading at this university."

Bentley stood up awkwardly. "I'm sorry," he said, "but I thought . . ."

"Sit down, Professor Bentley," Spofforth said. "I believe we can use this skill of yours, for the summer."

Bentley seated himself. He was clearly nervous; Spofforth knew that his own presence was overwhelming.

Spofforth leaned back in his chair, stretched, and smiled at Bentley amiably. "Tell me," he asked. "How did you learn to read?"

The man blinked at him a moment. Then he said, "From cards. Reading cards. And four little books: *First Reader*, and *Roberto and Consuela and Their Dog Biff*, and . . ."

"Where did you get such things?" Spofforth asked.

"It was strange," Bentley said. "The university has a collection of ancient porno films. I was trying to cull material for a course, when I came upon a sealed box of old film. With it were the four little books and the set of cards. When I played the film it was not porno at all. It showed a woman talking to children in a classroom. There was a black wall behind her and she would make marks on it that were white. For example, she would make what I later learned was the word 'woman,' and then the children would all say 'woman' together. She did the same for 'teacher' and 'tree' and 'water' and 'sky.' I remembered just having looked through the cards and seeing a picture of a woman. It had the same marks she had made under it. There were more pictures, more white marks on the black wall, more words spoken by the teacher and by the class." Bentley blinked, remembering. "The teacher was wearing a blue dress and her hair was white. She seemed to smile all the time . . ."

"And then you did what?" Spofforth said.

"Yes." Bentley shook his head, as if trying to shake away the memory. "I played the film again, and then again. I was fascinated by it, by something that was going on in it that I felt was . . . was . . ." He stopped, helpless for a word.

"Important?" Spofforth asked.

"Yes. *Important.*" Bentley looked at Spofforth's eyes for a brief moment, against the rule of Mandatory Politeness. Then he looked away, toward the window, outside of which the stoned graduate students still sat silent, their heads nodding occasionally.

"And then?" Spofforth said.

"I played the film over, more times than I could count. Slowly I began to realize, as though I had known it all along but hadn't known that I knew it, that the teacher and the class were looking at the marks and saying words that were represented by the marks. The marks were like pictures. Pictures of words. A person could look at them and say the words aloud. Later I was to learn that you could look at the marks and *hear* the words silently. The same words and words like them were in the books I had found."

"And you learned to understand other words?" Spofforth said. His voice was neutral, quiet.

"Yes. That took a long time. I had to realize that the words were made of *letters.* Letters made sounds that were always the same. I spent days and days at it. I did not want to stop. There was a pleasure in finding the things that the books could *say* within my mind . . ." He looked down at the floor. "I did not stop until I knew every word in the four books. It was only later, when I found three more books, that I discovered that what I was doing was called 'reading.'" He became silent and then, after a few moments, looked shyly up toward Spofforth's face.

Spofforth stared at him for a long moment, and then nodded his head slightly. "I see," he said. "Bentley, have you ever heard of silent films?"

"*Silent* films?" Bentley said. "No."

Spofforth smiled slightly. "I don't think many people have heard of them. They're very ancient. A great many were found recently, during a demolition."

"Oh?" Bentley said politely, not understanding.

"The thing about silent films, Professor Bentley," Spofforth said slowly, "is that the speeches of the actors in them are not spoken but written." He smiled again, gently. "To be understood, they must be read."

BENTLEY

Spofforth suggested I do this. Talk into the recorder at nights, after work, and discuss what I had done during the day. He gave me extra BB's just for this.

The work is dreary at times; but it may have its rewards. I have been at it five days now; this is the first on which I have felt at ease enough with the little recording machine to begin talking about myself into it. And what is there to say about myself? I am not an interesting person.

The films are brittle and must be handled with the greatest of care. When they break—as they frequently do—I must spend a careful time splicing them back together: I tried to get Dean Spofforth to assign me a technician robot, perhaps a moron robot trained as a dentist or in some kind of precision work, but Spofforth merely said, "That would be too expensive." And I'm certain he's right. So I thread the films into strange old machines called "projectors" and make certain they are adjusted properly and then I begin projecting them on a little screen on my bed-and-desk. The projector is always noisy. But even my footsteps seem terribly loud down here in the basement of the old library. Nobody ever comes here, and moss grows on the ancient stainless-steel walls.

Then, when words appear in print on the screen I stop the projector and read them aloud into a recorder. Sometimes this only takes a moment, as with lines like "No!" or "The End," where only the slightest hesitation is needed before pronouncing them. But at other times harder phrases and spellings occur, and then I must study for a long time before I am certain of the wording. One of my most difficult was on one of those black backgrounds on the screen after a highly emotional scene where a young woman had expressed worry. It read, in full: "If Dr. Carrothers does not arrive presently, Mother is certain to take leave of her senses." You can imagine the trouble I had with that one! And another went: "Only the mockingbird sings at the edge of the woods," spoken by an old man to a young girl.

The films themselves are at times fascinating. I have already gone through more of them than I know how to count and more than those remain. All of them are black and white, and they have the kind of jerky motions of the huge ape in *Kong Returns*. Everything about them is strange, not just the way the characters move and react. There is the—how can I say this?—the sense of involvement to them, the sense that great waves of feelingfulness wash over them. Yet to my understanding they are sometimes as blank and meaningless as the polished surface of a stone. Of course I do not know what a "mockingbird" is. Or what "Dr." means. But it is more than that which disturbs me, more even than the strangeness, the sense of antiquity about the life that they convey. It is the hint of emotions that are wholly unknown to me—emotions that *every member* of the ancient audience of these films once felt, and that are now lost forever. It is sadness that I feel most often. Sadness. "Only the mockingbird sings at the edge of the woods." Sadness.

Often I eat lunch at my bed-and-desk. A cup of lentil soup with monkey bacon. Or a soybar. The servo janitor has been programmed to feed me what I ask for from the school cafeteria. I will sit, sometimes, and play a film section over and over again, eating slowly, trying to feel my way into that dim past. Some things I see there I cannot forget. Sometimes it will be a scene of a small girl crying over a grave in a field. Or of a horse standing on the city street, with a crumpled hat on its head and the ears sticking through, or of old men drinking from large glass mugs and laughing in silence on the screen. Sometimes, watching these things, I find myself in tears.

And then for days at a time all the feeling goes and I merely drudge on, going through a whole two-reel film from beginning to end in a kind of mechanical way: "Biograph Pictures presents *Margaret's Lament.* Directed by John W. Kiley. Starring Mary Pickford . . ." And so on, until "The End." Then I shut off my recorder and remove the little steel ball and place it in its compartment in the black air-sealed case that holds the film. And then on to the next.

That is the drudgery part, and I sustain myself with marijuana and naps when it gets to be more than I can bear.

DAY THREE

I saw a group immolation today, for the first time in my life. Two young men and a woman had seated themselves in front of a building that made and dispensed shoes along Fifth Avenue. They had apparently poured some flammable liquid over themselves, because they looked wet. I saw them just as the woman applied a cigarette lighter to the hem of her denim skirt and pale flames began to engulf them like a yellow blossom of gauze. They must have been filled with all the right drugs, because there was no sign of pain on any of their faces—only a kind of smiling—as the flame, pale in the sunlight, began first to redden them, then to make them black. Several passersby stopped and watched. Gradually a bad smell began to fill the area, and I left.

I had heard of such immolations, always in groups of three, but I had never seen one before. They are said to happen frequently in New York.

I have found a book—a real book! Not one of the slim readers that I studied from in Ohio and that only told of Roberto and of Consuela and of their dog Biff, but a real, thick palpable book.

It was simple. I merely opened one of the hundreds of doors along the vast stainless-steel hallway outside my office and there, in the center of a small bare room, in a glass case, sat this large, fat book. I lifted the top of the case, which was thick with dust, and picked it up. It was heavy, and its pages were dry to the touch and yellow. The book is called *Dictionary*. It contains a forest of words.

DAY FIVE

Now that I have begun keeping this journal I find myself paying more attention to oddities during the day than I used to—so that I may record them here at night in the archives, I suppose. Noticing and thinking are sometimes a strain and a bafflement and I wonder if the Designers were aware of that when they made it almost impossible for the ordinary citizen to make use of a recorder. Or when they had us all taught that earliest learned wisdom: "When in doubt, forget it."

For example, I have been noticing an odd thing at the Bronx Zoo, or several odd things. I have been taking a thought bus out to the zoo on Wednesdays for over a month and I find that I always see only five children there—and they always seem to be the same children. They all wear white shirts and they are always eating ice-cream cones and—perhaps most odd—they always seem terribly excited and filled with fun to be at the zoo. The other zoo visitors, my age or older, often look at them dreamily and smile, and, when looked at, the children point toward an animal, an elephant, say, and shout, "Look at the big elephant!" and the older people smile at one another, as if reassured. Something seems sinister about this. I wonder if the children are robots?

And more sinister, if they are robots, where are the *real* children?

Every time I go into the House of Reptiles I see a woman in a red dress. Sometimes she is lying on a bench near the iguanas, asleep. Other times she may be pacing around idly. Today she was holding a sandwich in her hand and watching the python as it slid through branches of a synthetic tree, behind the glass of its cage. Putting that down now, I wonder about the python. It is always sliding through those branches. Yet I seem to remember from the time long ago when I was a child (how long ago that was, I of course have no way of knowing) that the big snakes in zoos were usually asleep, or bunched up into dormant lumps on a corner of their cases, looking nearly dead. But the python at the Bronx Zoo is always sliding and darting its tongue and provoking gasps from the people who come into the House of Reptiles to see it. Could it be a robot?

DAY ELEVEN

Things have begun to flood over me. I feel shaken as I write this, shaken to report what I thought of today. Yet it was so obvious, so clear, once I saw it. Why have I never thought of it before?

It was during a film. An old woman was sitting on the front porch (if that's what it is called) of a dark little house. She was in what was called a "rocking chair" and holding a tiny baby in her lap. Then, looking worried, she held the baby up and the picture ended momentarily, as they do, and these words appeared on the screen "Ellen's baby has the croup!" And when the word "baby" appeared on the screen I suddenly realized that I had not seen a real baby for longer than can be known! Yellows, blues, reds: years beyond numberings, and I had not seen a baby.

Where have the babies gone? And has anyone else asked this question?

And then the voice in me that comes from my childhood training says, "Don't ask—relax."

But I can't relax.

I will lay this aside and take some sopors.

DAY NINETEEN

Nineteen. This is the highest number I can ever remember using. Nothing in my life has ever been worth this high a counting before.

Yet it would be possible, I suppose, to count the blues and yellows of one's life. Useless, of course, but, it could be done.

Often in films I see large numbers. Often they are associated with war. The number 1918 seems especially common. I have no idea what to make of it. Could there have been a war that was fought for 1918 days? But nothing lasts that long. The mind reels to think of anything that long or that large or that extensive.

"Don't ask—relax." Yes, I must relax.

I must remember to eat some soybars and gravy before I take a sopor. For two nights together I have forgotten to eat.

Sometimes at night I study *Dictionary*, to learn new words, and at times that helps me become sleepy. But then at other times I find words that excite me. Often those are words the definitions of which elude me—like "disease" or "algebra." I turn them over in my mind, and I read over their definitions. But those almost always contain other infathomable words, which then excite me further. And I am forced to take a sopor after all.

I don't know how to relax.

The zoo used to help, but I haven't gone there lately because of those children. I have nothing against robots, of course. But those children ...

DAY TWENTY-ONE

I went to the zoo today and spoke to the woman in red. She was sitting on the bench by the iguanas and I sat beside her and said, "Is the python a robot?"

She turned and looked at me. There was something strange, mystical, about her eyes—like those of someone under hypnosis. Yet I could see that she was thinking, and that she wasn't drugged. She said nothing for a long time and I began to think she was not going to answer and would pull back into her Privacy the way we are all taught to do when we are troubled by strangers. But just as I started to shrug and get up she said, "I think they are *all* robots."

I looked at her, astonished. Nobody ever talked quite that way. And yet it was the way that I had been thinking, for days. It was so disturbing that I got up and left, without thanking her.

Leaving the House of Reptiles I saw the five children. They were all together, all holding ice-cream cones, their eyes wide with excitement. They all looked at me, smiling. I looked away . . .

DAY TWENTY-TWO

One compelling thing that keeps appearing in the films is a collection of people called a "family." It seems to have been a very common arrangement in ancient times. A "family" is a group of people that are often together, that even appear to live all together. There are always a man and a woman—unless one of them is dead; and even then that one is often spoken of, and images of the dead one ("photographs") are to be found near the living, on walls and the like. And then there are the younger ones, children of different ages. And the surprising thing, the thing that seems characteristic of these "families," is that the man and woman are always *the mother and the father of all of the children!* And there are older people sometimes too, and always they seem to be the mothers and fathers of either the man or the woman! I hardly know what to make of it. *Everyone seems to be related.*

And further, much of the sense of feelingfulness that these films have seems profoundly connected with this being related. And it seems to be presented in the films as *good.*

I know, of course, not to try being a moral judge of anyone. And certainly not of people from another time. I know the life in the films is contrary to the dictum "Alone is best"; but that is not what bothers me. After all, I have spent days at a time with other people—have even seen the same students every day for weeks. It is not the Mistake of Proximity that bothers me about those "families." I think it may be a kind of shock that the people take such *risks*. They seem to feel so much for one another.

I am shocked and saddened by it.

And they *talk* so much to one another. Their lips are moving all the time, even though no audible words come out.

DAY TWENTY-THREE

I had gone to bed last night thinking of those risks the people long ago were taking in their "families" and then the first thing this morning I went through a film that showed just how serious those risks could be.

On the screen an old man was dying. He lay in a strange old-fashioned bed at his home—not in a hospital dying center—and he was surrounded by his family. A clock with a pendulum was on the wall. There were girls, boys, men, women, old people—more than I could count. And they were all unhappy, all crying. And then when he died, two of the younger girls threw their bodies across his and heaved with silent sobbing. There was a dog at the foot of the bed, and when the man died it laid its head on its paws and seemed to grieve. And the clock stopped.

The whole spectacle of unnecessary pain upset me so that I left the film unfinished and went to the zoo.

I went directly to the House of Reptiles and the woman was

there. She was alone in the building except for two old men in gray sweaters and sandals who were smoking dope and nodding over the crocodiles at the pool in the center of the room. She was walking about carrying a sandwich and not seeming to look at anything.

I was still disturbed—by the film, by everything that had been happening since I began this journal—and impulsively I walked up to her and said, "Why are you always here?"

She stopped in her tracks and turned and looked at me in that penetrating, mystical way. It passed through me that she might be insane. But that was impossible, the Detectors would have found out if that were the case, and she would be off on a Reservation, agape with Time-Release Valium and gin. No, she had to be sane. Everybody who walked among others was sane.

"I live here," she said.

Nobody lived at zoos. Not as far as I knew. And all the zoo's work would be done, as it was in all Public Institutions, by robots of one kind or another.

"Why?" I said. That was Privacy Invasion. But somehow I didn't feel as though that edict applied. Maybe it was all those reptiles slithering and wriggling around in the glass cases that surrounded us. And the heavy, green, wet-looking artificial foliage on the artificial trees.

"Why not?" she said. And then, "*You* seem to be around here a lot."

I felt myself blushing. "That's true. I come here when I feel . . . upset."

She stared at me. "You don't take pills?"

"Certainly," I said. And then, "But I come to the zoo anyway."

"Well," she said, "I don't take pills."

Now I stared at *her*. It was an incredible thought. "You don't take pills?"

"I did. But now they make me sick." Her face softened a bit. "I mean, I vomit when I take pills."

"But isn't there a pill for that? I mean, a drug robot could . . ."

"I suppose so," she said, "but wouldn't I vomit up an anti-vomit pill?"

I didn't know whether I should smile at that but I did. Even though it all had a shocking ring to it.

"You could take an injection . . ." I said.

"Forget it," she said. "Relax." Abruptly she turned and looked toward the iguana cage. The iguanas were, as always, lively. They jumped around like toads in their glass cage. She bit her sandwich and began chewing.

"And you live here. At the zoo?" I said.

"Right," she said between bites.

"Doesn't it get . . . boring?" I said.

"Jesus, yes."

"Then why do you stay?"

She looked at me as though she wasn't going to answer. All she would have to do, of course, would be to shrug her shoulders and close her eyes, and Mandatory Politeness would require that I leave her alone. You can't go around interfering with Individualism with impunity.

But apparently she decided to answer me, and I felt grateful—I don't know why—when I saw that she was going to speak. "I live at the zoo," she said, "because I don't have a job and I have nowhere else to live."

I must have stared at her for a full minute. And then I said, "Why don't you drop out?"

"I did. I lived on a Drop-out Reservation for at least two yellows. Until I started vomiting from smoking dope and taking pills."

I had heard of the dope at Drop-out Reservations, of course; it was cultivated in vast fields by automatic equipment and was supposed to have a potency almost beyond belief. But I had never heard of anyone becoming sick from it.

"But when you dropped in again . . . shouldn't you have been assigned a job?"

"I didn't drop in again."

"You didn't . . . ?"

"Nope." Then she finished off her sandwich, turning her head away from me and toward the iguana cage again, chewing. For a moment I felt not bafflement but anger. Those stupid, leapfrogging iguanas!

Then I thought, *I should report her.* But I knew as I thought it that I wouldn't. I should have reported that group immolation too, as any responsible person is supposed to. But I hadn't. Probably no one had. You never heard of people being reported anymore.

When she had finished eating she turned to me and said, "I just left the dormitory and walked here. Nobody seemed to notice."

"But how do you live?" I said.

"Oh. It's easy." Her eyes had lost some of their intensity. "Outside this building, for instance, there's a sandwich machine. The kind you operate with a credit card. And every morning a servo robot comes to fill it with fresh sandwiches. I found out when I first came here, half a yellow ago, that the robot always brings five more sandwiches than the machine holds. He's a moron robot, so he just stands there holding the five extra sandwiches. And I take them from him. That's what I eat during the day. I drink from the water fountains."

"And you don't work?"

She stared at me. "You know what work is these days. They have to deactivate robots to find things to pay us for doing."

I knew that was true. Everybody did, I suppose. But no one ever actually said it. "You could garden . . ." I said.

"I don't *like* to garden," she said.

I walked over and sat on the bench by the python cage. The two old men had left, and we were alone. I didn't look at her. "What do you *do*?" I said. "What do you do when you are bored? There's no TV out here. And you can't use the Fun Facilities in New York without credit. And there's no way to get credit without a job . . ."

There was no answer, and for a minute I thought she hadn't heard me. But then I heard her footsteps and in a moment she was sitting beside me. "Lately," she said, "I've been trying to memorize my life."

"Memorize my life." The phrase was so odd that I said nothing. I just looked at the python writhing through the branches, none of it real.

"You should try it sometime," she said. "First you remember a thing that happened, and then you go over it and over it. That's 'memorizing.' If I keep it up long enough I'll have it all and I'll know it like a story or a song."

My God! I thought. *She can't be sane!* But here she was, and the Detectors had left her alone. And then I thought, *It's the not taking drugs.* What could have happened to her *mind . . . ?*

I got up from the bench, excused myself, and left.

DAY TWENTY-FOUR

"Memorize my life." I couldn't get the phrase out of my mind. All the way back from the Bronx to Manhattan and to the library on the bus, I looked at the face of the pleasant, shy, innocuous people who sat, carefully distanced from one another, on the bus seats, or moving up and down avenues, careful to avoid one another's eyes. And I kept thinking, *Memorize my life.* I couldn't let it alone, even though I hardly understood it.

And then, as the bus got close to the library and I sent it the wish signal to stop at the front escalator, I saw a large number of people on the streets and suddenly another phrase replaced the one that had been going so insistently through my mind: *Where are all the young people?*

For there was nobody young. Everybody was at least as old as I. And I am older than many of the fathers in the films. I am older than Douglas Fairbanks in *Captain Blood*—much older.

Why is no one any younger than I? The films are full of young people. In fact, they predominate.

Is something wrong?

DAY TWENTY-FIVE

As I grew up in the dormitory, along with the other boys and girls in my class, there was no group of younger children behind us. We were the youngest. I do not know how many of us there were in that big old cluster of Permoplastic buildings near Toledo, since we were never counted and did not ourselves know how to count.

I remember that there was a quiet old building called the Preteen Chapel where we would go for Privacy Drill and Serenity Training for about an hour each day. The idea was to sit there in a room full of children of your own age and become oblivious of their presence while watching moving lights and colors on a huge television screen at the front of the room. Weak sopors would be served by a moron robot— a Make Two—at the beginning of each session. I remember developing myself there to the point where I could enter after breakfast, stay for an hour after letting my sweet flavored sopor dissolve in my mouth, and leave for my next class without ever being aware of the presence of anyone else—even though there must have been a hundred other children with me.

That building was demolished by a crew of large machines and Make Three robots when we graduated from it and moved up to Teen Training. And when I was moved to the Sleep Center for Big People about a blue later, our old Sleep Center for Preteens was demolished too.

We must have been the last generation of children, ever.

DAY TWENTY-SIX

I saw another immolation today, at noon.

It was at the Burger Chef on Fifth Avenue. I often go there for lunch, since my NYU credit card quite generously permits more extra expenses than I really need. I had finished my algae-burger and was having a second glass of tea from the samovar when I felt a kind of rush of air behind me and heard someone say, "Oh, my!" I turned around, holding my tea glass, and there at the other end of the restaurant were three people, seated in a booth, in flames. The flames seemed very bright in the somewhat darkened room, and at first it was hard to see the people who were burning. But gradually I made them out, just as their faces began to twist and darken. They were all old people—women, I thought. And of course there was no sign of pain. They might have been playing gin rummy, except there they were, burning to death.

I wanted to scream; but of course I didn't. And I thought of throwing my glass of tea on their poor old burning bodies, but their Privacy of course forbade that. So I merely stood there and watched.

Two servos came out from the kitchen and stood near them—making sure, I suppose, that the fire didn't spread. Nobody moved. Nobody said anything.

Finally, when the smell had become unbearable, I left the Burger Chef. But I stopped when I saw a man staring from outside through the window at the people in flames. I stood next to him for a moment. Then I said, "I don't understand it."

The man looked at me, blankly at first. And then he frowned with a look of distaste and shrugged his shoulders and closed his eyes.

And I began to blush from embarrassment as I realized that I was crying. Crying. In public.

DAY TWENTY-NINE

I have begun actually to write this down. This is one of my days off and I have not looked at the films today. What I did was get sheets of drawing paper and a pen from the Self-expression Department and begin to write down the words from my recorded journal, using the large letters from the first page of *Dictionary* as a guide. At first it was so difficult that I felt I could never keep it up; I would replay from my recorder a few words and then print them down on paper. But it soon became an ordeal. And trying to spell the larger words is most difficult. Some of them I have learned from the films and, fortunately, some of the really big ones I have recently learned from *Dictionary* and I usually can find them there, although it takes some searching.

I believe there is some kind of principle of arranging the words in *Dictionary*—perhaps so they can be found easily—but I do not understand it. For pages, all of the words begin with the same letter, and then, abruptly, they start beginning with another, wholly different letter.

After a few hours of writing my hand began to ache and I could no longer hold the pen. I had to take pain pills; but when I did I discovered that they made it more difficult to pay attention to what I was doing, and I would miss whole words and phrases.

I had suspected that drugs might affect a person this way; but I had never had so convincing a proof before.

DAY THIRTY-ONE

I did not go to the zoo today.

I've printed words on paper constantly all day. Through lunchtime until now, when it's beginning to get dark outside. The pain in my hand became intense but I did not take pain pills and after a while I seemed even to forget about it. In fact, there was—how shall I say it?—something *rewarding* about the experience of sitting there at my desk, my hand and wrist filled with pain, printing words onto a piece of paper. I finished my journal up until day twenty-nine, and although I am here recording this now, into the voice recorder, I am anxious to pick up paper tomorrow and return to the task of printing the words.

There is something in my mind that will not stop insisting itself. That is the phrase "Memorize my life," which the woman at the House of Reptiles had spoken the other day. Writing it

down as I did about an hour ago, I could see something in the
words, something that took me a moment to grasp entirely.
What I was doing myself was memorizing my life. Putting these
words on paper, unlike just reading them into a recorder, was a
mental act—what the woman called "memorizing." I stopped
my work after I had written down the words "Memorize my
life," and I decided to do a little thing. I took *Dictionary* and
kept going through all the pages until I came to all the words
that together began with the letter "M" and then I began to
look through those. After a while I realized it was a sort of pattern, because words that started with the letter "M" followed by
an "E" were all together. I looked through that group of words
until finally, after some searching, I discovered the word "memorize." And this was the definition given: "To learn by heart,"
and how strange that was—heart, to learn by heart. I could
not understand it all. And yet the word "heart" seems somehow
right, for I know that my heart has always beaten. Always.

I have never in my life seemed to see and hear and think
so clearly. Can it be because I have not used drugs this day?
Or is it this act of writing? The two are so new and have come
together so closely that I cannot be sure of which it is. It is
extremely strange to feel like this. There is exhilaration to it,
but the sense of risk is almost terrifying.

DAY THIRTY-THREE

Last night I could not sleep. I lay in bed awake, staring at the
stainless-steel ceiling of my room in the archives. Several times
I started to call for the servo robot and ask for sopors but I was
determined not to. In a sense I enjoyed the feeling of sleepless-
ness. I got up for a while and began to walk around the room.
It is a bright room with a thick, heavy, lavender carpet. There is

a desk that is combined with my bed and on the desk is *Dictionary*. I spent about an hour turning through the book looking at the words. What meanings are locked in those words, and what a sense of the past!

I decided to go out. It was very late. There was no one in the streets, and although New York is certainly safe, I felt tense and a bit frightened. I had something on my mind and I could not let it go and I was determined not to take a sopor. I summoned a thought bus and told it to take me to the Bronx Zoo.

I was alone on the bus. I watched out its windows as it went winding the long way between the bungalows and empty lots of Manhattan. I looked at the lights in the buildings where some people still sat watching their television. New York is very peaceful, and especially at night, but I thought of all those people, those lives, watching television, and I kept thinking, *They know nothing of the past, not of their own past, nor of anyone else's past.* And of course it was true and I had known it all my life. But here at night, alone on the bus going through New York toward the zoo, I felt it most strongly and the strangeness of it began to overwhelm me.

The House of Reptiles was dark but it was not locked. I made noise when I came in the door and I heard the girl, startled, say, "Who's there?"

I said, "Only me."

And I heard her gasp and say, "My God! At night now, too."

"I guess so," I said, and then I saw the flash of her striking a light with a cigarette lighter and then the light steadied and I saw that she had lit a candle. She must have taken it from her pocket. She set it on the bench.

"Well," I said, "I'm glad you have light."

She must have been asleep on the bench, for she stretched

herself, and then she said, "Come on. You might as well sit down here."

So I went over and sat beside her. I could feel my hands trembling. I hoped she didn't notice. For some time we were silent, sitting on the bench. I could not see the reptiles in their glass cases, nor did they make any sounds. The room was silent. The light from the candle flame moved on her face. Finally she spoke.

"You're not supposed to be at the zoo at night," she said.

I looked at her. "Neither are you."

She looked down at her hands, which were folded in her lap. There was something nice about the gesture. I had seen it in the old films many times. Mary Pickford. She looked up at me. The intensity of her stare was softened a bit by the candlelight.

"Why did you come here?" she said.

I looked at her a long time before speaking and then I said, "It was the words you used the other day. I have not been able to get them out of my mind. You said you were going to memorize your life."

She nodded.

"At first I didn't know what that meant," I said, "but now I think I do. In fact, I think I am trying to do the same thing or something like it. Not my early life, not my childhood or in the dormitories or when I was in college, but the life that I am living now, have been living for some time. I am trying to memorize that." I stopped. I didn't know exactly how to go on. She was looking at my face closely.

"Then I'm not the only one," she said, "Maybe I've started something."

"Yes," I said, "maybe you have. But I have something that you may find helpful. Do you know what a recorder is?"

"I think so," she said. "Don't you say things into it and it says them back? Like when you call a library for information and the voice that gives it to you is not a person speaking then, but a person who spoke some time ago."

"Yes," I said. "That's the idea. I have a recorder. I thought you might like to try it."

"Do you have it with you now?" she said.

"Yes," I said.

"Good," she said. "That would be interesting, but we'll need light." She got up from the bench and walked across the room out of the light from the candle flame and I heard her opening something. And then I heard a click and the room was flooded with brightness. The glass from all of the cases glowed at me and there in them all of the reptiles, the iguanas, python, the green monitor lizards, the massive brown crocodiles in the cages, there they all sat, not moving, silent in all of that synthetic vegetation. She came back over to the bench and sat beside me. I could see now that her hair was badly mussed and there were creases in her face from sleeping on the bench. Yet even so she looked fresh and very much awake.

"Let's see this recorder," she said.

I fumbled in my pocket and pulled it out. "Here it is," I said. "I'll show you how it works."

We must have been there for over an hour. She was fascinated by the recorder and asked if she could keep it awhile but I told her it was impossible, that I had to use it in my work and they were very difficult to obtain. For a moment I almost told her about reading and writing but something restrained me from doing so. Maybe I would tell her at another time. When I told her it was time for me to return to where I stayed, she said, "Where do you stay? Where do you work?"

"At New York University," I said. "I only work there temporarily for this summer. I live in Ohio."

"What do you do at the university?" she said.

"I work with ancient films," I told her. "Do you know what films are?"

"Films? No," she said.

"Well, films are like video records. A way of recording images that move. They were used before the invention of television."

Her eyes widened. "Before the invention of television?"

"Yes," I said, "there was a time once when television had not been invented."

"My God," she said. "How do you know that?" Actually, of course, I didn't know that, but I had guessed from the films that I had seen that they came before television because the people in those families' houses in the films never had television sets. The idea of the sequence of events and circumstances—that things had not always been the same—was one of the strange and striking things that had occurred to me as I had become aware of what I can only call the past.

"That's very odd," the girl said, "to think that there may not have been television once. But I feel I can understand that. I feel that I understand a good many things since I have begun to memorize my life. You get the sense that one thing comes after another and that there is change."

I looked at her. "Good God, yes," I said. "I know what you mean." Then I took my recorder and left the room. The thought bus was waiting. It was beginning to become daylight. Some birds were singing and I thought, *Only the mockingbird sings at the edge of the woods.* But this time thinking it, I felt no sadness.

When I started to walk toward the bus I somehow felt awkward. I felt as though she had done me a great service. The nervousness that had driven me out here to the zoo in the middle of the night was now as dissipated as though I had taken two tabs of Nembucaine . . . But I did not know how to thank her, so I merely stepped back into the building and said, "Good night" and started to leave again.

"Wait," she said, and I turned around to face her.

"Why don't you take me with you?"

That came as a shock. "Why?" I said. "For sex?"

"Maybe," she said. "Not necessarily. I would . . . like to use your recorder."

"I don't know," I said. "I have an agreement with the university. I'm not sure . . ."

Suddenly her face changed. It became frighteningly twisted in anger—anger as great as on the faces of some of the actors in the films. "I thought you were different." Her voice was trembling, but controlled. "I thought you didn't care about making Mistakes. About Rules."

Her anger was very upsetting. Showing anger in public—and this was, in a sense, a public thing—was one of the worst of Mistakes itself. Almost as bad as my crying outside the Burger Chef had been. And then I thought to myself, of my crying, and I did not know what to say.

She must have interpreted my silence as disapproval, or as the beginning of a Retreat into Privacy, because suddenly she said, "Wait."

She walked quickly out of the House of Reptiles as I stood there, not knowing what else to do. In a moment she returned. She was carrying a rock as big as her hand. She must have taken it from one of the flower borders outside. I watched her, fascinated.

"Let me show you about Mistakes and Rules of Behavior,"

she said. She drew back and hurtled the rock right into the glass front of the python's case. It was astonishing. There was first a loud noise and the front of the case caved in. A large triangle of glass crashed to the floor at my feet and broke. While I stood there horrified, she walked up to the case, reached in with both hands, and pulled out the python. I shuddered; her confidence was overwhelming. What if the snake were not a robot?

She dragged the creature over headfirst, pulling open its mouth as she did so and bending to peer down into it. Then she held the head out toward me, with the broad, evil-looking mouth gaping wide. We had been right. About a foot or so down the throat was the unmistakable nuclear battery pack of a Class D robot.

I was too horrified by what she had done to be able to say anything.

And as we stood there in what must have looked like a "tableau" in the old movies, she triumphantly holding the serpent and I watching in horror at the magnitude of what she had done, there was a sudden noise behind me and I turned just as the door between two of the reptile cases in the wall opened and a tall, fierce Security robot came striding out. As he came toward us his voice boomed: "You are under arrest. You have a right to remain silent, you may ..."

The woman had been looking up coolly at the robot, who towered over her. And then she interrupted him sharply. "Bug off, robot," she said. "Bug off and shut up."

The robot stopped talking. He was immobile.

"Robot," she said. "Take this damn snake and get it fixed."

And the robot reached out, took the snake from her into its arms, and quietly walked out of the room into the night.

I hardly knew what I felt, seeing it all. It was a little like watching those violent scenes in some of the films, like the one in *Intolerance* where the great stone buildings came crashing down. You just stare at it all and feel nothing.

But then I began to think, and I said, "The Detectors . . ."

She looked at me. Her face was surprisingly calm. "You have to handle robots like that. They were made to serve people, and nobody knows it anymore."

To serve people? It sounded as though it might be true. "But what about the Detectors?"

"The Detectors don't detect anymore," she said. "Look at me. They haven't detected me. For stealing sandwiches. For sleeping in a Public Place. For leaving the Drop-out Reservation without Re-entry."

I said nothing, but the shock must have shown on my face.

"The Detectors don't detect *anything*," she said. "Maybe they never did. They don't have to. Everybody is so conditioned from childhood that nobody ever *does* anything."

"People burn themselves to death," I said. "Often."

"And do the Detectors stop that?" she said. "Why don't the Detectors know that people are thinking unbalanced, suicidal thoughts, and restrain them?"

I could only nod. She had to be right, of course.

I looked at the broken glass on the floor and then at the broken case with the plastic tree in it, now empty of movement. Then I looked at her, standing there in the House of Reptiles in the bright artificial light, calm, undrugged, and—I was afraid—totally out of her head.

She was looking toward the python's case. From one of the higher branches of the tree inside there was hanging some sort of fruit. Abruptly, she reached her arm inside the cage and stretched up toward the fruit, clearly intending to pick it.

I stared at her. The branch was quite high, and she had to stand tiptoed and reach as far up as she could reach, just to catch the bottom of the fruit with her fingertips. With the strong light from the inside of the case coming through her dress her body was outlined clearly; it was beautiful.

She plucked the fruit, and stood there poised like a dancer with it for a moment. Then she brought it down level with her breasts and, turning it over in her hand, looked at it. It was hard to tell what kind of fruit it was; it seemed to be some kind of mango. For a moment I thought she was going to try to eat it, even though I was certain it was plastic, but then she stretched her arm out and handed the thing to me. "This certainly can't be eaten," she said. Her voice was surprisingly calm, resigned.

I took it from her. "Why did you pick it?" I said.

"I don't know," she said. "It seemed to be the thing to do."

I looked at her for a long time, saying nothing. Despite the age lines and sleep lines in her face, and despite the uncombed look of her hair, she was very beautiful. And yet I felt no desire for her—only a kind of awe. And a slight sense of fear.

Then I stuffed the plastic fruit into my pocket and said, "I'm going back to the library and take some sopors."

She turned away, looking back toward the empty case. "Okay," she said. "Good night."

When I got back I put the fruit on top of *Dictionary* that sat on my bed-and-desk. Then I took three sopors. And slept until noon today.

The fruit is still sitting there. I want it to mean something; but it doesn't.

DAY THIRTY-SEVEN

Four days without pills. And only two joints a day—one after supper and one before going to bed. It is all very strange. I feel tense and, somehow, excited.

I am often restless and must have taken to walking up and down in the halls outside my room in the library basement. The halls are endless, labyrinthine, mossy and gently damp. I pass doorways and, occasionally, open a door and look in, remembering when I found *Dictionary*, apprehensive, almost, that I may find something. I'm not certain that I want to find anything. I have had enough new things since I came to this place.

But there is never anything in the rooms. Some have shelves in them, from floor to ceiling, but there is never anything on the shelves. I look around, then close the door and continue down the hall. The halls always smell musty.

The doors of the rooms are of different colors, so that you may tell them apart. My room has a lavender door, to match the carpet inside.

When I first moved in here, the feeling of walking about in this vast, empty building was frightening. But now I derive a kind of comfort from it.

I no longer take naps, as I once did.

DAY FORTY

Forty days. It is all written out and on my desk in front of me, on seventy-two pages of art paper. All of it printed by me.

It is the greatest achievement of my life. Yes, I have used that word: a great *achievement*. My learning to read was an achievement. Nobody knows that but me. Spofforth doesn't know it. But then Spofforth is a robot; and a robot might just know anything. But robots can achieve nothing; they have been constructed to do what they do, and cannot change.

I did seven films today, and hardly remember a word that I read into the machine.

I cannot get her off my mind. I see her with the trees and ferns in their glass cases behind her, holding the plastic fruit out to me.

DAY FORTY-ONE

Most Burger Chefs are small Permoplastic buildings, but the one on Fifth Avenue is larger and made of stainless steel. It has red lamps on the tables in the shape of tulips and its Soul Muzak from the speaker walls is the music of balalaikas. There are big brass samovars at each end of the red serving counter and the waitresses—Make Four robots of a female clone— wear red bandannas on their heads.

I was there this morning for a breakfast of synthetic scrambled eggs and hot tea. While I was waiting in line to be served, the man in front of me, a short man in a brown jump suit and with a face of blank serenity, was trying to get himself served an order of Golden Brown Fries for his breakfast. He had his credit card in his hand and I saw that it was orange, which meant that he was someone of importance.

The robot waitress behind the counter told him that Golden Brown Fries were forbidden with breakfast. Abruptly his look of serenity vanished, and he said, "What do you mean? I'm not eating breakfast."

She stared stupidly down at the counter and said, "Golden Brown Fries come only with the Super Shef." Then she looked over to the robot with identical features who was standing next to her. On both of them the eyebrows grew together right above the nose. "Only with the Super Shef. Isn't that right, Marge?"

I looked behind the counter and saw that there were stacks of fries sitting there in little plastic bags.

Marge said, "Golden Brown Fries come only with the Super Shef."

The first robot looked back at the man, briefly and then cast her eyes down again. "Golden Brown Fries come only with the Super Shef," she said.

The man looked furious. "All right," he said. "Then give me a Super Shef with them."

"With the Golden Brown Fries?"

"Yes."

"I'm sorry, sir, but the Super Shef machine is not working properly today. We have Syn-eggs and monkey bacon, and Golden Brown Toast."

For a moment the man looked as though he would scream. But instead he reached into his breast pocket, took out a little silver pill holder, and swallowed three green sopors. After a moment his face became serene again and he ordered toast.

DAY FORTY-TWO

I have her here at the library! She is sleeping now, on the thick carpet in an empty room down the hall.

Let me put down how it happened.

I had resolved never to go back to the zoo. But yesterday I could not stop thinking about her. It was not sex, or that idea called "love" that so many films are about. The only way I can explain it to myself is to say that she was the most *interesting* person I had ever met.

I think if I had not learned how to read I would not have been interested in her. Only frightened.

Yesterday after lunch I took the bus out to the zoo. It was a Thursday, so it was raining. There was no one in the streets except for a few moron robots emptying garbage and trimming hedges and working in the parks and city gardens.

She was not in the House of Reptiles when I got there. And I was stunned—frightened that she might have left and I would never see her again. I tried to sit down and wait for her, but I was so restless that I had to walk. First I looked at some of the reptiles. The python cage had been repaired; but the python was not in it. Instead there were four or five diamond-backed rattlesnakes, shaking their rattles enthusiastically, with the same kind of zeal as the child with the ice-cream cone that I had seen outside.

After a while I tired of looking at all those overbusy creatures and, seeing that the rain had stopped, I went outside.

The child, or one of the others just like it, was out there on one of the paths. Since there were almost no people at the zoo on a rain day, the child must have decided to concentrate its attention on doing some kind of performance for me alone. It walked up to me and said, "Hi there, mister. Isn't it fun to watch all the animals?"

I walked on by it, not answering. I could hear it tagging along behind me as I walked down a path toward a moated island that had zebras on it.

"Boy!" the child said. "The zebras sure look lively today."

Something about that made me feel a thing I hadn't allowed myself to feel since I was a child: anger. I spun and stared down at the chubby little freckle-faced creature, furious. "Bug off, robot," I said.

He did not look at me. "The zebras . . ." he said.

"Bug off."

And then he turned and, abruptly, began to hop and skip away down another path.

I felt fine about it. Even though I wasn't completely sure he *was* a robot. Robots are supposed to be identified by their colored earlobes, but like everyone else, I had heard all my life rumors that that wasn't always the case.

I tried to pay attention to the zebras for a while. But I couldn't keep my mind on them, because of all the various feelings I was experiencing: a kind of exultation from silencing that child—or whatever it was—and a whole group of mixed feelings about the woman, the most important of which was a dread that she might be gone. Or could she have been detected, after all?

The zebras were none too animated; perhaps that meant they were real.

After a while I began walking again and then I looked up the path ahead of me, toward a small gray fountain, and there she was in her red dress, walking toward me, carrying a bunch of yellow jonquils in her hand. I stopped walking, and for a moment it felt as though my heart had stopped beating.

She walked up to me carrying the flowers and smiling. "Hello, there," she said.

"Hello," I said. And then, "My name's Paul."

"I'm Mary," she said. "Mary Lou Borne."

"Where've you been? I went to the House of Reptiles."

"Walking. I went for a walk before lunch and I got caught in the rain."

And then I saw that her red dress and her hair were wet. "Oh," I said. "I was afraid you were . . . gone."

"Detected?" She laughed. "Let's go back to the snake house and have a sandwich."

"I've already had lunch," I said, "and you should put on some dry clothes."

"I don't have any dry clothes," she said. "This dress is all I have."

I hesitated a moment before I spoke. And then I said it. I don't know where it came from; but I said it. "Come back to Manhattan with me and I'll buy a dress."

She seemed hardly surprised at all. "I'll just get a sandwich . . ."

I bought her a dress from a machine on Fifth Avenue—a yellow dress of a handsome, rough fabric called Synlon. By the time we got there on the bus her hair had dried, and she looked stunning. She still had the flowers, and they matched the dress.

I got that word "stunning" from a Theda Bara film. A nobleman and a servant were watching Miss Bara, in a black dress, carrying white flowers, come down a curved staircase. The servant said, as the words showed, "Pretty. Mighty pretty," and the nobleman nodded slightly and said, "She is *stunning*."

We had not talked much on the bus. When I got her to my bedroom-office she sat on the black plastic sofa and looked around her. The room is large and colorfully furnished—lavender rug, bright floral prints on the steel walls, and gentle lighting—and I was really proud of it. I would have liked a window; but it was a basement—a fifth sub-basement, in fact—and far too deep in the ground for that.

"How do you like it?" I said.

She got up and straightened a picture of some flowers. "It's a little like a Chicago whorehouse," she said. "But I like it."

I did not understand that. "What's a Chicago whorehouse?" I said.

She looked at me and smiled. "I don't know. It's something my father used to say."

"Your *father*?" I said. "You had a father?"

"Sort of. When I ran away from the dormitory a very old man took care of me. Out in the desert. His name was Simon, and whenever he saw anything that was very bright—like a sunset—he would say, 'Just like a Chicago whorehouse.'"

She had been looking at the picture she had straightened. Then she turned her back on it and went to her seat on the sofa. "I could use a drink," she said.

"Liquor doesn't make you sick?"

"Not Syn-gin," she said. "Not if I don't drink much of it."

"All right," I said. "I think I can get some." I pressed the button on my desk for the servo robot and when he came, almost immediately, I told him to bring us two glasses of Syn-gin and ice.

As he turned to leave she said, "Wait a minute, robot," and then looked at me. "All right if I get something to eat? I'm awfully sick of the zoo's sandwiches."

"Of course," I said. "I'm sorry I didn't think of it." I was a bit put off by the way she seemed to be taking over, but I was pleased at the same time to be her host—especially since I had a great deal of unused credit on my NYU card. "The cafeteria machinery makes good monkey bacon and tomato sandwiches."

She frowned. "I never could eat monkey bacon," she said. "My father used to think monkey food was disgusting. How about roast beef? But not a sandwich."

I turned to the robot. "Can you get a plate of sliced roast beef?"

"Yeah," the robot said. "Sure."

"Good," I said, "and bring me some radishes and lettuce with my drink."

The robot left, and for a minute there was an awkward silence in the room. I was surprised at that, and actually a bit pleased in a way. Sometimes Mary Lou seemed to have no sensitivity at all.

I broke the silence. "You ran away from the dormitory?"

"Around puberty time. I've run away from a lot of places." I had never even thought that anyone might *think* of running away from a dormitory. No, that wasn't true. I remembered, as a child, hearing boys boast of how they were going to "run away," because they had been treated unfairly by a robot-teacher or something. But no one had ever done it. Except Mary Lou, it seemed.

"And you weren't detected?"

"At first I was sure I would be." She leaned back on the couch, relaxing. "I was terribly scared. I had walked for half a day down an old road and then found an empty old town in the desert. But the Detectors never came." She shook her head slowly from side to side. "That was when I began to realize that the Detectors didn't really work. And that you didn't have to obey robots."

I winced, remembering a thing that had happened to me in the dormitory, when a robot had put me in Coventry.

"You know," she said, "they teach you that robots are made to serve humans. But the way they say that word 'serve' it sounds like 'control.' My father—Simon—called it 'politician talk.'"

"Politician talk?"

"Some special way of lying," she said. "Simon was very old when I met him. He died only a couple of yellows after I moved in with him, and his teeth were all gone, and he could barely hear. He said a lot of things that he had learned from *his* father—or somebody—and that were very old."

"Was he trained in a dormitory?"

"I don't know. I never thought of asking him."

The robot came back with our food and drinks. She took her plate of roast beef in one hand, her drink of Syn-gin in the other, and made herself comfortable on the sofa. She took a deep sip of the gin, swallowed it with a small shudder, and then took a slice of the meat with her fingers and ate it in a very natural way that was new to me—I had never seen anyone eat with her fingers before.

"You know," she said, "Simon was probably the one who made a beef eater out of me. He used to rustle cattle from the big automatic ranches, or sometimes just hunt wild ones."

I had never heard of such a thing. "Does 'rustle' mean '*steal*'?" I said.

She nodded. "I suppose so." She took another slice of beef from the plate and then set the plate on the sofa beside her. She held the meat in her fingers and took another sip from the drink in her hand. "Don't ask about the Detectors," she said. "Because there weren't any." Then she finished her drink in one swallow. "Simon said that in his whole life he had never seen a Detector or heard of anyone being detected."

It was terribly shocking, but it sounded true. I was not young and I had never seen one or known anyone who had been detected. But then I had never known anyone, before, to even risk it.

We stopped talking for a while then, and she concentrated on finishing the meat on her plate. I just watched her eat, still quietly astonished by her, by how interesting she was—and how physically attractive—and how I myself had got her to come here to stay with me.

I wondered about sex, of course, but I felt that would not happen for a while. I hoped it wouldn't, since I am shyer than most people about it, and though she was powerfully attractive—a fact that seemed more evident than ever to me after I had finished my gin—I was too apprehensive now for anything of that kind.

Then after what seemed a long while, she said, "Let me see your recorder again," and I said, "Certainly," and went to my desk to get it. Next to the recorder was sitting the imitation fruit that she had picked from the python cage; she had not seemed to notice it since she had come to the room.

I left the fruit alone and took the recorder from my desk and gave it to her.

She remembered how to work it. "Do you mind," she said, "if I record something?"

I told her to go ahead. Then I had the robot bring us each another Syn-gin and ice and I lay back in my bed and listened while she talked into the recorder.

It took me a moment before I realized what she was doing. She spoke in a kind of slow, hypnotized way and said the words without any apparent feeling. What she was doing, I realized eventually, was saying her "life" as she had "memorized" it—repeating the words as she had learned to repeat them by practice:

"I remember a chair by my bed. I remember a green dress that I wore to my classes. Everybody tried to dress differently from everybody else, to show our Individuality. But I think we all looked the same.

"I was very smart in my classes, but I hated them.

"I remember a girl named Sarah, with awful pimples on her face. She was the first to tell me about sex. She had done it already, while some other children watched. It sounded . . . wrong.

"There was desert all around the place where we all lived, and Gila monsters sometimes came into the dormitories to sleep. The robots would pick them up and carry them out. I felt sorry for the big, stupid lizards. In the House of Reptiles they do not have any Gila monsters, but I think they should have . . ."

And on it went. At first I was interested, but after a while I became very sleepy. It had been a long day. And I was not used to drinking like that.

Somewhere during her talking into the recorder I fell asleep.

When I woke up this morning she was gone. At first I was alarmed to think she might have left. But I looked in the rooms along the hallway and, after opening a few that were empty, found her. She was curled up in the center of the room, on the heavy orange carpet, sleeping like a child. My heart warmed toward her. I felt like . . . like a *father*. And a lover too.

Then I came back to my office and had breakfast, and began writing this.

When I finish I will wake her up and we will go out to a restaurant for lunch.

DAY FORTY-THREE

After I woke her up I took her up Fifth Avenue on the conveyor belt and we had lunch at a vegetable restaurant. We had
spinach and beans.

The two of us had not taken any pills or smoked any dope
and it was surprising to notice how dazed and drugged everyone else seemed to be. Except, of course, for the robots who
waited on us. An older couple at a table nearby kept repeating
themselves in a kind of aimless imitation of a conversation.
He would say, "Florida's the best place," and she would say,
"I didn't catch your name," and he would say, "I like Florida,"
and she would say, "It's Arthur, isn't it?" and it just went on like
that throughout the meal. They must have had a sexual connection, but could not connect any other way. Such talk had
never been uncommon, but there with Mary Lou, where we
each had things to say to the other, and with our heads clear
and wide-awake, it was especially noticeable. And saddening.

DAY FORTY-SIX

Mary Lou has been here three days now. For the first two of
them she slept until noon, after telling me not to disturb her.
I spent the mornings working on a film about men who were
bare to the waist and who lived on the kind of sailboats that
could cross an ocean. Mostly the men fought one another with
knives and swords. They would say things like "Zounds!" and "I
am master of the seas." It was interesting; but Mary Lou was
too much in my thoughts for me to pay it close attention.

I worked only in the mornings for those two days, since I
was for some reason reluctant to let her see me at work. I don't
know why; but I did not want her to know about the reading.

And then on the third morning she came into my room and

she was carrying a book in her hand. The sight of her was striking: she was wearing a pair of the pajamas I had given her, and the top was unbuttoned so that I could see the place between her breasts. She was wearing a cross around her neck. I could see her navel. "Hey, look!" she said. "Look what I found." She held the book out to me.

Her pajama top adjusted itself to the gesture, and one of her nipples was briefly visible. I was confused, and must have looked like a fool standing there trying not to stare. I noticed that she was barefoot.

"Take it," she said, and practically forced the book into my hand.

After another moment of confusion I took it. It was a small book, without the stiff cover that I thought books were supposed to have.

I looked at the cover. The picture on it—faded yellow and blue—made no sense. It was a pattern of dark and light squares, with odd-looking shapes sitting on some of them. The title was *Basic Chess Endings* and the author's name was Reuben Fine.

I opened it up. The paper was yellow, and there were little diagrams of black and white squares and a lot of writing that did not seem to make sense.

I looked back to Mary Lou, having regained my calmness a bit. She must have noticed the way I had acted, because she had buttoned her pajama top. She was running her fingers through her hair, trying to comb it.

"Where did you get this?" I said.

She looked at me thoughtfully. Then she said, "Is it . . . Is it a *book*?"

"Yes," I said. "Where did you find it?"

She was staring at it, in my hands. Then she said, "Jesus Christ!"

"What?"

"It's just an expression," she said. Then she took my hand and said, "Come on. I'll show you where I found it."

I followed along with her like a child, holding her hand. I was embarrassed by her touch and wanted to let go but did not know how. She seemed full of purpose and strength; I was confused and disoriented.

She took me down the hall farther than I had ever been before, around a corner and through a double door and then down another hall. There were doorways all along, and some of them were open. The rooms seemed to be empty.

She seemed to guess what I was thinking. "Have you been down this far before?" she said.

Somehow I felt ashamed that I hadn't. But I had never thought of looking in all those rooms. It didn't seem proper. I didn't answer and she said, "I'll close those doors later," and then, "I couldn't sleep last night, so I got up after a while and started exploring." She laughed. "Simon always said, 'Check out your surroundings, sweetheart.' So I've been wandering around the halls like Lady Macbeth opening doors. Most of the rooms were empty."

"What's Lady Macbeth?" I said, trying to make conversation.

"A person who walks around in pajamas," she said.

At the end of the new hall we were in was a big red door, standing open. She led me to it, and as we walked into the room, finally let go of my hand.

I stared around me. The steel walls of the room were covered with shelves that were apparently made for books. I had seen a room somewhat like this in a film—except that there were big pictures on one of the walls of that room and tables and lamps. This one had nothing in it but shelves. Most of them were empty and covered with thick dust. There was a red carpet on the floor, with big spots of mold. But one wall, at the back of the room, had what must have been a hundred books.

"Look!" Mary Lou said, and ran over to the shelf. She ran a hand, very gently, along one of them. "Simon told me there were books. But I had no idea that there were so many."

Since I knew something about books already, it made me feel more comfortable—more in charge of things—to go over slowly and inspect them. I took one out of a shelf. The cover had a different version of that same pattern of squares, and the title read: *Paul Morphy and the Golden Age of Chess.* Inside were the same diagrams as in the first, but more writing of the ordinary kind.

I was holding the book open, trying to guess at what the word "chess" might mean, when Mary Lou spoke. "What is it exactly that you *do* with a book?"

"You read it."

"Oh," she said. And then, "What does 'read' mean?"

I nodded. Then I began turning the pages of the book I was holding and said, "Some of these markings here represent sounds. And the sounds make words. You look at the marks and sounds come into your mind and, after you practice long enough, they begin to sound like hearing a person talking. Talking—but silently."

She stared at me for a long time. Then she took a book from the shelf, somewhat awkwardly, and opened it. She was finding it a strange and complicated thing to handle, as I had a yellow before. She looked at the pages, felt of them with her fingers, and then handed the book back to me, her face blank. "I don't understand," she said.

I started to explain it again. Then I said, "I can say aloud what I am reading. It's what I do in my work—reading and then saying it aloud."

She frowned. "I still don't understand." She looked at me and then at the books on the steel shelves, and then at the moldy carpet on the floor at her feet. "Your work is . . . reading. Books?"

"No. I read something else. Something called silent films." I took the book from her. "I'll say aloud, if I can, what I read. Maybe that will make it understandable."

She nodded and I opened to the middle and began. "Mostly preferred is five B to B four, followed by the Lasker Variation, for, while White may regain his pawn, he obtains no great attack. It will be seen that, after the ninth move of White, a well-known position is arrived at, and most authorities consider it all in favor of the White side."

I thought I read it well, hardly stumbling over the unfamiliar words. I had no idea what it meant.

Mary Lou had moved next to me, pressing her body against mine, while I was reading. She was staring at the page. Then she looked into my face and said, "Were you saying things that you heard in your mind from just *looking* at that book?"

"That's right," I said.

Her face was uncomfortably close to mine. She seemed to have forgotten all the rules of Privacy—if she ever knew them. "And how long would it take to say aloud everything . . ." She squeezed my arm and I had to fight to keep from jumping and pulling away from her. Her eyes had become terribly intense, the way they sometimes disturbingly became. "To say aloud everything you hear in your mind from looking at all the sheets of paper in that book?"

I cleared my throat, and pulled slightly back from her. "A whole daytime, I think. When the book is easy and you don't say it aloud you can do it faster."

She took the book out of my hand and held it in front of her face, staring at it so intensely that I half expected her to start saying the words aloud by sheer force of concentration. But she did not. What she said was: "Jesus! There is that much ... that much silent BB recording in this? That much ... information?"

"Yes," I said.

"My God," she said, "we should do it with them all. What's the word?"

"Read."

"That's it. We should *read* them all."

She began to gather up an armful of books and I meekly did the same. We carried them down the hallways to my room.

DAY FORTY-EIGHT

I spent the rest of that morning reading to her from different books. But it was difficult for me to continue paying attention; I had almost no idea of what was being said. Several times we changed books, but it was still chess.

After several hours of this she interrupted to say, "Why are all books about chess?" and I said, "I have books at my home in Ohio that are about other things. Some of them tell stories." And then, suddenly, I thought of something I should have thought of before and I said, "I can look the word 'chess' up in *Dictionary*." I opened up the cabinet in my desk and took it out and began leafing through it until I found the words that began with "C." I found it almost right away. "Chess: a board game between two players." And there was a picture of two men seated at a table. On the table was one of those black-and-white arrangements with what my reading had taught me were called "pieces" sitting on it. "It's some kind of a game." I said. "Chess is a game."

Mary Lou looked at the picture. "There are pictures of people in books?" she said. "Like on Simon's walls?"

"Some books are full of pictures of people and things," I said. "The easy books, like the ones I learned to read with, have big pictures on each page."

She nodded. And then she looked at me intensely. "Would you teach me to read?" she said. "From those books with the big pictures in them?"

"I don't have them here," I said. "They're in Ohio."

Her face fell. "Do you only have books about . . . about chess?"

I shook my head. Then I said, "There might be more. Here in the library."

"You mean books about people?"

"That's right."

Her face lit up again. "Let's go look."

"I'm tired." I *was* tired, from all that reading and running around.

"*Come on*," she said. "This is *important*."

So I agreed to go search more rooms with her.

We must have spent over an hour going down hallways and opening doors. The rooms were all empty, although some of them had shelves along the walls. Once, Mary Lou asked me, "What are all these empty rooms *for*?" and I said, "Dean Spofforth told me the library is scheduled for demolition. I think that's why the rooms are empty." I supposed she knew that buildings all over New York had been scheduled for demolition long before we were born, but nothing happened to them.

"Yes," she said, "half of the buildings at the zoo are that way, too. But what are all these rooms *for*?"

"I don't know," I said. "Books?"

"That many books?"

"I don't know."

And then, at the end of a long, especially mossy hallway, where some of the overhead lights were dim, we came to a gray door that had a sign saying: STORAGE. We pushed the door open with some difficulty; it was a much heavier door than the others and it had some kind of seal around it. We got it open by pushing together and I was immediately surprised by two things. The air inside smelled strange—it smelled *old*—and there were steps going down. I had thought we were on the lowest floor of the library already. We took the steps, and I almost slipped and fell. They were heavily layered with some kind of slippery, yellowish dust. I caught myself just in time.

As we descended, the air smelled even stronger, older.

At the bottom of the stairs was a hallway. There were overhead lights, but they were very dim. The hallway was short, and at the end of it were two doors. One said: EQUIPMENT, and the other said: BOOKS, and below this in smaller letters: TO BE RECYCLED. We pushed the door open. There was at first nothing but darkness and sweet-smelling air behind the door. Then, suddenly, lights flickered on and Mary Lou gasped. "Jesus Christ!" she said.

The room was huge and there were books everywhere.

You could not see any walls because of the shelves filled

with books. And books were stacked up on their sides in the middle of the room, and in piles along the walls in front of the full shelves. They were of every color and size.

I stood there not knowing what to do or say. I was feeling something that was like what some of the films had made me feel—a sense that I was in the presence of great waves of feeling that had once been felt by people who were now dead and who understood things that I did not.

I knew that there had been books in the ancient world, of course, and that most of them were probably from that time before television, but I had no idea there were that many.

While I stood there, feeling what I have no name for, Mary Lou walked toward a pile of big, thin books that was not as high as the others. She reached up, the way I had seen her reach up for the inedible fruit in the python cage at the House of Reptiles, and took the top book down carefully. She held it awkwardly in both hands, and stared at its cover. Then very carefully she opened its pages. I could see that there were pictures. She stared at some of the pages for a long time. Then she said, "Flowers!" and closed the book and handed it to me. "Can you . . . say what you read on this?"

I took it from her and read the cover: *Wildflowers of North America.* I looked at her.

"Paul," she said softly, "I want you to teach me how to read."

SPOFFORTH

Every afternoon at two o'clock Spofforth took a walk, for about an hour. Like his habitual whistling, which was the only manifestation of his to-him-unknown ability to play the piano, the habit of taking walks had been, willy-nilly, copied into his metal brain from the start. It was not a compulsion; he could override it when he wished to; but he usually did not. His work at the university was so slight, so trivial to him, that he could easily spare the time. And there was no one with the authority to tell him not to.

He would walk through the city of New York, his arms swinging, his tread light, his head erect, usually looking neither to the right nor to the left. Sometimes he would look in the windows of the small automatic stores that distributed food and clothing to anyone with a credit card, or stop to watch a crew of Make Twos emptying garbage or working on the repair of ancient sewers. These matters concerned him; Spofforth knew far better than any human being did the impor-

tance of supplying food and clothing and removing waste.
The ineptitudes and malfunctions that plagued the rest of this
moribund city could not be allowed to stop those services. So
Spofforth would walk through a different part of Manhattan
every day and check to see if the food and clothing equipment
were functioning and if the wastes were being removed. He
was not a technician, but he was smart enough to repair ordinary breakdowns.

He generally did not look at the people he passed on the
street. Many of them would stare at him—at his size, his
physical vigor, his black earlobes—but he ignored them.

His walk this August day took him through midtown Manhattan, on the West Side. He walked through streets with
small Permoplastic houses, centuries old, some of them with
poorly tended flower gardens. Gardening, for some reason, was
taught in the dormitories. Probably hundreds of years before,
some Engineer-planner with a liking for flowers had decided
that flower gardening should be a part of the standard human
experience; because of that one casual idea, generations of
humanity had planted marigolds and zinnias and phlox and
yellow roses without really ever knowing why.

Sometimes Spofforth would stop and minutely examine
the equipment of a store, to see if its computers were working
properly, keeping supplies at the proper level, its Make One
unloaders ready and able to handle the morning's trucks, its
vending machines in good working order. He might go into
a clothing store, slip his special Unlimited credit card into a
slot, speak out loud into the Orderphone, saying, "I want a pair
of gray trousers that will fit me tightly." Then he would stand
in one of the little booths, just barely being able to fit into it,
let himself be measured by sound waves, and step out again

to watch the machines that would select the fabric from huge overhead bolts, cut it, and stitch his trousers together before returning his credit card. If something went wrong—and it often did—with the way the zipper was put in or the pockets were made or whatever, he would either repair the machine himself or try to commandeer a technician robot by telephone to repair it. If the telephone was working.

Or he would enter a sewer main and look around him to see what was cracking or jammed or rusting, and do what he could to get that repaired. Without him, New York might have no longer functioned at all. He sometimes wondered how other cities stayed alive, with no Make Nines, and no really effective humans around; he remembered the piles of garbage in the streets of Cleveland, and how poorly everyone had been dressed in St. Louis when he had served, briefly, as mayor of that city. And that had been almost a century before. No one in St. Louis had had pockets for years, and everyone's shirts had been too big, until Spofforth himself had repaired the sonic measuring equipment and removed a dead cat from the pocket machine of the city's only clothing store. They were probably not yet naked and starving in St. Louis; but what would happen in twenty blues, when everyone was old and weak, and there were no young people around with sense enough to go out and find a Make Seven to help in an emergency? Had he been able to he would have replicated himself, putting another hundred Make Nines into the world to keep things running in Baltimore and Los Angeles and Philadelphia and New Orleans. Not because he cared that much for humanity, but because he hated to see machinery that worked poorly. He thought of himself as a machine sometimes, and he felt responsible.

But had he been able to produce more Make Nines he

would have made certain they would come into the world without the ability to feel. And with the ability to die. With the gift of death.

On this hot August afternoon he did not stop anywhere until he came to a squat old building on Central Park West. He had a particular thing on his mind.

The building was one of the few in the city made of concrete, and it had columns in front of it and big, multi-paned windows and a dark, stained old wooden door. He opened the door, entered a dusty lobby with a glass chandelier hanging from a white ceiling, and walked up to a wooden counter with a scarred, gray plastic top.

Behind the counter a small man was hunched in an armchair, asleep.

Spofforth spoke to him sharply. "Are you the mayor of New York?"

The man opened his eyes sleepily. "Uh-huh," he said. "I'm the mayor."

"I want to talk to National Records," Spofforth said, allowing irritation to show in his voice. "I want the population for western America."

The man had wakened a bit. "Don't know about *that*," he said. "Nobody just comes in here off the street and talks to the records." He stood up and stretched, arrogantly. Then he looked at Spofforth more closely. "You a *robot*?" he said.

"That's right," Spofforth said. "Make Nine."

The man stared at him for a moment. Then he said, blinking, "Make *Nine*?"

"Ask your Control what to do. I want to talk to Government Records."

The man was peering at him now, with some interest. "They

call you Spofforth?" he said. "The one who tells City Council how high to keep the water pressure and when to get the tires for thought buses? Things like that?"

"I'm Spofforth and I can have you fired. Call your Computer Control."

"Okay," the man said. "Okay, sir." Then he flipped a switch on a table beside his armchair. A synthetic female voice from a speaker somewhere said, "This is Government."

"There's a Make Nine robot here. Name of Spofforth. Wants to talk to Government Records . . ."

"I see," the voice said, a trifle sweetly. "What may I help you with?"

"Does he have access?"

The speaker hummed a moment. Then the artificial voice said, "Of course he has access. If not he, who?"

The man flipped the switch off and then looked toward Spofforth. "Okay, sir," he said, trying to sound helpful.

"Well," Spofforth said, "where is the record?"

"The Population Record is . . . ah . . ." He began looking around the room. There was nothing in the room to look at, except the chandelier, and for a moment he stared at a distant wall. Then he shrugged, leaned over, and flipped the switch again, and the female voice again said, "This is Government."

"This is the mayor. Where's the National Population Record?"

"In New York," the voice said. "In Government Hall, Central Park West."

"That's where *I* am," the mayor said. "Where is it in the building?"

"Fifth floor. Second door on the left," the Government of the United States said.

As the man was turning the switch off again, Spofforth asked him where the elevator was.

"Don't work, sir. Not since I remember."

Spofforth looked at him a moment, wondering just how far back a human like that could remember. Probably no more than a blue. "Where are the stairs?" he said.

"All the way back and to the right," the mayor said. Then he fumbled in his shirt pocket, took out a joint and held it speculatively between his stubby fingers. "Tried to get that elevator fixed a lot of times. But you know how robots are ..."

"Yes," Spofforth said, heading for the stairs, "I know how robots are."

The Records console was a tarnished metal box about the size of a man's head, with a switch and a speaker. In front of it sat a metal chair. That was all there was in the room.

He turned the switch to the green "on" position and a rather cocky-sounding male voice said, "This is the record of the population of the world."

Suddenly, at this final annoyance, Spofforth became furious. "You're supposed to be for North America. I don't want the whole goddamn world."

Instantly the voice said brightly, "The population of the whole goddamn world is nineteen million four hundred thirty thousand seven hundred sixty-nine, as of noon, Greenwich Standard Time. By continent, alphabetically: Africa has approximately three million, ninety-three percent dormitory-trained, four percent free-loaders and the rest in institutions. Asia has about four and a half million souls, ninety-seven percent dormitory and almost all the others in institutions. Australia has been evacuated and has zero population. Europe is about the same ..."

"Shut *up!*" Spofforth said. "I don't want to know all that. I want to know about a person from North America. One person . . ."

The voice interrupted him. "Okay," it said, "*okay*. The goddamn population of North America is two million one hundred seventy-three thousand and twelve, with ninety-two percent dormitory-trained . . ."

"I don't care about that," Spofforth said. He had run into computers like this one before, but not for a long time. They dated from an era long before his own creation when it had been a fad to give machines "personality," when the techniques of Random Programming had first been worked out. One thing he didn't understand about the way the computer had been programmed, and he decided to ask. "Why do you say 'goddamn'?" he said.

"Because you did," the voice said affably. "I am programmed to reply in kind. I am a D 773 Intelligence, programmed to have personality."

Spofforth nearly laughed. "How old are you?" he said.

"I was programmed four hundred ninety goddamn yellows ago. In years, two hundred forty-five."

"Quit saying 'goddamn,'" Spofforth said. And then, "Do you have a name?"

"No."

"Do you have feelings?"

"Repeat the question please."

"You say you have personality. Do you have emotions too?"

"No. Goodness, no," the computer said.

Spofforth smiled wearily. "Are you ever bored?"

"No."

"All right," Spofforth said. "Now get my question right this time. And no cute answers." He looked around the empty room, noticing now the rotting plaster walls, the sagging ceiling. Then he said, "I want the available statistics on a human woman named Mary Lou Borne, from the Eastern New Mexico Dormitory. She is now about thirty years old. Sixty yellows."

Immediately the computer began to answer, its voice more mechanical, less bouncy than before. "Mary Lou Borne. Weight at birth seven pounds four ounces. Blood type seven. DNA code alpha delta niner oh oh six three seven four eight. High genetic indeterminacy. Candidate for Extinction at birth. Extinction not carried out. Reason unknown. Left-handed. Intelligence thirty-four. Eyesight ..."

"Repeat the intelligence," Spofforth said.

"Thirty-four, sir."

"On the Charles scale of intelligence?"

"Yes, sir. Thirty-four Charles."

That was surprising. He had never heard of a human being that intelligent before. Why hadn't she been destroyed before puberty? Probably for the same reason that pants in St. Louis didn't have zippers: malfunction.

"Tell me," Spofforth said. "When was she sterilized and when was her dormitory graduation?"

There was a long wait this time, as though the computer had been embarrassed by the question. Finally the voice said, "I have no record of sterilization, nor of supplementary birth control through sopors. I have no record of dormitory graduation."

"I thought so," Spofforth said grimly. "Search your memory. Do you have a record of any other female in North America without sterilization, birth control, and dormitory graduation? From either Thinker or Worker dormitories?"

The voice was silent for over a minute, making the search. Then it said, "No."

"What about the rest of the world?" Spofforth said. "What about the dormitories in China . . . ?"

"I will call Peking," the voice said.

"Don't bother," Spofforth said. "I don't want to think about it."

He turned the switch to red, consigning the World Population Record to whatever limbo its garrulous intelligence lived in, without boredom, between its rare evocations into speech.

Downstairs the mayor of New York was slumped in his plastic armchair with a blank smile on his face. Spofforth did not disturb him.

Outside the sun had began to shine. On his way back to his university office Spofforth walked through a small, robot-operated park and picked himself a yellow rose.

BENTLEY

It is nine days since I have written in this journal: nine days.
I have learned to add and subtract numbers. From one of the
books. But it was boring to learn what is called *Arithmetic for
Boys and Girls*, so we stopped after adding and subtracting. If
you have seven peaches and take away three you will have four
left. But what is a peach?

Mary Lou is learning very fast—so much faster than I did
that it is astonishing. But she has me to help her, and I had
no one.

I found some easy books with big print and pictures and I
would read slowly aloud to Mary Lou and have her say words
after me. And on the third day we made a discovery. It was in
the *Arithmetic for Boys and Girls* book. One problem began:
"There are twenty-six letters in the alphabet . . ." Mary Lou
said, "What's 'alphabet'?" and I decided to try to find it in *Dictionary*. And I did. And *Dictionary* said: "Alphabet: the letters

of a given language, arranged in the order fixed by custom. See facing page." I puzzled for a moment over what a "given" language might be, and a "facing" page, and then I looked at the page on the other side of the book and it was a chart, with the letter "A" at the top and the letter "Z" at the bottom. They were all familiar, and their order seemed familiar too. I counted them, and there were twenty-six, just as *Arithmetic for Boys and Girls* had said. "The order fixed by custom" seemed to mean the way people arranged them, like plants in a row. But people didn't arrange letters. Mary Lou and I were, as far as I knew, the only people who knew what a letter was. But of course people—perhaps everybody—had once known letters, and they must have put them into an order that was called an alphabet.

I looked at them and said them aloud: "A, B, C, D, E, F, G, H, I, J . . ." And then it struck me. That was the way the words were put into *Dictionary!* The "A" words were first, and then the "B" words!

I explained it to Mary Lou and she seemed to understand immediately. She took the book and leafed through it. I noticed that she had already become expert at handling books; her awkwardness with them was gone. After a minute she said, "We should memorize the alphabet."

Memorize. To learn by heart. "Why?" I said.

She looked up at my face. She was sitting cross-legged on the floor, in her yellow Synlon dress that I had bought her, and I was sitting at my bed-and-desk, with books piled on it in front of me. "I'm not sure," she said. She looked back down at the book in her lap. "Maybe it would help us use this book, if we could say the alphabet?"

I thought about that a moment. "All right," I said.

So we memorized it. And I was embarrassed because she

could say it long before I could. But she helped me learn to say it, and I finally did learn. It was difficult—especially the last part that went "W, X, Y, Z"—but I finally got it straight and said the whole twenty-six letters exactly right twice. When I finished Mary Lou laughed and said, "Now we know something together," and I laughed too. I didn't know why. It wasn't really funny.

She looked at my face for a moment, smiling. Then she said, "Come here and sit by me." And I found myself doing it, sitting on the rug next to her.

Then she said, "Let's say it one after the other," and she squeezed my arm and said, "A."

This time the touch of her did not embarrass me or make me self-conscious. Not at all. I said, "B."

She said, "C," and turned herself around to face me.

I said, "D," and watched her mouth, waiting for her to say her letter. She moistened her lips with her tongue, and said it softly. "E." It sounded like a sigh.

I said, "F," quickly. My heart was beginning to beat fast.

She turned her face and put her mouth next to my ear and said, "G." Then she giggled softly. And I felt something that almost made me jump. It was warm and wet, on my ear, and I realized it was her tongue. My heart almost stopped.

I did not know what to do, so I said, "H."

This time her tongue was actually in my ear. It made a shudder, a soft shudder, pass through my body, and something seemed to go loose in my stomach. And in my mind. With her tongue still in my ear she breathed, "I"—stretching it out so that it sounded: "aaaaiiiiiieeeeeeeee."

Frankly I had not had a sexual experience for blues and yellows. And what I was feeling now was something altogether new to me, and so exciting, so overwhelming, so shaking to my body and my imagination that I found myself sitting on the floor with her face against mine and I was crying. My face was becoming wet with tears.

And she whispered, "Jesus, Paul. You're crying. In front of me."

"Yes," I said. "I'm sorry. I shouldn't . . ."

"Do you feel bad?"

I wiped at my cheek with my hand, and it brushed against hers. I held still, with the back of my hand against her cheek, and then I felt her hand turning mine, ever so gently, until my palm was holding her cheek. I felt a wave of a new feeling, a soft, sweet feeling like that of a powerful drug, enter me. I looked at her face, at her wide and curious eyes, now somewhat sad. "No," I said. "No. I don't feel bad at all. I feel . . . something. I don't know." I was still crying. "It's a very *good* thing, what I feel."

Her face was very close to mine. She seemed to understand what I was saying, and she nodded her head. "Shall we finish saying the letters?"

I smiled. Then I said, "J." And I took my hand from her cheek and placed it on her back. "'J' is the next letter."

She smiled.

We did not get to the difficult part of the alphabet. The "W, X, Y and Z."

DAY FIFTY-NINE

Mary Lou has moved in with me! For two nights now we have slept together in my bed. By unfastening the desk part of it and setting it against the wall, she was able to make room for herself.

It was difficult for me to sleep with another person in the bed with me. I had heard of men and women sharing beds, but never to sleep in. But that was the way she wanted to do it, so I have done it.

I am self-conscious about her body, afraid to touch her or press against her. But I awoke this morning to find myself holding her in my arms. She was snoring lightly. I smelled her hair and kissed her lightly on the back of the neck and then just lay there, holding her sleeping body for a long, long time, until she woke.

She laughed when she woke and found me holding her and snuggled against me warmly. I became self-conscious again. But then we started talking and I forgot my self-consciousness. She talked about learning to read. She said she had dreamed she was reading—had dreamed that she had already read thousands and thousands of books and now knew everything there was to know about life.

"What is there to know about life?" I asked.

"Everything," she said. "They keep us so ignorant."

I wasn't certain I understood that—or who "they" were— so I said nothing.

"Let's have breakfast," she said. And I called the servo and we ate soybars and pig bacon. I felt very good, even though I had slept little.

During breakfast she leaned over the desk and kissed me. Just like that! I liked it.

After breakfast I decided to work on a film, and Mary Lou watched it with me. It was called *The Stock Broker* and its star was Buster Keaton. Buster Keaton is a very intense man who has many unusual difficulties in his films. They would be funny if they were not so sad.

Mary Lou was fascinated. She had never seen any films of any kind before and was only familiar with holographic TV, which she did not like.

Early in the first reel, when Buster Keaton was painting a house and kept painting the face of a man who would put his head out the window, Mary Lou said, "Paul, Buster Keaton looks exactly like you. He's so . . . *serious!*"

And she was right.

After the film we spent the day studying reading. She learns amazingly fast and asks interesting questions. I have had many students in the university where I teach, but none like her. And *my* reading is improving too.

Everything about her is delightful.

It is evening now, and Mary Lou is watching me write this at the desk propped against the wall. I explained to her about writing and she was excited and said that she must learn to do that too so that she could write down the memory of her life. "And write down other things I think of. So I can read them," she said.

That was interesting. Maybe that is the true reason that I write this—since I write so much more than Spofforth ever meant for me to record—I write it so I can read it. Reading it does something strange and exciting in my mind.

Perhaps one reason Mary Lou is bolder than I is that she lived in a Worker Dormitory before she ran away and I, of course, am a graduate of a Thinker Dormitory. Yet she is so fiercely intelligent! Why would she have been trained to be a Worker and not a Thinker? Perhaps the choices are made on some basis other than intelligence.

I must remember to get more paper, so that Mary Lou can learn to write and can begin to print out the memory of her life.

DAY SIXTY-FIVE

She has lived with me nine days now, against all principles of Individualism and Privacy. I feel guilty at times, compromising my Interior Development by the whims of another person, but I don't think about the immorality of that very often. In fact, these have been the happiest nine days of my life.

And she already reads nearly as well as I do! Amazing! And she has begun to write the memory of her life.

We are together constantly. It seems at times like Douglas Fairbanks and Mary Pickford—except they were too well-trained to have sex.

There is no sex at all in the old films, although many of the people live together in the most intimate and immoral ways. Porno, of the kind normally taught in Classics courses, was apparently undiscovered, like TV, at the time these silent films were made.

We make love as often as I am able. Sometimes it just happens while we are reading together, with her repeating the sentences after me. Once it took us almost all afternoon to finish a little book called *Making Paper Kites* because we kept stopping.

Neither of us smokes pot or takes pills. I am often very nervous and excited and feel that I cannot sit still. Sometimes we take short walks when that happens. And, although a part of me seems to cry out against the intensity of the way I am living and working and making love, I know that it is better this way than any other way that I have ever been.

Once, on a walk, we became excited and I suggested we go to a quick-sex bar at Times Square. So we did, and I used my NYU credit card to get the best cubicle they had. There were the usual big porno holographs in the lobby, and two robot doxies with naked breasts and black boots offered to assist us in an orgy, but Mary Lou, thank goodness, told them to bug off. And I turned down the offer of sex-up pills that the bartender made. We went to the cubicle alone, turned off the lights, and made love on the padded floor. But it was not really any good that way.

That was the way my lovemaking had always been before, and the way it is supposed to be. "Quick sex protects," as my Interpersonal Relations teacher used to say. But I wanted to be at my own place with Mary Lou, making love in my own bed and talking afterward. Except for the sex, I wanted to be like Mother and Father in one of the ancient films. I wanted to buy her flowers and to dance with her.

When we had finished Mary Lou said, "Let's get out of this sex factory," and then, as we were leaving, "I think that place is what Simon meant by a 'Chicago whorehouse.'"

And I *did* buy her flowers, at a vending machine. White carnations, like Gloria Swanson wore in *Queen of Them All.*

And before we went to bed that night I asked her to dance. I pinned a flower to her Synlon dress and I played the background music from a TV program, and we danced together. She had never heard of two people dancing together before, but any serious student of films knows about dancing. I had seen it many times. We were awkward and we stepped on each other's feet several times, but it was fun.

But when we went to bed something, I don't know what, frightened me. I held her close until she fell asleep. Then I lay awake for a long time, thinking. Something about the quick-sex place had frightened me, I think.

So I got out of bed and finished writing this. I am tired now, but I still feel frightened. Am I afraid she will leave? Am I afraid I will lose her?

DAY SEVENTY-SIX

She has been here eighteen days now, and I have not written anything down for the last nine.

My happiness has grown! I do not think about the immorality of our cohabitation, or of its being probably against the law. I think about Mary Lou and about what I see in films and what I read and what she reads.

All day yesterday she read a new kind of writing called poems. Some of them she read aloud. In places they were like chess—incomprehensible—and in other places they said strange and interesting things. She read this one to me twice:

> O Western wind, when wilt thou blow,
> That the small rain down can rain?
> Christ! That my love were in my arms
> And I in my bed again!

I had to look up "thou" in *Dictionary*. The second time she read the lines I felt the feeling I have felt in watching some of the strong scenes in films. An expansive feeling, painfully joyful, in my chest.

When she had finished I said, for some strange reason, "Only the mockingbird sings at the edge of the woods."

She looked up from the book and said, "What?" and I said it again: "Only the mockingbird sings at the edge of the woods."

"What does that mean?" she said.

"I don't know. It's from a film."

She pursed her lips. "It's like the words I just read, isn't it? It makes you feel something and you don't know what it is."

"Yes," I said, astonished, almost awed, to find that she had said what I wanted to say. "Yes. Exactly."

Then she read more poems, but none of them made me feel that way again. I liked hearing her read them anyway. I watched her sitting cross-legged on the floor, staring at the book, and listening to her serious and clear voice as she read to us both. She holds the book much closer to her face than I do, and there is something very touching about her when she reads.

We take walks together every day and have lunch in a different place.

DAY SEVENTY-SEVEN

Mary Lou went out this morning, as she often does, to buy some Quik-Serv food for us. She uses my credit card for this. When she was gone I started up the projector and began to watch a film with Lillian Gish and to read the dialogue from it into the recorder when suddenly the door opened and I looked up to see Spofforth standing there in the doorway. He was so tall and so powerful-looking that he seemed to fill up all the space just standing there. And yet I was not frightened by him this time. Spofforth is, after all, only a robot. I turned off the projector and invited him in. He came in and sat in the white plastic chair by the far wall, facing me. He was wearing khaki pants, sandals, and a white T-shirt. His face was unsmiling, but not harsh.

After we had sat silently for a while I said, "Have you been listening to my journal?" I hadn't seen him for a long time, and he had never been in my room before.

He nodded, "When I have time."

Something about this annoyed me, and I felt bold with him. "Why do you want to know about me?" I said. "Why do you want me to keep a journal of my life?"

He didn't answer. After a moment he said, "The teaching of reading is a crime. You could be sent to prison for it."

That did not frighten me. I thought of what Mary Lou had said about Detection, about how no one ever got detected. "Why?" I said. I was violating a Rule of Conduct: "Don't ask; relax." But I didn't care. I wanted to know why it should be a crime to teach someone to read. And why Spofforth hadn't told me this before, when I had first suggested teaching reading at NYU. "Why shouldn't I teach Mary Lou how to read?"

Spofforth leaned forward, putting his huge hands on his knees, staring at me. His stare was a bit frightening, but I did not look away from it.

"Reading is too intimate," Spofforth said. "It will put you too close to the feelings and the ideas of others. It will disturb and confuse you."

I was beginning to feel a bit frightened. It was not easy to be in Spofforth's presence, and to listen to his deep, authoritative voice and not want to be obedient, and unquestioning. But I remembered something I had read in a book: "Others can be wrong too, you know," and I held on to that. "Why should it be a crime to be disturbed and confused? And to know what others have thought and felt?"

Spofforth stared at me. "Don't you want to be happy?" he said.

I had heard that question asked before, by my robot-teachers at the dormitory; it had always seemed unanswerable. But now, here in my room with Mary Lou's things in it and with my projector and cans of film, and with my mind undrugged, it made me suddenly angry. "People who don't read are killing themselves, burning their bodies with fire. Are they happy?"

Spofforth stared at me. Then, suddenly, he looked away, toward the back of another chair where Mary Lou's red dress was lying, crumpled, with a pair of her sandals sitting on the seat by it. "It is also a crime," he said, but softer now, "to live for over a week with another person."

"What is a week?" I said.

"Seven days," Spofforth said.

"Why not seven days?" I said. "Or seven hundred? I am happy with Mary Lou. Happier than I ever was before, with dope and with quick sex."

"You're frightened," Spofforth said. "I can see that you're frightened right now."

Suddenly I stood up. "So what?" I said. "So what? It's better to be living than to be—to be a robot."

I *was* frightened. Frightened of Spofforth, frightened of the future. Frightened of my own anger. For a moment I had a strong desire, standing there silently, to take a sopor—to take a whole handful of them and to make myself calm, unruffled, unfeeling. But I *liked* being angry, and I was not ready to let go of it. "Why should you care if I'm happy?" I said. "What business is it of yours what I do? You're some kind of machine, anyway."

And then Spofforth did a surprising thing. He threw back his head and laughed, loud and deep, for a long time. And, crazily, I felt my anger going away and I began to laugh with him. Finally he stopped and said, "Okay, Bentley. Okay." He stood up. "You're more than I thought you were. Go on living with her." He walked toward the door and then turned around and faced me. "For a while."

I just looked at him and said nothing. He left, closing the door behind him.

When he was gone I sat down on my bed-and-desk again and found that my arms were trembling uncontrollably and that my heart was pounding. I had never talked like that to anyone before and certainly not to a robot. I was terribly frightened of myself. But, deeper, I was elated. It was strange. I had never felt that way before.

When Mary Lou returned I told her nothing about my visitor. But when she wanted to go on with our reading I made love to her instead. She was a little angry with that at first; but my desire for her was so strong, and we made love so powerfully, on the carpet on the floor, with my holding her body tightly and forcing myself into her strongly, that before long she was kissing me all over my face and laughing.

And afterward I felt so good, so relaxed, that I said, "Let's read for a while." And we did. And nothing happened. Spofforth did not return.

Mary Lou has been writing down the memory of her life at the same time that I have been writing this. I am at my desk and she is sitting in my extra chair, using a large book in her lap as a writing surface. She prints beautifully, methodically, in small, neat letters. I am embarrassed that after such a short time she can write better than I. Yet I was her teacher, and I am proud of that. I think now that in my years at the university I never taught anyone anything worth knowing; I have more pleasure from what I have taught Mary Lou than in all my work in Ohio.

DAY SEVENTY-EIGHT

We saw a group immolation today.

We decided to do a new thing and eat breakfast in the Burger Chef. It is a seven-block walk, and I mentioned that to her, telling her how I had got into the habit of counting things. At the dormitories everyone learns to count to ten, but counting is used mainly for the eight different prices of things a person can buy. A pair of pants costs two units and an algaeburger costs one unit and so on. And when you have used up all your units for the day your credit card turns pink and won't work anymore. Most things, of course, are free—like thought-bus rides and shoes and TV sets.

She counted the blocks and agreed that there were seven. "But I always counted my five sandwiches at the zoo," she said.

I thought of *Arithmetic for Boys and Girls*. "After you ate three sandwiches how many were left?" I said.

She laughed. "Two sandwiches." Then she stopped on the street and made herself look like the moron robot at the zoo. She held out her left hand stiffly as though it were holding five sandwiches. And she made her eyes blank and held her head cocked to the side and let her lips open slightly, like a moron robot's, and just stood there, staring stupidly at me.

At first I was shocked and didn't know what she was doing. Then I laughed aloud.

Some students passing by in denim robes stared at her and then looked away. I was a little embarrassed at her. Making a Spectacle; but I could not help laughing.

We went on to the Burger Chef, and there was an immolation already in progress.

It was exactly the same booth that I had seen it happen in before. It must have been almost over because the smell of burnt flesh in the room was pungent and you could feel the strong breeze from the exhaust fans that were trying to clear the air.

There were three people again—all women. Their bodies were burnt black, and in the breeze short flames flickered from what was left of their clothing and hair. Their faces were smiling.

I thought they were already dead when one of them spoke—or shouted. What she shouted was: "This is the ultimate inwardness, praise Jesus Christ our Lord!" Her mouth inside was black. Even her teeth were black.

Then she became silent. I supposed she was dead.

"My God!" Mary Lou said. "My God!"

I took her arm, not even caring if anyone saw me do it, and took her out the door. She walked to the curb and sat down facing the street.

She said nothing. Two thought buses and a Detection car went by in the street, and people passed her on the sidewalk, all ignoring her as she ignored them. I stood beside her, not knowing what to say or do.

Finally she said, still staring at the street, "Did they do it to themselves?"

"Yes," I said. "I think it happens often."

"My God," she said. "Why? Why would people do that?"

"I don't know," I said, "I don't know why they don't do it alone, either. Or in private."

"Yes," she said, "Maybe it's the drugs."

I didn't answer for a minute or so. Then I said, "Maybe it's the way they live."

She stood up, looked at me with a look of surprise, and reached out and held my right arm. "Yes," she said, "that's probably right."

DAY EIGHTY-THREE

I am in prison. I have been in prison five days. Just printing the word "prison" itself, on this coarse paper, is painful to me. I have never felt more alone in my life. I do not know how to live without Mary Lou.

There is a small window in my cell and if I look out it I can see the long, dirty green buildings of the compound, with their rusted metal roofs and heavily barred windows, under the late-afternoon sun. I have just come back from an afternoon working in the fields, and the blisters on my hands have opened and are wet, and the tight metal bracelets on my wrists sting the chafed skin beneath them. There is a bluish bruise on my side that is bigger than my hand where a moron guard clubbed me for losing time when I stumbled, my first day in the fields; and my feet ache from working in the heavy black shoes that were issued me when I first came here. I can hardly hold the pen that I am writing with, because of the cramping in my hand.

I do not know what has become of Mary Lou. The pains I can stand, for I know they could be worse and they will probably get better; but not knowing if I will ever see Mary Lou again and not knowing what has been done with her are more than I feel I can bear. I must find a way to die.

At first, without Mary Lou and with the shock of what had happened to me, I did not want to write again. Not ever. I was allowed to keep my pen and the pages of my journal, which

I stuffed into my jacket pocket without thinking when I was taken away. But I had no fresh paper to write on, and I made no effort to find any. I know I had started my journal with no reader in mind—for I was, then, the only person alive who could read. But I came to realize later that Mary Lou had become my audience. I was writing my journal for *her*. It seemed to me, then, that it was pointless to go on writing in prison, in this horrible place, without her.

I know I would not be writing now if a strange thing had not happened this noon, after I had finished my morning shift at the shoe factory and had gone to wash my face and hands before eating the wretched lunch of bread and protein soup they serve us here and that we are required to eat in silence. It happened in the little steel washroom with its three dirty washstands. I had washed my sore hands as well as I could with cold water and no soap and reached up to pull a paper towel out of the dispenser. As I touched the dispenser, awkwardly because my hands were stiff and cramped from yesterday's fieldwork, it fell open and a high stack of folded paper towels dropped into my hands. I grabbed them instinctively and then winced with the pain of it. But I held on to them, staring at them, and I realized that I was holding a stack of hundreds of sheets of strong, coarse paper. Paper that could be written on.

So much of what is important in my life seems to happen by accident. I found the reading film and books by accident, and I met Mary Lou by accident, and found *Dictionary* by accident. And the paper I am now writing on fell into my hands by accident. I do not know what to think about this; but I am glad to write again, even if no one will read it and even if I find a way to die tomorrow.

I will stop now. I have dropped the pen too many times. My hand will not hold it.

Mary Lou, Mary Lou. I cannot stand this.

DAY EIGHTY-EIGHT

It is five days since I last wrote. My hands are better now, stronger, and I can hold the pen fairly well. But my back and side still ache.

My feet are better. After several days here I noticed that many of my fellow prisoners were barefoot, and I reported for work the next morning without my shoes. My feet are still sore, but they are healing. And my muscles are beginning to feel stronger, tighter.

I am not happy. I am very unhappy, but I no longer am certain that I want to die. Drowning is a possibility. But I will wait awhile before I decide.

The robot guards are horrible. One has beaten me, and I see them beat other prisoners. I know it is terribly wrong of me, but I would like to kill the one who beat me, before I die. I am shocked at myself for wanting that, but it is one of the things that make me want to live. He has tiny red eyes like some hateful and cruel animal, and heavy muscles that bulge under his brown uniform. I could smash his face with a brick.

And, before I die, I want to bring my journal up to now. It is still daylight outside. If I work steadily I think I can write about how I came to be sent here before I must go to sleep.

For several days Mary Lou and I had been coming back, over and over, to the book of poems. We would read them aloud to one another, only barely understanding them. One poem we kept coming back to is called "The Hollow Men."

Early one afternoon I was reading it aloud while sitting on the floor next to Mary Lou. I believe I can write the words down:

> We are the hollow men
> We are the stuffed men
> Leaning together
> Headpiece filled with straw. Alas!
> Our dried voices when
> We whisper together
> Are quiet and meaningless
> As wind in dry grass . . .

And that was as far as I got. The door opened and Dean Spofforth walked in. He stood over us hugely, folded his arms, and stared down. It was shocking to see him in my room like this. Mary Lou had never seen him before, and she was staring up at him with her eyes very wide.

There was something odd about his appearance and it took me a moment to tell what it was. And then I realized it; Spofforth was wearing a broad black armband with the white face of Privacy printed on it. I recognized it from a school lesson somewhere long ago; it was the armband of a Detector.

Mary Lou was the first to speak. "What do you want?" she said. She did not sound frightened.

"You are both under arrest," Spofforth said. And then, "I want you both to stand."

We stood up. I was still holding the book. "Well?" Mary Lou said.

Spofforth looked her steadily in the face. "I am a Detector, and you have been detected."

I could tell that she was shocked and trying not to show it.

I wanted to put my arm around her, to protect her somehow. But I just stood there.

Spofforth was much taller than either of us, and his dignity and force were overwhelming. I had always been afraid of him and now his saying that he was a Detector had me speechless.

"Detected doing what?" Mary Lou said. There was a slight trembling in her voice.

Spofforth stared at her, unblinking. "Detected in cohabitation. Detected in the teaching of reading and detected in the act of reading itself."

"But, Dean Spofforth," I broke in, "you already *knew* I could . . ."

"Yes," he said, "and I told you clearly that reading would not be taught at this university. The teaching of reading is a crime."

Something sank deep inside me. I felt the strength and excitement that had been so much of my life for recent days all go away and I was standing in front of this massive robot like a little child. "A *crime?*" I said.

"Yes, Bentley," he said. "Your hearing will be tomorrow. You are to remain in your room until I return in the morning."

Then he took Mary Lou by the arm and said, "You will come with me."

She tried to pull away from him and then, finding she could not break his grip, she said, "Bug off, robot. Bug off, for Christ's sake."

He looked at her and seemed to laugh. "That won't work," he said. But his voice softened and he added, "No harm will come to you."

And as he went out the door he turned and looked at me. "Don't be too unhappy, Bentley. This may all be for the best."

She went with him without a struggle, and he pulled the door shut behind himself.

No harm? What worse harm could there be than this separation? Where is she? Where is Mary Lou?

I am crying as I write. I cannot finish now. I will take sopors and sleep.

DAY EIGHTY-NINE

There is more to tell than I can say in the time that I have. But I will try.

Spofforth himself took me to court. I was handcuffed and he brought me on a black thought bus to a place in Central Park called Justice House. It was a two-story plastic building with dirty windows.

The courtroom was large. There were many pictures of strange-looking men on the walls. Some of them were wearing the suits and ties that I had seen in ancient films. One man stood in front of a bookcase, much like Douglas Fairbanks. And under his picture there was writing. It said: "*Sydney Fairfax, Chief Justice.*" And under this, in smaller print, were the numbers 1997–2014. I believe those numbers were what are called "dates."

There was a black-robed robot judge sitting in an armchair at the far end of the courtroom, facing the entranceway. I started when I saw him; I had seen his face before. It was the face of the Make Seven headmaster at the dormitory in Ohio where I had been educated. An Upper-Management Robot. I remembered hearing once, "All Make Sevens look alike." And I, being just a child, had said, "Why?" and the child I was talking to had said, "Don't ask; relax."

The judge was dormant when we came in. That is, his power

had been turned off. Next to him was sitting, also dormant, and in a lower, simpler chair, a Make Four clerk robot.

When we got closer I could see that there was yellowish dust, like that in the sealed-off part of the library, all over each of them. The intelligent-looking creases on the judge's face were filled with yellow dust. His hands were folded in his lap, and from his right forearm to his chin a spider had built a web, some time ago. There were holes in the web, and dust on it. A few tiny bodies of insects, like dried snot, hung on the remains of the web. There was no spider visible.

Behind the judge was the Great Seal of North America, just like the one in Piety House at the Thinker Dormitory. It too was covered with dust, which had settled thickly on the relief images of dove and heart; and the plasticasts of the twin Holy Goddesses of Individualism and Privacy, which flanked the Great Seal, were also covered with dust.

Spofforth placed me in the defendant's chair, which was made of something called wood and was uncomfortable. Then he removed my handcuffs, with a surprisingly gentle touch, and had me place my right hand in the Truth Hole that sat directly in front of me. He said quietly, "For each lie you tell, a finger will be severed. Answer the judge with care."

I had, of course, learned of Truth Holes, and of courts, in my Minimal Civics classes. But I had never seen these things before and I found myself trembling with fright. Perhaps the fright was made worse by the resemblance so many things bore to the dormitories, and to the time I was punished for Privacy Imposition as a child. I shifted my weight in the hard seat, tried to make myself comfortable, and waited.

Spofforth looked around the room as though he were study-ing the holes in the plaster, or the pictures of ancient men, or the empty wood benches. Then he walked over to the judge and ran a finger down the side of the robot's cheek and then looked at the little pile of dust on his finger. "Inexcusable," he said

He turned to the clerk and said, in an authoritative voice, "Activate yourself, Clerk of the Court."

The clerk did not move except for his mouth. He said, "Who commands the court?"

"I am a Robot Rational. Make Nine. I command you to awaken."

Immediately the clerk stood. Some debris fell from his lap onto the floor. "Yes, your honor. I am awake and active."

"I want you to summon a cleaning crew and have the judge cleaned. Immediately." Then Spofforth looked at the bits of yellow dust and debris that were clinging to the clerk's lap and said, "Have yourself cleaned up too."

The clerk spoke respectfully. "The court servos and cleaning crew are no longer operable, your honor."

"Why not?"

"Dead batteries and general malfunction, your honor."

"Why haven't they been repaired?"

"There have been no repair crews in Central Park for sixty yellows, your honor."

"All right," Spofforth said. "Then get cleaning materials yourself and clean the two of you up."

"Yes, your honor." The clerk turned and walked slowly out of the room. He limped badly, with one of his legs almost dragging behind him.

A few minutes later he returned with a pail of water and a sponge. He walked up to the judge and, dipping the sponge in water, began wiping off the judge's face. Some of the yellow dust smeared, but most of it came off. Then he began cleaning the judge's hands, slowly and awkwardly.

Spofforth appeared impatient. I did not know that there was such a thing as an impatient robot; but Spofforth was tapping a foot audibly. Then, abruptly, he strode to the seated judge, stooped, picked up the hem of the judge's robe, and shook it vigorously. Dust flew everywhere. As it began to settle I saw that the spider web was gone.

Then Spofforth stood back and faced the judge. He told the clerk to stop and he stopped immediately, leaving a greenish stain on the judge's left hand, still folded in his lap.

"Your services will not be needed for this hearing," Spofforth told the clerk. "I will record the proceedings myself. While the hearing is in progress you may phone General Maintenance to send a City Cleaning and a City Repair robot immediately."

The clerk looked at Spofforth stupidly. I think he was a Make Three—green lobes—and they are only a bit above moron robots. "The telephone doesn't work," he said.

"Then *walk* to General Maintenance. It's about five blocks from here."

"Walk?" the robot said.

"You clearly know how. Do you know where to go?"

"Yes, sir." The clerk turned and began to limp toward the door. Spofforth said, "Wait," and then, "Come here."

The clerk turned around, came to him, and stood facing him. Spofforth bent down, took the clerk's left leg in his hand, felt of it a moment, and then gave it an abrupt wrench. Something inside it made a heavy scraping sound. Spofforth stood up. "Now go," he said.

And the clerk walked out of the court with his gait perfectly normal.

Spofforth turned and faced the judge again. The judge was cleaner now, but a bit streaked and rumpled.

"I call the court to session," Spofforth said, just as our Civics class had taught us any citizen could do. They had never said anything about robots doing it, though. They had told us how important courts were for protecting our sacred rights to Privacy and Individuality, and how helpful a judge could be, but you somehow got the idea that it was a good idea to stay away from courts altogether.

The judge's head came awake, although the rest of him remained motionless. "Who calls the court?" he said, in a deep, grave voice.

"I am a Make Nine robot," Spofforth said quietly, "programmed for Detection and so empowered by the Government of North America."

The rest of the judge woke up at that. He adjusted his robe, ran fingers through his grayish hair, then placed his chin in his hand and said, "The court is in session. What is the citizen robot's request?"

Citizen robot? I had never heard that term before.

"A criminal case, Judge," Spofforth said. "The defendant will give his name." He turned to me. "Say your name, title, and place of residence." And then, nodding toward the Truth Hole, "Be careful."

I had almost forgotten about the Truth Hole. I avoided looking at it and said carefully, "My name is Paul Bentley. I am Professor of Mental Arts at Southeast Ohio University and my official residence is at Professor House on campus. Currently I live at the Arts Library of New York University, where I am temporarily employed by the Dean of Faculties." I did not know whether I should say that Spofforth was the dean I worked for, but I did not.

"Very good, son," the judge said. He looked at Spofforth. "What is the criminal charge?"

"There are three charges," Spofforth said, "Cohabitation, Reading, and the Teaching of Reading."

The judge looked at him blankly. "What is Reading?" he said.

Spofforth said nothing for a moment. Then he said, "You are a Make Seven, designed in the Fourth Age. Your Legal Program would not contain the charge. Consult your archives."

"Yes," the judge said. He flipped a switch on the arm of his huge chair and a voice somewhere said, "This is the Archives of Law for North America," and the judge said, "Is there a civil crime called Reading? And is it a different crime to teach the first crime?"

The archives voice was a long time replying. I had never heard a computer take so long. Or maybe it was merely the way I felt. Finally the voice came back and said, "Reading is the subtle and thorough sharing of ideas and feelings by under-handed means. It is a gross invasion of Privacy and a direct violation of the Constitutions of the Third, Fourth, and Fifth ages. The Teaching of Reading is equally a crime against Privacy and Personhood. One to five years on each count."

The judge switched off the computer. Then he said, "This is clearly a grave business, young man. And you are charged with Cohabitation also." Then, to Spofforth, "With what has he cohabited? Man, woman, robot, or beast?"

"With a woman. They have lived together for seven weeks."

The judge nodded and turned to me. "That is not as grave as the other, young man. But it is a serious risking of Individuality and Personhood and it has been known often to lead to far more serious behavior."

"Yes, Judge," I said. I started to say that I was sorry, but I realized just in time that I was not at all sorry—just frightened. I could have lost a finger.

"Is there anything else?" the judge asked Spofforth.

"No."

The judge looked at me. "Take your hand from the Honesty Regulator and rise and face the court."

I took my hand out of the Truth Hole and stood.

"How do you plead, guilty or not guilty?" the judge said.

No longer having my hand in the box, I could have lied. But then I supposed my hand would be put back in if I said "not guilty" and we proceeded to have a trial. And, indeed, I have found out from another prisoner here that that is exactly the case. Almost everyone pleads guilty.

I looked at the judge and said, "Guilty."

"The court commends your honesty," the judge said. "You are sentenced to six years in the North American Penitentiary, at hard labor for the first two years." The judge lowered his head slightly and looked at me sternly. "Come forward," he said.

I walked up to his chair. He rose, slowly, and then reached out his arms. His large hands, one still with the green stain, grasped my shoulders. I felt something stinging my skin, like a drug injection. And I went unconscious.

I awoke in this prison.

That is all I can write today. My writing hand and arm ache from what I have already written. Besides, it is late and I must do physical work tomorrow.

DAY NINETY

My room—or "cell"—at the prison is not much bigger than a small thought bus, but it is comfortable and private. I have a bed, a chair, a lamp and a TV wall with a small library of recordings. The only recording I have played so far is of a dance-and-exercise program, but I did not feel like dancing and took the BB out of the holder before the program was finished.

There are about fifty other prisoners in identical cells in the same building; we all leave for work together after breakfast. In the mornings I work in a prison shoe factory. I am one of fourteen inmate inspectors. The shoes are made, of course, by automatic equipment; my job is to examine one shoe out of each fourteen for flaws. A moron robot watches over us and I have been warned that if I do not pick up a shoe after the man on my left picks one up, each time, I will be punished. I have found that it is not really necessary to *look at* the shoe, so I do not. I merely pick up one out of each fourteen.

Since I am trained at Mental Arts it is easy for me to spend much of the shoe-inspection time in gentle hallucinating, but I am dismayed at times to find that there is one aspect of my hallucinations over which I have no control; images of Mary Lou will come, with shocking vividness, into my mind. I will be trying to amuse myself with hallucinated abstractions—colors and free-form shapes—when, without warning, I will see Mary Lou's face, with that intense and puzzled stare. Or Mary Lou sitting cross-legged on the floor of my office with a book in her lap, reading.

When I was teaching, I used to make a little joke during my hallucinating-to-orgasm lecture. I would say to my classes, "This would be a good technique to learn in case you are ever sent to prison." It never got much of a laugh, since I suppose you have to be well-educated in Classics—James Cagney films, for instance—to understand the prison reference. Anyway, that was a joke I used to make. But I do not now hallucinate to orgasm—even though I am expert at the technique. At night in my cell I masturbate—as I suppose the other prisoners do. I want to save my most intimate thoughts of Mary Lou for when I am alone at night.

We are given two joints and two sopors with our evening meal but I have been saving mine. After supper I can smell the sweet smell of marijuana in the big prison dormitory and hear the music of erotic TV coming from the other cells, and imagine the synthetic bliss on the faces of the other prisoners. Somehow the thought of that, writing it now, makes me shudder. I want Mary Lou here with me, I want to hear her voice. I want to laugh with her. I want her to comfort me.

A year ago I would not have known what I was feeling. But after all those films I know what it is: I am in love with Mary Lou.

It feels terrible. Being in love feels terrible.

I don't know where this prison is. Somewhere by the ocean. I was brought here unconscious and woke to find myself being given a blue uniform by a robot. I could not sleep the first night, wanting her with me.

I want her. Nothing else is real.

DAY NINETY-ONE

In the afternoons I work in a field at the edge of the ocean. The field is vast, with about two miles of shoreline; it is full of a coarse synthetic plant called Protein 4. The plants are big ugly things, about the size and shape of a man's head, purple-green in color and with a rancid smell. Even out in the sunny fields, the smell is sometimes almost overpowering. My job is feeding them individually with chemicals that are prescribed by a computer each day. I have a little squirt gun that is loaded with pellets by a computer terminal at the end of each long row, and I hold it to a little plastic mouth that is imbedded in the yellow soil at the base of each plant and squeeze a pellet in.

It is backbreaking to do, under the hot sun, keeping up the fast tempo that is created by the constant music in the field. Forty of us work there, with a five-minute break each hour. We all perspire constantly.

Ten moron robots could do this work. But we are being rehabilitated.

Or that is what the television we must watch during our after-lunch social time tells us. We are not allowed to talk during social time, so I do not know if the others feel as angry as I do, and as weary.

Two robots in brown uniforms watch over us while we work. They are short, heavy, and ugly, and whenever I look toward the one who has beaten me he seems to be staring at me, unblinking, with his android's mouth hanging slightly open, as if he is about to drool.

My hand is still so tired and sore from squeezing the trigger on that pistol that I cannot write any more.

Mary Lou. I only hope that you are not as unhappy as I. And I hope that you think of me, from time to time.

MARY LOU

One

Reading gets to be a bore sometimes, but every now and then I find out something that I enjoy knowing about. I'm sitting in an armchair by the window as I write this, holding a board in my lap to write on, and for a long time before starting I just sat and stared at the snow coming down. Big, heavy, clumped-together flakes falling straight down from the sky. Bob has told me to take it easy so I won't get a backache from carrying around this stuck-out belly. So I watched the snow for a long time. And I began to think of something I'd read a few days ago about the water cycle, about how the whole elaborate business of evaporation and condensation and winds and air really works. I watched the snow coming down and thought about how those white clumps had recently been the surface water of the Atlantic Ocean, turned to vapor by the heat of the sun. I could visualize clouds moving together far above the water, and the water in them crystallizing into snowflakes, and those flakes falling and clumping and falling further until I could see them, outside this window in New York.

Something makes me feel very good about just *knowing* things like that.

When I was a little girl Simon talked to me about things like the water cycle and the precession of the equinoxes. He had an old piece of blackboard and chalk; I remember him drawing me a picture of the planet Saturn with its rings. When I asked him how he knew about such things he told me he had learned them from his father. His grandfather had, as a boy, looked at the night sky through a celestial telescope, way back in the days not long after what Simon called "the death of intellectual curiosity."

Although he couldn't read or write and had never been to school, Simon had some knowledge of the past. Not just of Chicago whorehouses but of the Roman Empire and of China and Greece and Persia. I can remember him in our little wooden shack, a marijuana cigarette hanging from his toothless mouth while he stood at the wood stove stirring rabbit stew or bean soup, and saying, "There used to be big men in the world, men of mind and power and imagination. There was St. Paul and Einstein and Shakespeare . . ." He had several lists of names from the past that he would rattle off grandly at such times, and they always gave me a sense of wonder to hear. "There was Julius Caesar and Tolstoy and Immanuel Kant. But now it's all robots. Robots and the pleasure principle. Everybody's head is a cheap movie show."

Jesus. I miss Simon, almost as much as I miss Paul. I wish he were here in New York with me, during the hours in the morning when Bob is at work at the university. While I was writing the first part of this journal, this memorizing of my life, when Paul and I were living together, I wanted Simon to be able to answer questions for me about the days when I first showed up at his place in the desert. About how I looked as a girl, and whether I was pretty and smart and whether I really learned things as fast as he said I did. Now I wish I had him for his sense of humor, and his wildness. He was an old, old man; but he was far wilder and far funnier than either of the two I have lived with since.

Paul was *pathetically* serious. It's comical just to remember how his face looked when I threw the rock at the glass on the python cage, or how gravely he went about teaching me how to read. And he used to read over the first parts of this journal, when we were living at the library, and purse his lips, and frown—even at the parts I thought were funny.

Bob is hardly better. It would be silly to expect a robot to have a sense of humor, but it is still hard to take his gravity and his sensitivity. Especially when he tells me about that dream he keeps having and that he has had all of his long life. At first I was interested, but I eventually became bored with it.

I suppose that dream has much to do with my living here in this three-room apartment with him. It was almost certainly the beginning of his desire to live and act like an ordinary human being of a long time ago, to try to live a life like the life of the dream's original dreamer.

So I am the wife or mistress he would have had. And we play out some kind of game of domesticity, because Bob wants it that way.

I think he's insane.

And how does he know his brain wasn't copied from a bachelor's? Or a woman's?

He won't listen to any of my objections. What he says is: "Do you really mind it, Mary?"

And I guess I don't. I miss Paul. I think I loved Paul in some small way. But when I get right down to it I don't really mind this life, this being the companion of a brown-skinned robot.

What the hell, I used to live at the *zoo*, for Christ's sake. I'll make out.

It's still snowing outside the window. I'm going to finish this entry in my memory journal and then just sit for an hour and drink beer and watch the snow and wait for Bob to come home.

Sure, it would be nice to have Paul back. But as Simon said, you can't win them all. I'll make out.

Two

Bob has been telling me about his dream again, and as usual I can do little but smile politely at him when he talks and try to be sympathetic. He dreams of a white woman, but she is nothing like me. I am dark-haired and physically strong, with good, solid hips and thighs. She is blonde and tall and thin. "Esthetic," he says. And I am not that—although the word might well fit Paul. The woman in Bob's dream is always standing by a pool of black water, and she wears a bathrobe. I don't think I have ever worn a bathrobe in my life, and I am not inclined to stand by pools of anything for very long at a time.

I think what I'm trying to say is that he is in love with her and not with me. And, further, it is for the best.

I certainly don't love Bob—hated him, in fact, when he took Paul away from me and had him sent to prison. Cried and hit him, a lot of times, after the initial shock. And one of the hardest things to get used to was that he really is a Detector—that, in fact, there really *are* Detectors after all. It didn't bother me that he was a robot, or black; the main thing about the experience was in discovering that I could be *detected*. It took away a thing that had given me a great deal of strength all my life: the feeling that I wasn't being fooled by this society-for-idiots I live in. It hurt some of the confidence that Simon had given me—Simon, the only person I've ever loved, or am ever likely to love.

Well. Paul was a dear, sweet man, and I worry for him. I have tried to make Bob have him released from whatever prison he was sent to, but Bob will not even discuss it with me. He merely says, "No one will hurt him," and that's all he will say. There were times, at first, when I felt like crying for Paul; I missed his sweetness and his naïveté, and the childish way he liked to buy me things. But I never really shed tears for him.

Bob, on the other hand, is a creature of consequence. He is, I know, very old—older than Simon would be if he were still living; yet that seems to be of no importance except that it gives him a world-weariness that is appealing. And his being a robot means nothing to me except a certain simplicity in our relationship because there can't be any sex between us. That was a disappointment when I first discovered it; but I have become used to it.

Three

It has been a half a year since Paul and I were separated and I have become comfortable living with Bob, if not altogether happy. It would be ridiculous to berate a robot for a lack of humanity and yet that is, after all, the problem. I do not mean that he lacks feelings—far from it. I must always remember to ask him to sit with me while I eat or his feelings will be hurt. When I am angry with him he looks genuinely baffled. Once when I was bored I taunted him with the name "Robot" and he became furious—frightening—and shouted at me, "I did not choose my incarnation." No. He is like Paul in that I must always be alert to his sensitivities. I am the one who is cool about other people.

But Bob is not human, and I cannot forget that. I forgot it a few times during our first months together. It was after my anger with his taking Paul from me had subsided, during the second month; I tried to seduce him. We were sitting at the kitchen table silently, while I was finishing a plate of scrambled eggs and my third glass of beer and he was sitting next to me, his handsome head inclined toward me, watching me eat. He seemed touchingly shy. I had long since become accustomed to the fact that he did not eat and had totally forgotten the implications of that simple fact. Maybe it was the beer, but I found myself seeing for the first time how really *good-looking* he was, with his soft brown, youthful skin, his short and curly and shiny black hair, his brown eyes. And how strong and sensitive his face was! I had a sudden rush of feeling then, not so much sexual as motherly, and I reached out and placed my hand on his arm, just above the wrist. It was warm, like anybody's arm.

He looked down toward the table top, and said nothing. We did not talk to one another very much back then anyway. He was wearing a short-sleeved beige Synlon shirt, and his brown—beautiful brown—arm was smooth, warm to my touch, and hairless. He was wearing khaki trousers. I set my glass down and slowly—as if in a dream—reached out my hand toward his thigh. And during the short moment it took, setting the glass down, pausing a moment in hesitation, and then reaching out to him while my other hand was still lightly gripping his arm, the whole thing had become specifically, excitingly sexual; I was suddenly aroused and was, for a moment, dizzy with it. I set my palm on the inside of his thigh.

We sat like that for what seemed a long time. I honestly did not know what to do next. My mind was totally without any calculation of the situation; the word "robot" did not for a moment enter it. Yet I did not go any further, as I might have with other . . . with other *men*.

Then he lifted his head and looked at me. His face was strange. Yet there seemed to be no expression at all on it. "What are you trying to do?" he said.

I just looked at him dumbly.

He inclined his head toward mine. "What in the hell are you trying to do?"

I said nothing.

Then he took my hand from his leg with his free hand. I took my hand from his arm. He stood up and began to take off his pants. I stared at him, not thinking of anything.

I had not even expected the point he was making. And when I saw, I was truly shocked. There was nothing between his legs. Only a simple crease in the smooth, brown flesh.

He was looking at me all this time. When he saw that his lower nakedness had registered with me he said, "I was made in a factory in Cleveland, Ohio, woman. I was not born. I am not a human being."

I looked away and, a moment later, heard him putting his pants back on.

I took a thought bus to the zoo. A few days afterward I discovered that I was pregnant.

Four

Instead of talking about his dream last night, Bob began talking about artificial intelligences.

Bob says his brain is not at all like the telepathic one of a thought bus. They receive instructions and drive themselves by what he calls an "intention signal receiver and route seeker." He says neither he nor any of the other six or seven Detectors left in North America have any telepathic ability whatever. Telepathy would be too much of a burden for their "human model" intelligences.

Bob is a Make Nine robot. He says Make Nines, of which he may be the last one remaining, were of a very special "copied intelligence" type and the last series of robots ever made. They were designed to be industrial managers and senior executives; Bob himself ran the automobile monopoly until private cars ceased to exist. He tells me that not only were there private cars but there were machines, once, that flew through the air and carried people in them. It sounds impossible.

My way of getting used to being with Bob, after he insisted that we live together, was to ask him questions about the way things worked. He seemed to enjoy answering them.

I asked him why it was that thought buses weren't driven by robots.

"The real idea," he said, "was to make the ultimate machine. It was the same kind of idea that had led to me—to my kind of robot."

"What's ultimate about a thought bus?" I said. They seemed to me such ordinary things, always around, with their comfortable seats and with never more than three or four passengers. Sturdy, gray, four-wheeled aluminum vehicles and one of the few mechanical things that always worked and that did not require a credit card to use.

Bob was sitting in a dusty Plexiglas armchair in the kitchen of our apartment; I was boiling synthetic eggs at the nuclear stove, on the one burner that worked. Over the stove a portion of the wall covering had fallen away years before to reveal copies of a green-jacketed book that had been nailed there by some long-gone former tenants, for insulation.

"Well, they always *work*, for one thing," he said grimly. "They don't need spare parts. The brain of a thought bus is so good at finding wear and stress points in the machinery, and making critical adjustments to distribute the wear and tear, that it just wasn't necessary to make any." He was looking out the window, at snow falling. "My body works the same way," he said. "I don't need spare parts either." He became silent.

He seemed to have drifted off the point. I had noticed him doing it before and had called it to his attention. "Just getting senile," he had said. "Robot brains wear out like anybody else's." But apparently, thought-bus brains did not wear out.

I think Bob is too obsessed by that dream of his, and by his attempt to "resurrect his lost self"—the attempt that led him to send Paul away and take me as his wife. Rob wants to find out whose brain he has and to recover its memories. I think it's impossible. I think *he* knows it's impossible. The brain he has is an *erased* copy of a very intelligent person's brain. Erased completely, except for a few old dreams.

I've told him he should let it go. "When in doubt, forget it," as Paul says. But he says it's the only thing that keeps him sane—that interests him. In their first ten blues Make Nine had burned out their own circuits with household current and transformers, had smashed their brains in heavy plant equipment, or had merely freaked out and begun to drool like idiots, or had become erratic, screaming lunatics—had drowned themselves in rivers and buried themselves alive in agricultural fields. No more robots were made after the Make Nine series. Never.

Bob has a way, when he is thinking, of running his fingers through his black, kinky hair, over and over again. It is a very *human* gesture. I certainly have never seen another robot do it. And sometimes he *whistles*.

He told me once that he remembered part of a line of a poem from his brain's erased memory. It went: "Whose 'something' these are I think I know . . ." But he could not remember what the "something" was. A word like "tools or "dreams." Sometimes he would say it that way:

"Whose dreams these are I think I know . . . ?" But it did not satisfy him.

I asked him once why he thought he was any different from the other Make Nines, when he told me that as far as he knew none of the others had shared these "memories." What he said was: "I'm the only black one." And that was all.

When he drifted off like that on that snowy afternoon in our kitchen, I brought him back by asking, "Is self-maintenance the only 'ultimate' thing about a thought bus?"

"No," he said, and ran his fingers through his hair. "No." But instead of going on right away he said, "Get me a marijuana cigarette, will you, Mary?" He always calls me "Mary" instead of Mary Lou.

"Okay," I said. "But how can dope work on a robot?"

"Just get it," he said.

I got a joint from a package in my bedroom. They were a mild brand, called Nevada Grass, that were delivered with the

Pro-milk and synthetic eggs twice a week to the people in the apartment complex where we live. The people who have, as most of us do, the use of the yellow credit card. I say "people" because Bob is the only robot who lives here. He commutes to work by thought bus and is gone six hours a day. Most of that time I read books, or ancient magazines on microfilm. Bob brings me books from work almost every day. He gets them from some archives building that is even older than the one I lived in with Paul. He brought me a microfilm projector after I asked him once if there were other things to read besides books. Bob can be very helpful—although, come to think of it, I believe all robots were originally programmed that way: to help people.

I am certainly wandering in this account, in this continuation of my plan to memorize my life. Maybe I'm getting senile—like Bob.

No, I'm not senile. I'm just excited to be memorizing my life again. Before I started this I was merely bored—as bored as I had been after Simon died in New Mexico, as bored and freaky as I was getting at the Bronx Zoo before Paul first showed up, looking so childlike and simple, and appealing . . .

I'd better quit thinking about Paul.

I brought Bob his joint and he lit it and inhaled deeply. Then, trying to be friendly, he said, "Don't you *ever* smoke? Or take pills?"

"No," I said. "They make me sick, physically. And I don't like the idea of them anyway. I like being wide awake."

"Yes, you do," he said. "I envy you."

"Why envy me?" I said. "I'm human and subject to diseases, and aging, and broken bones . . ."

He ignored that. "I was programmed to be wide awake and

fully aware twenty-three hours a day. It has only been in the last few years, since I've begun to allow myself to concentrate on thinking about my dreams, about my former personality and its erased feelings and memories, that I've learned to . . . to relax my mind and let it wander." He took another puff from the joint. "I never *liked* being wide awake. I certainly don't like it now."

I thought about that for a minute. "I doubt if that marijuana could affect a metal brain. Why don't you try programming yourself for a high? Can't you alter some circuits somewhere and make yourself euphoric, or drunk?"

"I tried it. Back in Dearborn. And later, when I was first assigned by Government to this nonsense of being a university dean. The second time I tried harder than the first because I was furious at the pretense of learning that the university was committed to—the learning of nothing by students who come here to learn nothing except some kind of inwardness. But I didn't get high. I got hung-over."

He stood up from his chair and walked over to the window and watched the snow for a while. I took my eggs off the fire and began to peel them.

Then he spoke again. "Maybe it was the buried memory of a classical education in my brain that made me feel so furious. Or maybe it was just that I had been really *trained* to do my job. I know and understand engineering. Not one of my students knows any of the laws of thermodynamics or vector analysis or solid geometry or statistical analysis. I know all these disciplines and more. They are not magnetic memories built into my brain, either. I *learned* them by playing library tapes over and over again, studying along with every other Make Nine robot, in Cleveland. And I learned to be a Detector . . ." He shook his head, and turned away from the window to face me. "But that doesn't matter anymore, either. Your father was right. There aren't many working Detectors anymore. There is no need for them. When the children stopped being born . . ."

"The children?" I said.

"Yes," he said. Then he sat down again. "Let me tell you about thought buses."

"But what about children?" I said. "Paul told me once . . ."

He looked at me strangely. "Mary," he said, "I don't know why children aren't being born. It's something to do with the population control equipment."

"If no one gets born," I said, "there won't be any more people on the earth."

He was silent for a minute. Then he looked at me. "Do you care?" he said. "Do you really care?"

I looked back at him. I didn't know what to say. I didn't know if I *did* care.

Five

We moved into this apartment a week after Paul was sent away and over the months I have grown to like it fairly well. Bob has tried to get repair and maintenance robots in to fix the peeling walls and put on new wallpaper and repair the burners on the stove and reupholster the couch, but so far he has had no luck. He is probably the highest-ranking power in New York; at least I don't know of any creature with more authority. But he can't get much done. Simon used to say to me when I was a little girl that things were all falling apart and good riddance. "The Age of Technology has rusted," he would say. Well, it's gotten worse in the forty yellows since Simon died. Still, it's not too bad here. I wash the windows and clean the floors myself, and there is plenty of food.

I have learned to enjoy drinking beer during my pregnancy and Bob knows a place where there is an inexhaustible supply that comes from an automated brewery. Every third or fourth can turns out to be rancid, but it's easy enough to pour those down the toilet. The sink drain is too stopped up.

The other day Bob brought me a hand-painted ancient picture from the archives to hang over a big ugly spot on the living-room wall. There was a little brass plaque on the frame, and I could read it: "Pieter Bruegel. *Landscape with the Fall of Icarus.*" It is very good-looking. I can see it when I look up from the table where I am writing this. There is a body of water in the picture—an ocean or a large lake—and sticking up out of the water is a leg. I don't understand it; but I like the stillness of the rest of the scene. Except for that leg, which is splashing in the water. I might try to get some blue paint someday and paint over it.

Bob has a way of picking up on a conversation days after I thought we had finished with it. I suppose it has to do with the way his mind stores information. He says he is incapable of forgetting anything. But if that is true why was it necessary for him to labor at learning things during his early training?

This morning while I was eating breakfast and he was sitting with me he started talking about thought buses again. I suppose he had been thinking about it while I was asleep. Sometimes it seems spooky to me when I get out of bed in the morning and find him sitting in the living room with his hands folded under his chin or pacing around in the kitchen.

I offered, once, to teach him to read so that he would have something to *do* all night, but he just said, "I know too much already, Mary." I didn't pursue it.

I was eating a bowl of synthetic protein flakes and not liking the taste of them much when Bob said, apropos of nothing, "A thought bus brain isn't really awake all the time. Just receptive. It might not be too bad to have a brain like that. Just receptiveness and a limited sense of purpose."

"I've met people like that," I said, chewing the tough flakes. I didn't look at him; I was still, rather sleepily, staring at the bright identification picture on the side of the cereal box. It showed a face that everyone presumably trusted—but whose name almost no one knew—a face smiling over a big bowl of what were clearly synthetic protein flakes. The picture of the cereal was, of course, necessary to let people know what was in the box, but I had been wondering about the meaning of the man's picture. One thing I have to say about Paul is that he gets you wondering about things like that. He has more curiosity about the *meanings* of things and how they make you *feel* than anyone I have ever known. I must have picked up some of it from him.

The face on the box was, Paul had told me, the face of Jesus Christ. It was used to sell a lot of things. "Vestigial reverence" was the term Paul read somewhere that was supposed to be the idea, probably a hundred or more blues ago, when such things were all planned out.

"All the brain of a bus does," Bob was saying, "is read the mind of a passenger who has a destination thought out, and then work out a way to drive him there without any accidents. And to fit his destination in with those of the other passengers. It probably isn't a bad life."

I looked up at him. "If you like rolling around on wheels," I said.

"The first models of thought buses that were made at the Ford works were *two-way* telepaths. They would broadcast music or pleasant thoughts into the heads of their passengers. Some of the night runs would send out erotic thoughts."

"Why don't they do that anymore? The equipment broke down?"

"No," he said. "As I told you, thought buses are different from the rest of the junk. They don't break down. What happened was that nobody would get *off* the buses."

I nodded. Then I said, "*I* might have."

"But you're different," he said. "You're the only unprogrammed woman in North America. And certainly the only pregnant one."

"Why would I be pregnant if no one else is?" I said.

"Because you don't use pills or marijuana. Most drugs for the past thirty years have contained a fertility-inhibiting agent. I checked some control tapes at the library after the subject came up between us the other day. There was a Directed Plan to cut back population for a year. A computer decision. But something went wrong with it, and the population was never turned back on again."

That was a shocker. I just sat there for a moment, thinking about it. Another equipment malfunction, or another burned-out computer, and no more babies. Ever.

"Could you do anything about it? Fix it, I mean?"

"Maybe," he said. "But I'm not programmed for repair."

"Oh, come on, Bob," I said, suddenly irritated. "I bet you could paint these walls and fix the sink if you really wanted to."

He said nothing.

I was feeling strange, annoyed. Something about our conversation about the lack of children in the world—a thing I had never noticed until Paul had pointed it out to me—was bothering me.

I looked at him hard—with that look that Paul calls mystical and says he loves me for. "Are robots able to lie?" I said.

He didn't answer.

Six

Yesterday afternoon Bob came home early from the university. I'm seven months pregnant now, and I loaf around the apartment a lot, just letting the time pass by and watching the snow falling. Sometimes I read a little, and sometimes I just sit. Yesterday when Bob came in I was bored and restless and I told him, "If I had a decent coat I'd take a walk."

He looked at me strangely a moment. Then he said, "I'll get you a coat," and he turned around and walked out the door.

It must have been two hours before he got back. By that time I was even more bored, and impatient with him for taking so long.

He had a package with him and held it a minute, standing in front of me, before he gave it to me. There was something odd about his face. He looked very serious and—how can I say this?—vulnerable. Yes, big as he is, and powerful, he looked vulnerable to me, like a child, as he handed me the box.

I opened it. In it was a bright red coat with a black velvet collar. I took it out and tried it on. It was certainly *red*. And I didn't much like the collar. But it sure was warm.

"Where did you get this?" I said. "And what took you so long?"

"I searched the inventories of five warehouses," he said, staring at me, "before I found it."

I raised my eyebrows but said nothing. The coat fit pretty well as long as I didn't try to button it over my belly. "How do you like it?" I said, turning around in front of him.

He said nothing, but stared at me thoughtfully for a long moment. Then he said, "It's all right. It might look better if you had black hair."

That was an odd thing for him to say. And he had never given any sign before that he ever noticed how I looked. "Should I have the color changed?" I said. My hair is brown. Just plain brown, with no particular character to it. Where I have it is in the figure. And the eyes. I like my eyes.

"No," he said. "I don't want you to dye your hair." There was something sad about the way he said it. And then he said another strange thing: "Would you like to take a walk with me?"

I looked up at him, not letting myself blink for a moment. Then I said, "Sure."

And when we were out on the street he took my hand. Surprised hell out of me. He began to whistle. We walked like that for about an hour on the nearly empty streets in the snow and through Washington Square, where only a few zonked old ladies sat smoking their joints in silence. Bob was careful to walk slowly so that I could keep up with him—he really is enormous—but he said nothing the whole time. He would stop whistling every now and then and look down at me, as if he were studying my face; but he did not say a word.

It was strange. Yet I felt somehow pleased with it. I felt there was something important to him about the red coat and the walking and the holding of my hand, and I didn't really feel it necessary to know exactly what it was. If he had wanted me to know he would have told me. Somehow I felt *needed* by him, and for a while very important. It was a good feeling. I wish he had put his arm around me.

Sometimes the thought that I will soon be a mother frightens me and makes me feel alone. I've never talked to Bob about this, would not know how to talk to him; he seems so absorbed in his own longings.

I have read a book about having babies and taking care of them. But I have no idea of what it will feel like to *be* a mother. I have never seen one.

Seven

Here in New York, when walking by myself through the snow I watch the faces. They are not always bland, not always empty, not stupid. Some are frowning in concentration, as if difficult thought were trying to burst out in speech. I see middle-aged men with lean bodies and gray hair and bright clothing, their eyes glazed, lost in thought. Suicides by immolation abound in this city. Are the men thinking of death? I never ask them. One doesn't.

Why don't we talk to one another? Why don't we huddle together against the cold wind that blows down the empty streets of this city? Once, long ago, there were private telephones in New York. People talked to one another then—perhaps distantly, strangely, with their voices made thin and artificial by electronics; but they talked. Of the price of groceries, the presidential elections, the sexual behavior of their teenage children, their fear of the weather and their fear of death. And they *read*, hearing the voices of the living and the dead speaking to them in eloquent silence, in touch with a babble of human talk that must have filled the mind in a manner that said: *I am human. I talk and I listen and I read.*

Why can no one *read*? What happened?

I have a copy of the last book ever published by Random House, once a place of business that caused books to be printed and sold by the millions. The book is called *Heavy Rape*; it was published in 2189. On the flyleaf is a statement that begins: "With this novel, fifth in a series, Random House closes its editorial doors. The abolition of reading programs in the schools during the past twenty years has helped bring this about. It is with regret . . ." And so on.

Bob seems to know almost everything; but he doesn't know when or why people stopped reading. "Most people are too lazy," he said. "They only want distractions."

Maybe he is right, but I don't really *feel* that he is. In the basement of the apartment building we live in, a very old building that has been restored many times, is a crudely lettered phrase on the wall near the reactor: WRITING SUCKS. The wall is painted in an institutional green, and scratched into the paint are crude drawings of penises and women's breasts and of couples engaged in oral sex or hitting one another, but those are the only words: WRITING SUCKS. There is no *laziness* in that statement, nor in the impulse to *write* it by scratching into tough paint with the point of a nail or a knife. What I think of when I read that harsh, declarative phrase is how much *hatred* there is in it.

Perhaps the grimness and coldness that I see everywhere exist because there are no children. No one is young anymore. In my whole life I have never seen anyone younger than I am.

My only idea of childhood comes from memory, and from the obscene charade of those robot children at the zoo.

I must be at least thirty. When my child comes he will have no playmates. He will be alone in a world of old and tired people who have lost the gift for living.

Eight

There must have been a period in the ancient world when there were still television writers who wrote their scripts, even though none of the actors could read them. And, although there were some writers who would use tape recorders to write with—especially for the sex-and-pain shows that were popular at the time—many refused to out of a kind of snobbery and would continue to type their scripts. Although the manufacturing of typewriters had ceased years before and spare parts and ribbons were almost impossible to find, typewritten scripts continued to be turned out. Every studio therefore had to have a *reader*—a person whose job it was to read aloud the typed scripts into a tape recorder so the director could understand them and the actors could learn their parts. Alfred Fain, whose book was used to insulate the walls of our apartment against the cold weather after the Death of Oil, was both a scriptwriter and a reader during the last days of story-television—or Literal-Video. His book is called *The Last Autobiography* and it starts like this:

> When I was a young man reading was still taught in the public schools, as an elective. I can clearly remember the group of twelve-year-olds in Miss Warburton's read-

ing class back in St. Louis. There were seventeen of us and we thought of ourselves proudly as an intellectual elite. The other thousands of students in the school, who could only spell words like "fuck" and "shit"—scrawling them on the walls of the sports arenas and gymnasiums and TV rooms that made up most of the space in the school—treated us with a kind of grudging awe. Even though they bullied us at times—and I still shudder to remember the hockey player who used to bloody my nose regularly after our class in Mind Tripping—they seemed secretly to envy us. And they had a pretty fair idea of what reading *was*.

But that was a long time ago, and I am fifty now: The young people I work with—porno stars, hot young directors of game shows, pleasure experts, emotion manipulators, admen—neither understand nor care about what reading *is*. One day on a set we were dealing with a script written by an old-timer that called for a book to be thrown by a young girl at an older woman. The scene was part of a Good-Feeling Religion story, adapted from some forgotten ancient, and it took place in the waiting room of a clinic. The crew had put together a pretty convincing waiting room with plastic chairs and a shag rug, but when the director arrived the prop man had a quick conference with him, telling him he "didn't quite follow that thing about the *book*." And the director, clearly unsure what a book was but not wanting to admit he didn't know, asked me what it was for. I told him it established the girl who was reading it as an intellectual and somewhat antisocial. He pretended to consider this, although he probably did not recognize the word "intellectual" either, and then he said, "Let's use a glass ashtray. And some blood, when it cuts her. The scene's too flat anyhow."

I was too shocked to quarrel with him. I hadn't really realized until then how far we had come.

And that leads me to this question: why am I writing this? And the answer is only that I have always wanted to. Back in school, learning to read, all of us thought we would someday write books and that *somebody* would read them. I know now that I waited too long to start this; but I'll go on with it anyway.

That script, ironically, won the director an award. It told the story of a married woman who brings her husband, Claude, to a clinic because of impotence. While waiting for the doctors to assess Claude's problem, she is hit in the face with an ashtray by a sex-starved young lesbian and goes into a coma, during which she has a religious awakening, with visions.

I remember getting on mescaline and gin at the party where the award was given and trying to explain to a bare-breasted actress who sat on a sofa next to me that the only standards of the television industry were monetary, that there was no real motive in television beyond the making of money. She smiled at me all the time I talked, and occasionally ran her fingertips lightly across her nipples. And when I got finished she said, "But money is fulfillment too."

I got drunk and took her to a motel.

Writing a book, I feel as a Talmudic scholar or an Egyptologist might have felt at Disneyland in the twentieth century. Except, I suppose, I do not really have to wonder if there is anyone who wants to hear what I have to say; I *know* there is no one. I can only wonder how many people are left alive who can read. Possibly a few thousand. A friend of mine who works part time as the head of a publishing house says the average book finds about eighty readers. I've asked him why they don't stop publishing altogether. He says he frankly doesn't know, but that his publishing company is such a tiny division of the recreation corporation that owns it that they have probably forgotten about its existence. He doesn't know how to read himself, but he respects books because his mother had been a kind of recluse who read almost constantly, and he loved her deeply. He is, by the way, one of the few people I know who were brought up in a family. Most of my friends have come out of the dormitories. I was reared in a kibbutz, out in Nebraska. But then I'm Jewish, and that, too, is a pretty rare thing these days: to be Jewish and to know it. I was one of the last members of the kibbutz; it was converted into a state-operated Thinker Dormitory when I was in my twenties.

I was born in 2137 . . .

Reading that date I was immediately curious about how long ago Alfred Fain had lived, and I asked Bob. He said, "About two hundred years."

Then I said, "Is there a date now? Does this year have a number?"

He looked at me coldly. "No," he said. "There is no date."

I would like to know the date. I would like for my child to have a birth date.

BENTLEY

I am not so tired now. The work is getting easier to do, and I feel stronger.

I am sleeping better at nights, now that I have decided to take my sopors. And the food is passable now and I eat a great deal. More than I have ever eaten before in my life.

I do not exactly *like* the effect of sopors anymore; but they are necessary if I am to sleep properly. They stop some of the pain of my thoughts.

Today I tripped and fell between the rows of plants, and another prisoner who was nearby ran over and helped me up. He was a tall, gray-haired man whom I had noticed before because of the way he whistles at times.

He helped me brush myself off and then looked at me closely and said, "You all right, buddy?"

All of this was terribly intimate—almost obscene—but I did not mind, really. "Yes," I said. "I'm all right." And then one of the robots shouted, "No talking. Invasion of Privacy!" and the man looked at me, grinned broadly, and shrugged. We both went back to work. But as he walked away I heard him mutter, "Stupid goddamn robots!" and I was shocked at the strength of unashamed feeling in his voice.

I have seen other prisoners whispering together in the rows. It is often several minutes before a robot notices and stops them.

The robots walk between the rows with us; but they stop before going close to the low cliff at the end of the field. Perhaps they are programmed that way so they will not fall—or be pushed—over the cliff. Anyway they are far enough back by the time I arrive at the seaward end of the row so that there is a short time when they cannot see me, because of a dip in the ground before it comes to the edge of the cliff.

I have learned to speed up, doing two squirts of the gun to each beat of music, toward the end of each row. This gives me time to stand at the edge of the ocean for sixteen beats—and I am thankful I learned to determine this from *Arithmetic for Boys and Girls.* I stand and look out over the ocean. It is wonderful to look at—broad and huge and serene. Something deep in my self seems to respond to it, with a feeling I cannot name. But I am learning again to welcome strange feelings. Sometimes there are birds over the ocean, their curved wings outspread, sailing in the air in smooth broad arcs, above my world of men and machines, inscrutable, and breathtaking to see. Looking at them I say sometimes to myself a word I learned from a film: "Splendid!"

I said I am learning to welcome strange feelings, and this is true. How different I now seem from what I was, far less than a yellow ago, when I first began to feel those feelings while watching silent films at my bed-and-desk. I know that I am being disobedient to all that I was taught about feelings toward things outside myself when I was a child, but I do not care. In fact, I enjoy doing what was forbidden once.

I have nothing to lose.

I think the ocean means most to me on rain days, when the water and sky are gray. There is a sandy beach below the cliff; its tan color looks beautiful against the gray water. And the white birds in the gray sky! My heart beats noticeably when I even imagine it, here in my cell. And it is sad, like the horse with the hat on its head in the old film, like King Kong falling— so slowly, so softly, so far—and like the words that I now say aloud: "Only the mockingbird sings at the edge of the woods." Like remembering Mary Lou, cross-legged on the floor, her eyes on her book.

Sadness. Sadness. But I will embrace the sadness, and make it a part of this life that I am memorizing.

I have nothing to lose.

DAY NINETY-SEVEN

An astonishing thing happened today, out in the field.

I had been working for about two hours; it was nearly time for the second break. I heard a rustling sound behind me where the robot overseer normally stood and I looked around and there the robot was, staggering jerkily in the row. Just as I looked his heavy foot came down on a Protein 4 plant. The plant split open with a disgusting noise and covered his foot with purple juice.

The robot's mouth was grimly set and his eyes stared upward. He staggered for a few more moments, stepped on another plant, and then stood completely still for a moment, as if dormant. Then he fell flat to the ground like a dead weight. The other robot walked over to him, looked down at his inert body, and said, "Rise." But the other did not move. The standing robot bent down and picked up the fallen one and began to carry him back toward the prison buildings.

A minute later I heard a loud voice in the field shout, "Malfunction, boys!" There were the sounds of running. I looked in astonishment and saw a group of blue-uniformed prisoners running between the rows and then, suddenly, there was an arm around my shoulder—a thing that had never happened before in my life: a stranger putting an arm around my shoulder!—and it was the man with gray hair and he was saying, "Come on, buddy! To the beach," and I found myself running, following him. And I was feeling frightened. Frightened but good.

There was a place where the cliff was low and there was a cleft in the rock where you could climb down worn old steps, themselves made of rock. As I was going down with the others, astonished at the back-slapping and friendly shouting among them—a thing I had never seen even as a child—I noticed a strange thing on one of the cliff rocks beside the stairs. There was writing, in faded white paint. It said: "John loves Julie, Class of '94."

Everything was so strange that I felt almost hypnotized by it. Men were saying things to one another and laughing, just as in pirate films. Or, for that matter, in some prison films. But seeing it in a film and then actually seeing it happen are two very different things.

And yet, thinking about it now in my cell, I can see that I was not upset as I might have been, possibly because I *had* seen such intimacy in the films.

Some of the men gathered together pieces of driftwood and built a fire on the beach. I had never seen an open fire before and I liked it. Then some of the men actually took off their clothes, ran laughing down the beach and into the water. Some splashed and played in the shallow waters; others went out deeper and began to swim, just as though they were in a Health and Fitness pool. I noticed that they stayed in little groups, both those who were playing and those swimming, and they seemed to want it that way.

The rest of us sat in a circle around the fire. The gray-haired man pulled a joint from his shirt pocket and took a twig from the fire and lit it. He seemed to be accustomed to fires—in fact, all of them seemed to have done this many times before.

One man, smiling, said to the man next to him, "Charlie, how long since the last malfunction?" and Charlie said, "It's been a while. We were overdue." And the other laughed and said, "Yeah!"

The gray-haired man came over and sat by me. He offered me the joint but I shook my head, so he shrugged and gave it to the man on the other side of me. Then he said, "We've got at least an hour. Repair on robots is slow here."

"Where are we?" I asked.

"I'm not sure," he said. "Everybody gets knocked out in court and they don't wake him up till he gets here. But one guy told me once he thought it was North Carolina." He spoke to the man who had taken the joint. The man was passing it to the next man. "Is that right, Foreman? North Carolina?"

Foreman turned around. "I heard South," he said, "South Carolina."

"Well, somewhere in there," the gray-haired man said.

For a while we were all silent around the fire, watching its flames in the afternoon air, listening to the sound of the surf against the beach and hearing the occasional cry of a gull overhead. Then one of the older men spoke to me. "What they put you in for? Kill somebody?"

I was embarrassed and didn't know what to say. He would not have understood about reading. "I was living with someone," I said finally. "A woman . . ."

The man's face brightened for a moment and then almost immediately went sad. "I lived with a woman once. For over a blue."

"Oh?" I said.

"Yeah. A blue and a yellow. At least. That isn't what they put me here for, though. Shit, I'm a thief is why. But I sure do remember . . ." He was wrinkled and thin and bent; there were only a few hairs on his head, and his hands shook as he took the joint and inhaled from it and then passed it to the younger man next to him.

"Women," the gray-haired man beside me said, breaking the silence.

Something about that one word seemed to open up the older man. "I used to fix coffee for her," he said, "and we'd drink it in bed. Real coffee with real milk in it, and sometimes when I could find it a piece of fruit. An orange, maybe. She'd drink that coffee out of a gray mug and I'd just sit at the other end of the bed facing her and pretend to be thinking about my own coffee but what I was really doing was watching her. God, I could watch that woman." He shook his head.

I could feel his sadness. There were goose bumps on my arms and legs from hearing him talk like that. I had never heard another person speak for *me* like that before. He had said what I felt and, sad as I was, there was relief for me in it.

Someone else said softly, "What become of her?"

For a while the old man didn't answer. Then he said, "Don't know. One day I come home from the mill and she wasn't there. Never saw her again."

There was silence for a moment and then one of the younger prisoners spoke up. He was trying, I suppose, to be helpful. "Well, quick sex is best," he said philosophically.

The old man turned his head slowly and stared at the man who had just spoken. And then he said to him, strongly and evenly, "Fuck that. You can just fuck that."

The younger man looked flustered, and turned his face away. "I didn't mean . . ."

"Fuck it," the old man said. "Fuck your quick sex, I know what my life's been like." Then he turned toward the ocean again and said softly, repeating himself, "I know what my life's been like."

Hearing this and seeing the way the old man looked toward the ocean with his thin shoulders squared under his faded blue prison shirt and the breeze blowing the few wisps of hair on his old, tight-skinned head, I felt such sadness that it was beyond tears. And I was thinking of Mary Lou and of the way she had looked in the mornings sometimes, drinking tea. Or of her hand on the back of my neck and the way that, sometimes, she would stare at me and stare, and then smile . . .

I must have sat there thinking these things about Mary Lou and feeling my own grief for a long while, looking out toward the ocean, past the old man. And then I heard the gray-haired man next to me say softly. "You wanta swim?" I looked up at him, startled, and said, "No," perhaps too quickly. But the thought of getting naked with all those strangers had brought me back to the present with a start.

Yet I love to swim.

In the Thinker Dormitories, each child has the pool to himself for ten minutes. Dormitories are very strict about Individualism.

I was thinking about this when the gray-haired man suddenly said, "My name's Belasco."

I looked down at the sand at my feet. "Hello," I said.

And then, a moment later, he said, "What's your *name*, buddy?"

"Oh," I said, still looking at the sand. "Bentley." And I felt his hand on my shoulder and looked, startled, at his face. He was grinning at me. "Good to know you, Bentley," he said.

After a while I got up and walked down to the water's edge but away from the swimmers. I know that I have changed much since I left Ohio; but all that intimacy and feeling were more than I could stand at once. And I wanted to be alone with my thoughts of Mary Lou.

At the water's edge I found a hermit crab, in a small, curled whelk shell. I knew it was a hermit crab from a picture in a book Mary Lou had found: *Sea-shore Creatures of North America.*

There was a strong, briny, clean smell along the edge of the water, and the waves, gently rolling in along the wet sands, made a sound like I had never heard before. I stood there in the sun watching, and smelling the smell, and listening to the water-sound, until Belasco's voice called me back. "Time to go, Bentley. They'll have him fixed before long."

We all climbed silently up the stairs and went back to our positions in the fields and waited.

After a while the robots came back. They did not notice that we had made no progress in their absence. Stupid robots.

I bent to work, in time to music.

When I got to the seaward end of the row, I looked down at the beach. Our fire was still burning.

I realized that I have just written "*our* fire." How strange, that I should think of it as belonging to all of us—to us as a group!

As we were going back to the fields from the beach I walked beside the white-haired old man. I wanted, for a moment, to say something kind to him, to thank him for making my own sadness more bearable, or, even to put my arm around his frail-looking old shoulders. But I did none of these. I do not know how to do such things. I wish I knew how; I sincerely wish it. But I do not.

DAY NINETY-NINE

Alone in my cell at night I think a great deal. I think sometimes of the things I have read in books, or about my boyhood, or about my three blues as a professor in Ohio. Sometimes I think about that time when I first learned to read, over two yellows ago, when I found the box with the film and the flash cards and the little books with pictures. The words on the box said: "*Beginning Readers' Kit.*" They were the first printed words I had ever seen, and of course I could not read them. Whatever gave me the patience to persist until I learned to read words from a book?

If I had not learned to read in Ohio and then come to New York to try to become a professor of reading, I would not be in prison now. And I would not have met Mary Lou. I would not be filled with this sadness.

I think of her more than I think of any other thing. I see her trying not to look frightened, as Spofforth took her out the door of my room at the library. That was the last time I saw her. I do not know where Spofforth took her, or what has become of her. She is probably in a prison for women, but I'm not certain of that.

I tried to get Spofforth to tell me what would become of her, while we were riding in the thought bus to my hearing; but he would not answer me.

I have tried to draw a picture of her face on my sheets of drawing paper, using colored crayons. But it is no good; I was never able to draw.

Yellows and blues ago there was a boy in my dormitory who could draw beautifully. One time he put some of his drawings on my desk in a classroom and I looked at them with awe. There were pictures of birds and of cows and of people and trees and of the robot who monitored the hall outside the classroom. They were remarkable pictures, with clear lines and with amazing accuracy.

I did not know what to do with the pictures. Taking or giving private things to others was a terrible thing to do and could cause high punishment. So I left them on my desk and the next day they were gone. And a few days after that the boy who drew them was also gone. I do not know what became of him. Nobody spoke of him.

Will it be the same with Mary Lou? Is it all over, and will there be no mention of her in the world again?

Tonight I have taken four sopors. I do not want to remember so much.

DAY ONE HUNDRED FOUR

After supper this evening Belasco came to my cell! And he had a small gray-and-white animal in his arm.

I was sitting in my chair, thinking about Mary Lou and remembering the sound of her voice when she read aloud, when suddenly I saw my door come open. And there Belasco stood, grinning at me, with that animal under his arm.

"How . . . ?" I said.

He held a finger to his lips and then said softly, "None of the doors are locked tonight, Bentley. You might call it another malfunction." He pushed the door shut and then set the animal on the floor. It sat and looked at me with a kind of bored curiosity; then it began scratching its ear with a hind foot. It was something like a dog, but smaller.

"The doors are locked at night by a computer; but sometimes the computer forgets to lock them."

"Oh," I said, still watching the little animal. Then I said, "What is it?"

"What is what?" Belasco said.

"The animal."

He stared at me with great surprise. "You don't know what a *cat* is, Bentley?"

"I never saw one before."

He shook his head. Then he reached down and stroked the animal a few times. "This is a cat. It's a pet."

"A pet?" I said.

Belasco shook his head, grinning. "Boy! You don't know anything they don't teach in school, do you? A pet is an animal you keep for yourself. It's a friend."

Of course, I thought. Like Roberto and Consuela and their dog Biff, in the book I had learned to read from. Biff was the pet of Roberto and Consuela. And the book had said, "Roberto is Consuela's friend," and that was what a friend was. Somebody you were more than a person should be with anyone else. Apparently an animal could be a friend, too.

I wanted to bend down and touch the cat, but I was afraid to. "Does it have a name?"

"No," Belasco said. He walked over and sat on the edge of my bed, still speaking only barely above a whisper. "No. I just call it 'cat.'" He pulled a joint out of his shirt pocket and put it in his mouth. His blue prison jacket sleeves were rolled up and I could see that he had some kind of decorations that looked as if they were printed in blue ink on each of his forearms, just above the bracelets on his wrists. On his right arm was a heart and on his left the outline of a naked woman.

He lit the joint. "You can give the cat a name if you want to, Bentley."

"You mean I can just decide what to call it?"

"That's right." He passed me the joint and I took it quite casually—considering that I knew sharing was illegal—and drew a puff from it and passed it back.

Then, when I let the smoke out, I said, "All right. The cat's name will be Biff."

Belasco smiled. "Fine. The beast has been needing a name. Now it's got one." He looked down at the cat, who was walking slowly around, exploring the room. "Right, Biff?"

Bentley and Belasco and their cat Biff, I thought.

DAY ONE HUNDRED FIVE

The prison buildings are, I believe, the most ancient structures I have ever seen. There are five of them, built of large green-painted blocks of stone, with dirty windows with rusted bars on them. I have only been in two of the five buildings—the dormitory with the barred cells where I sleep, and the shoe factory building where I work in the mornings. I do not know what is in the other three buildings. One of them, which sits a bit apart from the others, seems to be even older than the rest, and its windows have been boarded up, like the summer house in *Angel on a String*, with Gloria Swanson. I have walked over to this building during the after-lunch exercise period and looked at it more closely. Its stones are covered with a smooth, wet moss, and its big metal doors are always locked.

Around all of the buildings is a very high double fence of thick wire mesh, once painted red but now faded to pink. There is a gateway in the fence through which we pass to work in the fields. There are four moron robot guards at this gateway at all times. As we pass through on our way to work they check the metal bands that are permanently fastened to our wrists before we are let through.

I was given a five-minute orientation lecture by the warden—a large, beefy Make Six—when I first was issued my uniforms. Among other things he explained that if a prisoner left without having his wristbands deactivated by the guards the bands would become like white-hot wires and would burn his hands off at the wrists if he did not return to within the gates immediately.

The bands are narrow and tight; they are made of an extremely hard, dull, silvery metal. I do not know how they were put on. They were around my wrists when I awoke in prison.

I think it is near to wintertime, because the air outside is cold. But the field around the plants is heated somehow, and the sun continues to shine. The ground is warm beneath my feet as I fertilize the obscene plants, and yet the air is cold on my body. And the stupid music never stops, never malfunctions, and the robots stare and stare. It is like a dream.

DAY ONE HUNDRED SIXTEEN

It has been eleven days since I have written anything about my life. I would have lost count of the days if I had not thought to make a crayon mark on the wall every evening after supper. The marks are under the huge TV screen that fills up most of the back wall of my cell, and which my chair, bolted to the floor, permanently faces. I can see the marks now when I raise my head from the paper on the drawing board in my lap; they look like a design of neat gray stripes on the wall, under the TV.

I am losing interest in writing. I feel, sometimes, that if I do not get my books back or see any more silent films I will forget how to read and will not want to write.

Belasco has not been back since the first night. I suppose it is because the computer has not forgotten to lock the doors after supper. After I make the mark on the wall I always check the door and it is always locked.

I do not think of Mary Lou all of the time, as I once did. I do not think of very much at all. I take my sopors and smoke my dope and watch erotic fantasies and death fantasies in life-sized three dimensions on the TV and go to sleep early.

The same shows are repeated every eight or nine days on the TV, or I can watch Self-improvement and Rehabilitation shows from a file of thirty recorded BB's that are issued to each prisoner at his orientation. But I do not play the BB's. I watch whatever is on. I am not interested in watching television *shows*; I only watch television.

This is enough writing. I am tired of it.

DAY ONE HUNDRED NINETEEN

There was a storm this afternoon, while we were at work out in the field. For a long time the robot guards seemed confused by the wind and the heavy rain and they did not call to us when we found ourselves standing at the edge of the cliff with rain blowing on our bodies, staring at the sky and the ocean. The sky would go quickly from gray to black and back to gray again. Lightning kept flashing in it almost constantly. And below us the ocean pounded and roared. Its waves would inundate the beach and slap heavily at the base of the cliff and then recede for only a moment before they would be back—dark, almost black, foaming, loud.

All of us watched, and no one tried to speak. The noise, of thunder and of the ocean, was deafening.

And then, as it began to quiet down a bit, we all turned and began to head back toward the dormitory. And as I was walking through the Protein 4 field and the rain, gentler now, was still hitting my face and my drenched clothing, I realized that I was cold and shivering and suddenly these words came into my mind:

> O Western wind, when wilt thou blow,
> That the small rain down can rain?
> Christ! That my love were in my arms
> And I in my bed again!

And I fell down on my knees in the field and wept, dumbly, for Mary Lou and for the life that I had, for a time, lived, when my mind and my imagination were, so briefly, alive.

There were no guards near. Belasco came back for me. He

helped me up silently and, with his arm around me, helped me back into the dormitory. We did not speak to each other until I was at the open door of my cell. Then he took his arm away from me and looked me in the face. His eyes were grave, and reassuring. "Hell, Bentley," he said, "I think I know how you feel." Then he slapped me gently on the shoulder and turned and walked to his cell.

I stood leaning against the cold steel bars and watched the other prisoners, their hair wet and their clothing drenched, walk back to their cells. I wanted to put my arm around each of them. Whether I knew their names or not, they were, all of them, my *friends*.

DAY ONE HUNDRED TWENTY-ONE

I got into the boarded-up building today.

It was simple. I was out in the gravel yard between buildings during the exercise period after lunch. I saw two robot guards walk up the steps to the building, unlock the door, and go inside. After a few moments they came out, each carrying a box of the kind our toilet paper comes in. They carried their boxes over toward the dormitory building. The door stayed open. I went in.

Inside, the floors were of Permoplastic. The walls were of some other material, filthy and crumbling, and there was very little light since the windows were boarded up. I walked quickly through dark hallways, opening doors.

Some of the rooms were empty; others had things like soap and paper towels and toilet paper and food trays, stacked up on shelves. I took a stack of paper towels, for this journal. And then I saw a dim and faded sign over a pair of double doors at the end of a hall. It was the only other sign with writing I had ever seen except for the ones in the basement of the library in New York.

I could not make out the words at first; they were faded and covered with dirt. And the hallway was dark. But when I got up close and looked carefully I made them out: EAST WING LIBRARY.

I almost jumped at the word "Library." I just stood there, staring at the sign, and felt my heart pounding.

And then I tried the doors and found that they were locked. I pulled and pushed and tried to twist the knobs, but I could not make anything budge. It was horrible.

I became overwhelmed with anger and beat my fists against the door. But it did not move and I only hurt myself.

I slipped out of the building after I heard the guards return and go into one of the storage rooms.

I must get inside that library! I must have books again. If I cannot read and learn and have things that are worth thinking about, I would rather immolate myself than go on living.

Synthetic gasoline is used in the harvesting machines. I know that I could get some and burn myself.

I will stop writing now and watch TV.

DAY ONE HUNDRED THIRTY-TWO

For eleven days I have been despondent. In the afternoons I have not bothered to go to look at the ocean when I get to the end of my row, and I have not tried to write in the evenings. My mind is as blank as I can make it while I work— I concentrate only on the thick, rancid smell of the Protein 4 plants.

The guards say nothing, but I still hate them. It is all I really feel. Their thick, slow bodies and their slack faces are like the synthetic, rubbery plants I feed. They are—the phrase is from *Intolerance*—an abomination in my sight.

If I take four or five sopors it is not unpleasant to watch TV. My TV wall is a good one, and it always works.

My body no longer hurts. It is strong now, and my muscles are firm and hard. I am suntanned, and my eyes are clear. There are tough calluses on my hands and on the soles of my feet, and I work well and have not been beaten again. But the sadness in my heart has come back. It has come to me slowly, a day at a time, and I am more despairing than during my first days in prison. Everything seems hopeless.

Days pass, sometimes, without my thinking of Mary Lou. Hopeless.

DAY ONE HUNDRED THIRTY-THREE

I have seen where the synthetic gasoline is kept. It is in the computer shed at the edge of the field.

All prisoners have electronic cigarette lighters, for smoking marijuana.

DAY ONE HUNDRED THIRTY-SIX

Last night Belasco came to my cell again, and at first I did not want to see him. When I found the door to my cell was unlocked I became nervous. I did not want to leave, and I did not want anyone coming in.

But he walked in anyway and said, "Good to see you, Bentley."

I just looked at the floor at my feet. My TV was off, and I had been sitting like that for hours, on the edge of my bed.

He was silent for a while and I heard him seat himself in

my chair, but I still did not look up. I did not feel that I could even raise my head.

Finally he spoke again, softly. "I seen you in the fields the last few days, Bentley. You been looking like a robot." His voice was sympathetic, soothing.

I made myself speak. "I suppose so," I said.

We were quiet again. Then he said, "I know how it is, Bentley. You get to thinking about dying. Like they do in the cities, with gas and a lighter. Or here we got the ocean. I seen guys go out all the way. Hell, I used to think about it myself: just swim as far as I can and not look back . . ."

I looked up at him. "*You* felt like that?" I was astonished. "You seem so strong."

He laughed wryly and I looked up toward his face. "Shit," he said, "I'm like everybody else. This kind of living ain't much better than being dead." He laughed again, shaking his head from side to side. "And it ain't much better on the outside, to tell the truth. No real work to do, except the same kind of crap you do in here. At the Worker Dormitories they told us, 'Labor fulfills.' Horseshit." He took a joint from his pocket and lit it. "I was stealing credit cards the first blue after I graduated. Been in prison half my life. Wanted to die the first two or three stretches, but I didn't. Nowadays I got my cats, and I sneak around a little . . ." Then he interrupted himself. "Hey!" he said. "You want to have Biff?"

I stared at him. "For my own . . . pet?"

"Sure. Why not? I got four more. Pain in the ass to find food for sometimes, though. But I can teach you how."

"Thank you," I said. "I'd like that. I'd like to have a cat."

"We can go get her now," he said.

And I found myself leaving my cell easily. As we went

out the unlocked door I turned to Belasco and said, "I feel better."

He slapped me lightly on the back. "What are friends for?" he said.

I stood there a moment, not knowing what to say. And then, almost without thinking of the gesture, I reached out and put my hand on his forearm. And I thought of something. "There's a building I want to get in. Do you think it might be unlocked?"

He grinned at me. "That's more like it," he said. And then, "Let's go see."

We left the building. It was simple and there were no guards in sight.

We got into the deserted building with no trouble, but inside it was too dark to see, and we stumbled over boxes in the hallways. Then I heard Belasco say, "Sometimes these old places have a switch on the wall," and I heard him fumbling, heard him trip and curse, and then there was a *click* and a big overhead light came on in the hallway. For a moment I was frightened that the guards might see the light, but then I remembered the boarded-up windows and was relieved.

But when I found the library door it was still locked! I was tense enough already, and I could have screamed.

Belasco looked at me. "Is that where you want to go?"

I said, "Yes." Without even asking me what I wanted to get in the room for, he began to examine the lock. It was of a kind I had never seen before, and didn't even appear to be electronic.

Belasco whistled quietly. "Wow!" he said. "This bastard is *old.*" He began feeling in his pockets until he found his prison-issued lighter. Then he put it on the floor and stamped on it two or three times with his heel, until it was broken. He reached down, picked up the mess of wires and glass and plastic, and, after studying it a moment, pulled out a piece of stiff wire about as long as my thumb. I watched him silently, having no idea what he was doing this for.

He bent to the lock on the door carefully, placed the end of his wire into a slot in it, and began probing around. Every now and then a little clicking sound came from inside the lock somewhere. He cursed a couple of times, quietly, and continued. And then, just as I was about to ask him what he was trying to do, there was a softer sound inside the lock and Belasco grinned, took the doorknob in his hand, and opened the door!

It was dark inside, but Belasco found a switch on the wall again and two somewhat dim overhead lights came on.

I looked around me eagerly, hoping to find the walls lined with books. But they were empty. I stared for a long time, feeling almost sick. There were ancient wooden tables and chairs, and a few small boxes along one wall, but there were no shelves and the pock-marked walls were empty even of pictures.

"What's the problem?" Belasco said.

I looked at him. "I was hoping to find . . . books."

"Books?" He apparently didn't know the word. But he said, "What's in those boxes over there?"

I nodded, without much hope, and went over to look at the boxes by the wall. The first two I opened were filled with rusty spoons—so badly rusted that they were all frozen together in a reddish mass. But the third box was filled with books! I began taking them out eagerly. There were twelve of them. And at the bottom of the box was a pile of sheets of blank paper that was hardly yellow at all.

Excitedly I began to read the titles. The biggest was called *North Carolina Revised Statutes: 1992.* Another was called *Woodworking for Fun and Profit* and a third, also very thick, was called *Gone With the Wind*. It felt wonderful just to hold them and think of all the writing inside.

Belasco had been watching me with mild curiosity. Finally he spoke. "Are those things books?" he said.

"Yes."

He picked one up from the box and ran his finger through the dust on the cover. "Never heard of such a thing," he said.

I looked at him. "Let's get the cat and get these back to my cell."

"Sure," he said. "I'll help you."

We got Biff and carried the books back without any trouble at all.

It is very late now and Belasco has gone back to his cell. I will stop writing now and look through my books. I have them hidden between my water bed and the wall, near where Biff is sleeping.

DAY ONE HUNDRED THIRTY-NINE

I am very tired because I read almost all night last night and had to work all day today. But what excitement I have found! My tired mind was busy all day, with all of the new things I had to think about.

I think I will make a list of my new books:

North Carolina Revised Statutes: 1992
Woodworking for Fun and Profit
Gone With the Wind
Holy Bible
Audel's Robot Maintenance and Repair Guide
A Dictionary of the English Language
The Causes of Population Decline

Europe in the 18th and 19th Centuries
A Backpacker's Guide to the Carolina Coast
A Short History of the United States
Cooking Shore Dinners: Let's Have a Party!
The Causes of the Decline

I have been reading the history books, going from one to the other and to the dictionary to find the meaning of new words. The dictionary is a pleasure to use, now that I know the alphabet.

There is much in the history books that I do not understand, and it is hard for me to accept the idea that there have been so many people in the world. In the history that is about Europe there are pictures of Paris and Berlin and London, and the size of the buildings and the number of people are staggering.

Sometimes Biff jumps up into my lap while I am reading and goes to sleep there. I like that.

DAY ONE HUNDRED FORTY-NINE

For ten days now I have spent every moment that I can in reading. No one has bothered me; the guards either do not care or, more likely, their programming does not take into account the phenomenon. I even take a book to social time with me and no one seems to notice that I am reading it during the films.

My blue prison jacket—already a bit faded—has large pockets and I always carry one of my smaller books in it. *A Short History of the United States* and *The Causes of Population Decline* are both small, and they fit very comfortably. I read during my five-minute breaks at the shoe factory.

The first sentence of *The Causes of Population Decline* says: "In the first thirty years of the twenty-first century the population of the earth declined by one-half, and it is still declining." To read things like this, that consider the nature of all of human life, and at far-off times, fascinates me for reasons that I do not understand.

I do not know how long ago the twenty-first century was, although I understand that it is more recent than the eighteenth and nineteenth centuries that my history book is about. But I was never taught about "centuries" in the dormitory; I only know the meaning of the word from the dictionary: it divides up human history into groups of one hundred years—of two hundred yellows.

The twenty-first century must have been a long time ago. For one thing, there are no mentions of robots in the book.

Audel's Robot Maintenance and Repair Guide has the date 2135 on it, and I know from reading history that the date is from the twenty-second century.

Holy Bible begins: "In the beginning, God created the heavens and the earth." It does not give the century of the "beginning," nor is it clear who "God" is, or was. I am not certain whether *Holy Bible* is a book of history or maintenance or poetry. It names many strange people who do not seem real.

The robots in the Audel's book are shown in pictures and diagrams. They are all of a very simple kind made for elementary chores like fieldwork and record keeping.

Gone With the Wind resembles some of the films I know. It is, I think, a made-up story. It is about some silly people in big houses, and about a war. I don't think I will ever finish it, since it is very long.

Many of the other books make no sense at all to me. Still, they seem to fit into some larger, only dimly clear, pattern.

What I like most is the strange sensation I get in the little hairs at the back of my neck when I read certain sentences. And, oddly enough, there are sentences that are often quite unclear to me, or that make me sad. I still remember this one from my days in New York:

> My life is light, waiting for the death wind,
> Like a feather on the back of my hand.

I will stop writing now, and go back to reading. My life is very strange.

DAY ONE HUNDRED SIXTY-NINE

I read continuously, and take no sopors and smoke no marijuana. I read until I can stay awake no longer and fall in bed and lie there with my mind whirling and with faces and people and ideas from the past crowding and confusing me until, exhausted, I fall asleep.

And I am learning new words. Thirty or forty a day.

Long before robots and Privacy, mankind had a violent and astonishing history. I hardly know how to think or feel about some of the dead people I have read of, and of the great events. There is the Russian Revolution and the French Revolution and the Great Flood of Fire and World War III and the Denver Incident. I was taught as a child that all things before the Second Age were violent and destructive because of a failure to respect individual rights; but it was never more specific than that. We had never developed a sense of history as such; all we knew, if we ever thought about it, was that there had been others before us and that we were better than they. But no one was ever encouraged to *think* about anything outside of himself. "Don't ask; relax."

I am amazed to think of the number of people who must have screamed and died on battlefields in order to fulfill the ambitions of presidents and emperors. Or of the aggregation into the hands of some large groups of people, like the United States of America, great reserves of wealth and power, denied to most others.

And yet, despite all this, there seemed to have been good and kind men and women. And many of them happy.

DAY ONE HUNDRED SEVENTY-TWO

The back part of *Holy Bible* is about Jesus Christ. Some sentences in it have been underlined by a former reader.

Jesus Christ died violently when he was still young, but before he died he said and did a great many striking things. He cured many sick people and talked strangely to many others. Some of the underlined sayings resemble what I was taught in my Piety classes. "The kingdom of God is within you," for example, sounds much like our being taught to seek fulfillment only inwardly, through drugs and Privacy. But others of his sayings are quite different. "Ye must love one another" is one of these. Another one that is very strong is: "I am the way and the truth and the life." And another: "Come unto me all ye who are heavy laden and I will give you rest."

If someone should come to me and say, "I am the way and the truth and the life," I would want with all my strength to believe him. I want those things: a way, the truth, and life.

As well as I understand it, Jesus claimed to be the son of God, the one who was supposed to have made heaven and earth. That perplexes me and makes me feel that Jesus was unreliable. Still, he seems to have known things that others did not know and was not a silly person, like those in *Gone With the Wind*, or a murderously ambitious one, like the American presidents.

Whatever Jesus was, he was a thing called a "great man." I am not certain I like the idea of "great men", it makes me uncomfortable. "Great men" often have had very bloody plans for mankind.

I think my writing is improving. I know more words, and the making of sentences comes more easily.

DAY ONE HUNDRED SEVENTY-SEVEN

I have read all of my books, except for *Gone With the Wind* and *The Art of the Dance*, and I want more. Five nights ago the doors were unlocked again and Belasco and I went back to the abandoned building and searched it thoroughly, but we found no more books.

I must have more to read! When I think of all those books in the basement of the library in New York I hunger to be back there.

In New York I saw some films that showed prison escapes. And in those prisons the guards were human and vigilant, while here ours are only moron robots.

But there are these metal bracelets that cannot be deactivated for more than a half day at a time. And how would I get to New York if I escaped?

In the *Backpacking* book there is a map of what is called the Eastern Seaboard; North and South Carolina are on this map, and so is New York. If I walked along the beach, keeping the ocean on my right, I would come to New York. But I have no idea how far it is.

Cooking Shore Dinners tells about finding clams and other

things to eat on beaches. I could feed myself that way, if I escaped.

And I could copy this journal, in smaller writing, on the thin paper I found with the box of books and carry it with me in my pocket. But I could not carry all the books.

And there is no way to remove the bracelets. Unless there is something that would cut them.

DAY ONE HUNDRED SEVENTY-EIGHT

In the shoe factory there is a very large machine that cuts the sheets of plastic that the shoes are made from. It has a shining blade of adamant steel that cuts through about twenty sheets of tough plastic at a single stroke. There is a robot guard by the machine, and no human worker is supposed to go near it. But I have noticed that at times the guard seems dormant; he may be a nearly senile robot that has been assigned to the simple task of standing by a machine.

If, when I saw him looking dormant, I went to the machine and held my hands in exactly the right spot, the knife might be able to cut my bracelets.

If I made a mistake it would cut my hands off. Or it might not be able to cut through the metal and the blade would catch on it and twist my arms out of their sockets.

It is too frightening. I will stop thinking about it.

DAY ONE HUNDRED EIGHTY

The Causes of Population Decline says this interesting thing about the number of people in the world:

The reduction of the planet's inhabitants has been accounted for in a diverse and conflicting number of ways by contemporary demography. The most persuasive of these accounts usually suggest one or more of the following factors:

1. fears of overpopulation
2. the perfection of sterilization techniques
3. the disappearance of the family
4. the widespread concern with "inner" experiences
5. a loss of interest in children
6. a widespread desire to avoid responsibilities

The book then analyzes each of these things.

But nowhere does it speak of a possibility that there might be *no children at all*. And that, I think, is the way the world has come to be. I do not think there are any more children.

After we all die, there may be no others.

I do not know whether that is bad or good.

Yet I think it would be in many ways a good thing to be the father of a child, and to have Mary Lou be the mother. And I would like to live with her, and for us to be a family—despite the great risks to my Individuality.

What is my Individuality good for, anyway? And is it truly holy, or was I only taught that because the robots who taught me were programmed by someone, once, to say it?

DAY ONE HUNDRED EIGHTY-FOUR

Today the Protein 4 plants were harvested. When we went out in the field to work there were two huge yellow machines already there, noisily moving down the rows like giant thought buses, throwing up clouds of dust and scooping up the ripened plants twenty or thirty at a time and feeding them into hoppers, where I supposed they would be pulverized, to be made into soybars and synthetic protein flakes.

We kept our distance from the field because of the smell, which was far worse even than usual, and watched the machines in silence for a while.

Finally someone spoke. It was Belasco, and he said grimly, "There goes another season's work, boys."

Nobody said anything else. *Another season's work.* I looked around and behind me, looking at things closely for the first time in weeks. The trees on the hills beyond the prison buildings had all lost their leaves. The air was cold on my skin. I felt a tingling, thinking of the feeling of my skin, looking up at the pale blueness of the sky. At the edge of the hills a great crowd of birds was flying, wheeling, and turning in unison.

And I decided then that I must escape from this prison.

SPOFFORTH

Her face was not pretty, but it held his frightened gaze as it always did. She stood on the wet mud at the edge of the pond, as tall as he, her white feet not even sinking into it, her face puzzled and her arms tense, shaking slightly beneath her long robe as she held the thing out to him. What it was he could never tell, no matter how hard he tried to see it across the four or five feet that separated them. He stared and stared at what she was holding out to him and then, sadly, defeated, looked down. The mud was over his own white ankles, and he could not move. Nor, he felt, could she. He looked up again at her, still holding out the thing that would not focus for his eyes, and he tried to speak to her, to ask her what she wanted to give him, but he could not speak. He became more frightened. And he awoke.

Deep, deep he had known it was a dream. He always seemed to know. And afterward, sitting on the edge of his narrow bed in the apartment, he thought of the woman in the dream, as he always did afterward, and then he thought of the girl with the black hair and the red coat. He had never, in his long, long life, dreamed of her; it was always the woman in the robe—his secondhand dream, taken by accident from a life he had not lived and knew almost nothing of.

He had seen a few real women who looked something like her. Mary Borne was one of these, with her bright, strong eyes and her solid way of standing, although she was much stronger-looking, much more poised than the woman in the dream.

For years he had felt that if he could find a woman like her and live with that woman he might find a key to the other life that the consciousness he bore had lived—the life of whoever had been copied to make his brain. And now he was doing it. But he had found no key.

The dream, which happened every eight or ten days, was always disturbing, and he never became entirely accustomed to the fright he felt during it; but he accepted it as a part of his life. Sometimes there were other dreams, with subject matter from his own memory. And there were others that used subject matter he did not recognize—some involving the catching of fish, and some a battered upright piano.

He got off the bed and walked heavily to the window and looked out at the early morning. Distant and clear in the pale dawn it stood, higher than anything else outside: the Empire State Building, the high grave marker for the city of New York.

BENTLEY

I had no trouble finding Belasco's cell. I had watched him go there to get Biff for me, and I found it easily. When I pushed open the unlocked door and went in, Belasco was lying on his bunk, petting an orange cat. His TV was not on. There were three other cats asleep in a sort of pile in the corner. Photographs of naked women covered one wall, and on the others were pictures of trees and fields and of the ocean.

There was an armchair covered in pale green cloth, and a floor lamp—both of them gotten in some illegal way, I'm certain. Had Belasco known how to read he would have had a better place for it than I.

I did not sit down. I was too agitated.

When Belasco looked up at me he seemed surprised. "What you doing out of your cell, Bentley?" he said.

"They were open again." I ignored Mandatory Politeness and looked directly at his face. "I wanted to see you."

He sat up on his bed and gently dropped the cat to the floor.

It stretched and then joined the others in the corner. "You look worried," he said.

I kept looking at him. "I'm frightened, I have decided to escape."

He looked at me, started to say something, and then didn't. Finally he said, "How?"

"That big knife blade in the shoe factory. I think I can cut these off with it." I held my bracelets out toward him.

He shook his head and whistled softly. "Jesus! What if you miss?"

"I have to leave this place. Do you want to go with me?"

He looked at me for a long while. Then he said, "No." He pushed himself further upright in his bed. "Being on the outside doesn't mean that much to me. Not anymore. And I wouldn't have the guts to hold my hands under that knife." He began fumbling in his shirt pocket for a marijuana cigarette. "Are you sure you have?"

I let my breath out with a sigh, and then sat in the armchair and stared for a while at the manacles on my wrists. They were a little looser than when they were new; I had become leaner and harder from the work in the fields. "I don't know. I won't know until I try."

He lighted the joint and nodded. "If you do get out, what'll you eat? This place is far from any civilization."

"I can find clams along the beach. And maybe fields with things growing that I can eat . . ."

"Come *on*, Bentley. You can't live that way. What if you don't find any clams? And this is *winter*. You'd better wait till spring."

I looked at him. What he said made sense. But I knew, too, that I could not wait until spring. "No," I said. "I'll leave tomorrow."

He shook his head at me. "Okay. Okay." Then he got out of the bed, leaned down, pulled back the bedcover, and reached under. He slid out a large cardboard box and opened it. Inside were packages of cookies and bread, and soybars, all wrapped in clear plastic. "Take what you can carry of this."

"I don't want to . . ."

"*Take* it," he said. "I can get more." And then, "You'll need something to carry it with." He thought for a moment and then went to the door of his cell and shouted, "Larsen! Come here!" and a moment later a short man whom I recognized from the Protein 4 fields came walking up. "Larsen," Belasco said, "I need a backpack."

Larsen looked at him a minute. "That's a lot of work." he said. "A lot of stitchin." And you gotta get the canvas, and tubes for the frame . . ."

"You've already got one in your cell, the one you made out of a pair of pants. I saw it when we had that poker game, that time when all the robots were malfunctioning."

"Hell," Larsen said. "I can't let you have that one. That's for my escape."

"Horseshit," Belasco said. "You ain't going nowhere. That poker game was three or four yellows ago. And how are you going to get your bracelets off? With your teeth?"

"I could use a file . . ."

"That's horseshit too," Belasco said. "They may run this prison dumb, but they ain't that dumb. There ain't no hand tools hard enough to cut them bracelets, and you know it."

"Then how are you getting out?"

"Not me. Bentley here." Belasco reached out and put his hand on my shoulder. "He's gonna try using the big knife in the shoe factory."

Larsen stared at me. "*That's* a damn fool thing to do."

"It's his business, Larsen," Belasco said. "Can you let him have the backpack?"

Larsen thought a moment. Then he said, "What do I get for it?"

"Two of my pictures from the wall. Any two you pick."

Larsen looked at him narrowly. "And a cat?"

Belasco frowned. "Shit." Then, "Okay. The black one."

"The orange," Larsen said.

Belasco shook his head wearily. "Get the backpack," he said.

And he got it, and Belasco filled it with food for me and showed me how I could carry Biff in it if I needed to.

Without sopors, I did not sleep that night. I did not want the aftereffects of sopors when I went to the shoe factory in the morning. I was tormented by thoughts of what I planned to do: not only to risk grave injury under the knife but to face a life of bare survival, in winter, with no knowledge of the places I would be traveling through and with no training for the difficulties except for one thin book about shore dinners. Nothing in my education—my stupid, life-hating education—had prepared me for what I was about to do.

A part of me kept saying that I should wait. Wait until spring, wait until they told me my sentence was over. Life in prison wasn't really any worse than life in a Thinker Dormitory, and if I learned to be like Belasco I could make an easy life for myself here. There really was almost no discipline, once you learned how to avoid being beaten by the guards, just by keeping an eye out for them. Obviously, once the device of the metal bracelets had been invented, everything about running a prison had gone slack, as with so much else. There was plenty of dope, and I was used to the food and the labor. And there was TV, and Biff, my cat . . .

But that was only part of me. There was another, deeper part that said, "You must leave this place." And I knew, knew even to my terror, that I had to listen to that voice.

My old programming would say, "When in doubt, forget it." But I had to quiet that voice, too. Because it was *wrong*. If I was to continue to live a life that was worth the trouble of living it, I had to leave.

Whenever I would see that huge knife in my imagination, on the cold and empty beaches, I would think of Mary Lou throwing the rock into the python's cage. It made the night alone in my cell bearable.

In the morning I wore the backpack to breakfast and ate my protein flakes and black bread while wearing it. None of the guards even seemed to notice.

When I finished my breakfast I looked up to see Belasco walking over toward my little table. We were not supposed to speak at meals, but he said, "Here, Bentley. Eat this on the way to the factory," and he handed me his chunk of bread—which was far larger than mine had been. A guard shouted, "Invasion of Privacy!" from across the room, but I ignored him.

"Thanks," I said. Then I held out my hand, as men did in films. "Goodbye, Belasco," I said.

He understood the gesture, and took my hand firmly, looking me in the face. "Goodbye, Bentley," he said. "I think you're doing the right thing."

I nodded, squeezed his hand hard, and then turned and walked away.

When I filed into the doorway with the rest of my shift the

knife was already in operation. I stopped and let the others walk in past me and stared at it for a minute. It looked overwhelming to me and my stomach seemed to clamp tight inside me and my hands began to tremble, from just looking at it.

It was about the length of a man's leg, and broader. The metal was adamant steel, silvery gray, with a curved edge that was so sharp it hardly made any sound as it cleaved like a guillotine through twenty layers of thick polymeric shoe material. The material was fed to it on a conveyor belt, and held in position on a kind of anvil under the blade by a set of metal hands; they would hold a stack of material under the blade and the blade would drop from a height of five feet and shear noiselessly into the stack and then pull back up again. I could see light glitter on the edge of the blade when it was at its high point, and I thought of what would happen if it touched my wrists. And how could I be certain where to place them? And if I succeeded with one arm, I still would have to do the other. It was impossible. Standing there, I felt it wash over me like a wave: *I'll bleed to death. The blood will jet from my wrists like a fountain . . .*

And then I said aloud, "So what? I have nothing to lose."

I pushed myself through the other men who were taking up their positions on the assembly line and walked up to the machine. The only robot in the room was the one presiding over the blade, with his arms folded across his heavy chest and his eyes vacant. I walked up beside him. He shifted his eyes toward me but remained motionless, saying nothing.

The blade came down, glittering, with horrible speed. I stood there watching it, transfixed. This time I could hear the soft hiss of its slicing edge. I put my hands in my pockets to stop them from trembling.

I looked down at the belt, where the automatic hands were pushing the cut material into a hopper to be sent back for further cuts. And I saw something that made my heart beat even faster: there was a thin, dark line on the anvil where the edge of the blade had been touching it, probably for blues and yellows. It showed exactly where the blade would come down!

And then I thought of how I might do it. And without stopping to consider, to let myself think and become even more frightened, I went ahead.

When the next stack had been cut and before the hands could push it off the anvil, I reached out and took a handful of the half-pieces, keeping their freshly cut edges still lined up. The hand removed the others, and a fresh uncut stack was brought into position. There would be a few moments' hesitation before the knife came down. Not letting myself look up at or think about the blade, I pushed the new material onto the floor.

Immediately I saw, out of the edge of my vision, the robot by me move. He unfolded his arms. I ignored him and placed the stack of already cut pieces so that their straight new edges were exactly flush with the thin line on the anvil. Then I took the wire hook I had made, hooked it through the bracelet on my left hand, made a fist, and *then* looked up. The blade was poised above me, unmoving. Its edge, from directly beneath it, was like a perfect hairline under the thickness and heaviness of its heft.

I forced myself not to shudder and not to think. As fast as I could, I put my knuckles down on the belt about an inch from the thin line, pulled the bracelet with the hook with my right hand, steadying my right hand on the stack of material. There was a space of a half inch there, as I pulled the arm against the force of the hook, between the back of my wrist and the metal of the bracelet. I was holding my head back, away from the blade. My body felt like stone.

And then the robot shouted in my ear, "*Violation! Viola-tion!*" But I did not move.

And the blade came down, fanning my face, came down like a destroying angel, like a bullet. And I screamed out in pain.

I had closed my eyes. I forced them open. There was no blood! And a piece of the bracelet lay, severed, on the belt in front of me. Already the computer-controlled hands were pushing it into the bin. The robot was still shouting. I looked at him and said, "Bug off, robot."

He stared, unmoving, his hands now at his sides.

I looked at my left wrist. The metal of the bracelet, with a gap in it now, was twisted into the flesh. With my right hand I loosened it, ignoring the now-staring robot, and flexed my wrist. It hurt, but nothing was broken. Then I slipped one cut edge of the bracelet under the near edge of the anvil away from the blade and, using the hook, pulled up on the other side, and the bracelet, slowly, opened up until I could remove my hand. As I did so the blade came down again, missing me by about a foot.

I took a breath and then transferred the hook to the bracelet on my right hand.

I waited until another stack of material appeared and was cut and then took another handful as I had before. As I reached out to place my right fist on the belt I felt a hand clamp on my arm with a powerful grip. It was the robot.

Immediately, without thinking, I lowered my head and butted him in the chest as hard as I could, loosening his grip and pushing him back up against the belt. He doubled over forward. I pulled back and kicked him in the stomach. I was wearing my heavy prison boots and I kicked as hard as I could, with all of the strength a season's work in the Protein 4 fields had given my legs. He made no sound, but fell heavily to the floor. But immediately he was struggling to get up.

I turned my back on him and I looked up. The blade was just returning to its top, waiting position. Behind me I heard men's voices, and then the robot shouting again, "Violation! Violation!"

Not looking away, I held my right wrist under the blade, keeping my head well back, trying not to think of what would happen if the robot got to me and grabbed my arm just as the blade was coming down.

The wait seemed to last forever.

And then it happened. There was the glitter of adamant steel and the sudden fanning. And the pain. And just before I screamed again I heard a sound like the sound of a dry stick breaking.

I opened my eyes and looked down. The bracelet was cut, but my hand was bent strangely and I knew instantly what had happened. I had broken my wrist.

Yet, realizing that, I felt no further pain. There was a ringing in my ears, and I could remember the pain of the impact; but now there was no more pain. And my mind was clear—as clear as it has ever been.

And then I thought of the robot and looked over to where I had knocked him.

He was still on the floor. Larsen and the old man with white hair were sitting on him. And Belasco was standing over him holding a heavy wrench in one hand and my cat, Biff, in his other.

I stared.

"Here," Belasco said, grinning, "you forgot your cat."

Using the hook, I got the other bracelet off and put it in my pocket. Then I walked over to Belasco, and took Biff in my good hand.

"Do you know what a sling is?" Belasco said. After I took Biff, he began taking off his shirt, transferring the wrench from hand to hand, and keeping his eye on the now still robot.

"A sling?" I said.

"Just wait." He got the shirt off and then tore it in two. He tied a knot between sleeve and tail and put it around my neck, just above the backpack harness, and then showed me how to put my right arm in the broader part of the shirt. "After you get a little distance," he said, "soak your wrist in ocean water. Do it every now and then." He gripped my shoulder. "You're a brave son of a bitch," he said.

"Thank you," I said. "Thank you."

"Haul ass, Bentley," Belasco said.

And I did.

After I had run and walked for several miles north of the prison, keeping the ocean on my right, the pain began in earnest in my wrist. I stopped and put down Biff, who had clawed at me a few times and scratched, and meowed loudly, and finally gotten quiet. Then I lay down at the edge of the water, on my back, with my chest heaving painfully from the running, and from everything else, and I let my damaged wrist lie in the shallow and cold winter surf. Some of the water came up and lapped against my side. Biff began to meow plaintively. I said and did nothing and lay there as the tide came closer in and washed icily across me, making me finally get up and away from it. I had not lost the pain, although the cold water muted it. And I had not lost my fear of the journey ahead of me. But despite that there was jubilation in my heart. I was a free man.

For the first time in my entire life, I was a free man.

I went to the water's edge and, using my left hand, raised a handful of water to my mouth and drank it. And my throat constricted on it, gagged, and I spit the rest out. I did not know sea water was undrinkable. No one had ever told me.

Something in me suddenly gave way and I let myself fall to the beach and lie there, in pain and in thirst, crying. It was too much. It was all too much.

I lay there on the cold wet sand with a bitter wind blowing across me, with my whole right arm throbbing in pain and with my throat burning from the sea salt, not knowing where to find water. I did not know even where to begin looking for water, or how, really, to find clams, or any food, once the supply I had in my small backpack was eaten.

But then I sat up suddenly. There was something to drink. Belasco had given me three cans of liquid protein.

I took the backpack off, opened it where Larsen had sewn buttons on its top, and found a can and opened it carefully. And I drank only a few swallows of it, gave some to Biff, and then plugged the hole in the top of the can with my handkerchief. Some of my good feeling came back. I had enough to drink for a few days; I would find water somehow. I got up and began walking northward, with Biff keeping more or less at my side, or ahead of me or behind. The sand near the water's edge was easy to walk on and I kept up a brisk pace, swinging my good arm at my side.

After a while the sun came out from behind clouds. And

sandpipers appeared on the beach, and gulls began flying overhead, and there was the good, clean smell of the ocean in the
air. My arm was not uncomfortable in the sling and, although
it still hurt greatly when I allowed myself to think about it,
I know I could stand it. I had felt worse my first few days in
prison, and I had survived that—had, in fact, become stronger
for it. I would survive this.

That night I slept on the sand beside an old log that lay half
buried at the place where the beach began to have grass growing on it. I built myself a fire with a few sticks of driftwood,
lighting it with my prison lighter the way I had seen Belasco do
it that time that seemed so long before. I sat by the fire, leaning
against the log for a while, and held Biff in my lap, until the
sky became dark and the stars came out, very brightly, above us.
Then I lay down in the sand in my blue prison sweater, covering myself with my jacket, and fell soundly asleep.

I awoke at dawn. The fire was out and my body was cold and
stiff and my wrist throbbed painfully. The other wrist was sore
and stiff where the bracelet had been twisted on it. But I was
deeply rested from the long sleep, despite the pain in my body.
And I was not afraid.

Biff was curled against me. She woke when I did.

And I did find clams, for breakfast! I had no rake of the kind
the book showed in its pictures, but I used a long stick and
searched the beach for the little bubbles in the wet sand where
their necks stick up. I lost seven or eight before I learned to be
fast enough to flip one out of the hard-packed sand before it
burrowed in deeper. But I got four of them—all big ones.

For a while it seemed as if opening them was impossible.
I got the book out of my pocket—*Cooking Shore Dinners:
Let's Have a Party!*—and looked at the instructions, but they

weren't much help. They showed a special knife being used to "whisk the little fellow from his hiding place," as the book put it. But I had no knife. There were no sharp knives in the prison. But then I thought of something. I had put the two pieces of the second bracelet into my pocket after I got it off. I reached into my pocket, got out the larger piece of the metal, and, while Biff watched with only slight interest, used the sharp end that had been cut by the blade to pry open my first clam. It took a while, and I almost cut myself several times, but I managed it!

I ate the clam raw. I had never tasted anything like that before. It was delicious. And it was food and drink also; there was a good deal of drinkable liquid in each clam.

That day I walked a great many miles up the coast, still a bit apprehensive about being pursued. But I saw and heard no sign of anyone following me. Nor did I see any sign of human habitation. The weather was cold, and for a while in the afternoon a light snow fell; but my prison clothes were warm enough and I was not seriously bothered by it. I found more clams for lunch, and ate half a soybar with them and drank some more of the liquid protein. Biff took easily to eating clams, lapping and biting them out of their shells with great enthusiasm. I soon became proficient at finding and opening them.

From time to time I would go inland for some distance and try to find some high ground and look around me for fresh water—a lake, river, or irrigation ditch—but I saw none. I knew I would eventually need more than the clams and the liquid protein.

It was like that for days; I lost count of them. Gradually my wrist became better, and one night by my fire I tried an experiment that worked and that made me feel much more confident about the future. There happened to be a sizable patch of ice and frozen snow trapped under a rocky ledge a short distance from the beach. I had a metal prison bowl in my backpack, brought along for cooking my shore dinners in; and I went to the patch of ice and, using my broken bracelet, chipped some into the bowl. Then I built a small fire, let it burn down, and set the bowl on the hot coals. When the ice melted I found that I could drink it! And I did, letting Biff have some of it. Then I added a few sticks to my fire, put more ice in the bowl to melt, and dug a double handful of clams while it did so. Then I added the clams to the now-boiling water and after a few minutes I had a delicious hot clam stew.

I survived that way for a month, finding what shelter I could to sleep by, and eating the food Belasco had given me a little at a time. But eventually Belasco's food ran out, and I was forced to live on clams alone for days and days—I do not know how many, since I was not keeping this journal at the time—until I eventually found a frozen fish lying on the beach and cooked it. It gave me a change of diet for two days; but it was soon gone.

Biff caught herself several small shore birds, and I was able to get one of them away from her; but after that she would disappear up the beach to do her hunting. It would have been nice to make a hunting cat out of her, but I had no idea how to do that.

I knew, too, that the ocean was full of fish and crustaceans and other good things to eat; but I had no idea how to get any of them out of it. *Cooking Shore Dinners* spoke of berries and roots and potatoes, but there were none of these to be had. I kept making regular excursions inland in search of water and of fields like the one at the prison; I found nothing but wild, dead grass and weeds. There was no sense that the land had ever been cultivated, and no sign of any kind of life. I wondered if the Denver Incident had caused the land to be "stifled," as my history books put it, back at that time, or else during some later war after the death of literacy, unrecorded in books. When literacy died, so had history.

Toward the end of this time I must have gone twenty or more days with nothing to eat but clams, and sometimes even they were hard to find. I would wake up in the mornings with a metallic taste in my mouth and a cramping in my stomach, and I would find that after walking for only a short time I had to lie in the sand and rest. And my skin had become dry and itchy. I knew I needed something else in my diet, but there was nothing else to be had. I tried sneaking up on sleeping or resting gulls, but I was never able to get really close to one. Once, in a field of brown grass, I saw a snake and chased it, but it slithered away too fast for my tired legs to follow. I fell in the field exhausted; the snake would have made a meaty stew. Sometimes I would see a rabbit; but they were far too fast for me.

I began to get sick. My wrist was healed by then, although it was a bit crooked and stiff and would hurt when I picked up Biff with my right hand, but now my head began to ache furiously, and I would become terribly thirsty. I had to stop often to melt ice for water, and then sometimes I would throw it up. And one night I threw up my dinner and was too weak to cook anything more. I fell asleep, face down, by the remains of my fire, not really even sheltered from the weather.

When I awoke I was shivering terribly and my head was wet with perspiration. I was covered with a light blanket of snow; and the snow was still falling on me. The sky was a dark gray, and the sand around me had frozen. All of my joints ached.

I tried to get up, and could hardly stand. Eventually the best

I could do was to sit up on the beach and look around me for wood to build a fire with. But there was none around; I had gathered up all of the sticks in the area the night before. I needed a fire desperately.

Biff rubbed herself against my hip, crying softly.

In a dormitory or in prison a robot would have given me a single Med Pill and I would have been all right. But I had no pills with me whatever.

I must have sat there for over an hour, waiting for the sky to become lighter and for the day to become warmer. But that did not happen. The sky remained very dark, and a cold wind began to blow, blowing snow into my face and stinging my cheeks and eyes.

I knew that if I continued to sit there, or lay down, I would become sicker. I kept thinking of a line from a poem by T. S. Eliot:

> My life is light, waiting for the death wind,
> Like a feather on the back of my hand.

Finally I said the line aloud, into the wind, as strongly as I could. And I knew that if I did not get up I would probably die, that my lean flesh would be picked by gulls and that my bones would eventually roll in the winds and the water on that beach. And I did not want that to happen.

Moaning slightly, I pushed myself upright, and then fell on one knee. "Up!" I said aloud, and stood up again. I staggered for a moment, my head hanging over, too weak to hold it erect. The pain and the vertigo were powerful. But I got my head up and began walking. Several times I veered into the surf and staggered out again.

But eventually I found some wood and, shaking terribly, managed to make a fire. And I reserved a sturdy, long stick of driftwood to use as a walking staff.

My backpack was empty now, except for my bowl. I was able to slide the denim material it was made of from the light metal tubes, take off my coat and sweater; and, shaking violently with the cold, button the fabric around me like a vest. Then I quickly put the sweater and coat back on and after I warmed my body up again at the fire I was even better sheltered from the cold. A scarf and a cap would have been very useful; but I had grown a beard and that helped keep my face and neck warm. I could have killed Biff and eaten her and used her skin for a hat; but I did not want to kill Biff. I was a changed person from what I had been trained to be; I no longer wished to be alone, private, or even self-reliant. I needed Biff. Self-reliance was not just a matter of drugs and silence.

I managed to tie the bowl with a string to the frame of my backpack. I put the frame back over my shoulders, took up my walking staff, and, still feverish and dizzy, but stronger now, continued northward along the empty beach.

It continued to snow, and as the day wore on I became colder. I stopped twice to attempt a fire, but I wasn't able to get one lighted because of the wetness of what wood I could find and the way the wind kept blowing out my little lighter. When I became thirsty there was nothing to do but swallow handfuls of snow. The beach had become frozen too hard for me to be able to dig for clams. I kept moving ahead, slowly, and tried not to worry.

And then as I came around a curve in the beach toward evening, I saw in front of me, sitting on a low bluff back from the shore, a large old building, with lights in the windows. The snow was falling faster. The possibility of finding shelter, and warmth, gave me some strength, and I hurried forward, in a kind of limping half-run, until I came to the bottom of the bluff. But my heart sank. There were no stairs up to it—only loosely piled boulders all around, as a bulwark against the ocean.

I stood there for a while wondering what to do, until I realized that I *must* climb up there. I could not take the chance of sleeping on the beach and of being too weak and fevered in the morning even to sit up.

I began climbing, scrambling up a boulder, resting, and pushing myself slowly up the next one. Biff seemed to think I was playing, and ran up and down the rocks with ease, while my right wrist ached and my throat ached for water and the boulders scraped my legs and knees. It must have been immensely painful, but I do not think about the pain. I just kept clawing my way up those rocks, knowing that the snow-filled beach might be my death.

And I made it to the top and lay there, panting, while Biff snuggled against me. I patted her head. The palm of my hand was scratched and bleeding and there was a long gash in the sleeve of my jacket. But I was all right.

I had not been able to climb with my staff, so I had to half walk and half crawl to get to the door of the building. And it was, thank God, unlocked. I pushed it open and fell into light and warmth.

I sat on some kind of hard floor for a long time, leaning back against the door I had come in, holding my head in my hands. I was dizzy, and sick; but I was warm.

When the dizziness subsided I looked around me.

I was in a vast, powerfully lighted room, under a high ceiling.

In front of me and on either side were heavy gray machines, and a long conveyor belt and robots, their backs toward me, tending the machines. There was very little noise.

Strengthened by the warmth, I began to search the huge room for water. I found some almost immediately. One of the big machines was some sort of drill, with its bit cooled by a fine spray from a hose; the used water ran down a small trough in front of the conveyor belt and into a floor drain.

The robot who stood by the machine, doing nothing, ignored me and I ignored him. I kneeled by the belt, held my hands above the floor drain, caught the water and drank it from my hands. It was warm and slightly oily, but drinkable.

After I had my fill of it and while Biff was still lapping at the wetness around the floor drain, I washed my hands and face as best I could with the water. The oil in it seemed to soothe the scratched places on my skin.

Then I stood up, feeling better, and began to look more closely around me.

I now saw that there were actually three conveyor belts; one along each of three walls of the room. And moving along steadily on these belts were what I now recognized to be bright steel toasters. There had been toasters like them when I was a small child doing KP in the dormitory kitchen, but I hadn't seen one since.

They were being constructed and wired by machines as they passed along the belts. Some machines would add a part and weld it in place as the toaster passed by. Each machine was tended by a Make Two robot—a kind of shuffling imbecile of an android—who stood by it, watching it work. Sheet steel came from a huge roll at the start of the line; completed toasters came off the end of it. Toasters were being made at a rapid pace, there in that overlighted and cavernous room. Metal was being bent and formed by machine, with almost no noise, and parts were being made and added to the basic form. Standing there, finally warm but still half starved, I found myself wondering whatever became of the toasters and why it was that I had not seen one in thirty years. Whenever I wanted toast I had always stuck a fork in a slice of bread and held it over an open flame. I think that was what everybody did.

And then, walking toward the end of the line, I saw what was happening. A Make Three robot in a pale gray uniform was standing there. Unlike the others, he was rather deft in his movements. As each completed toaster came to him he would throw a switch on its side, just above the little nuclear battery, and when nothing happened—when no heating element became red hot—he would discard the toaster into a large, wheeled bin.

Like all of the other robots, he ignored my presence completely. I stood there, still a bit dazed by the warmth of the room, watching him for what seemed to be a long time. He would pick up each finished toaster as it came off the automatic production line, throw the switch, look inside, discover that it didn't work, and then drop it into the bin at his side.

The robot had a round face and eyes that bulged slightly; he looked a bit like Peter Lorre but without the intelligence. While I was standing there by him the bin filled up with shiny new toasters and, seeing this, he shouted, in a deep, mechanical voice, "Recycle time!" and then reached under the conveyor belt and threw the handle of a switch.

The toaster line stopped, and all of the robots stood at attention, in their gray uniforms. From the ones I could see, they all had faces like Peter Lorre.

The bin full of discarded toasters began to roll along the floor; I had to move quickly to get out of its way. It rolled smartly down to the end of the room where the production line began and stopped in front of a small doorway. The door opened and a robot came out and began taking the toasters from the bin, carrying them awkwardly in his arms. He took them into a small room behind the door and I could see him putting them into a hopper that fed them into a machine of a kind I had seen at the prison. It was a machine for converting junked steel into new steel. The toasters were being made into sheet metal again.

The factory was a closed system. Nothing came in and nothing went out. It could have been making and unmaking defective toasters for centuries, for all I knew. If there was a robot-repair station anywhere nearby, the sub-moron robots would last nearly forever. And, apparently, no new raw materials were needed.

I spent the rest of that night there, sitting against the wall and sleeping as well as I could. When I awoke in the morning, daylight was coming in the windows and the lights had dimmed themselves. Toasters were still moving along the production line there in the gray morning light and the robots were still standing where they had been the evening before. My body was stiff, and I was ravenous.

It was good to be warm again, and I decided to stay there in the factory for the rest of the winter, if I could just find food. And it turned out that there was food. The robots were of a very primitive make, somewhat like the ones diagrammed in my *Audel's Robot Maintenance and Repair Guide*. They had been made by selective cloning from living tissue, and they required food. Shortly after I awoke, the assembly line shut itself down automatically and all of the robots gathered in a sheeplike cluster by a doorway next to the recycling room, and the inspector robot, the one from the end of the line, opened the door. Inside was a large closet with three sets of shelves, two of them stacked high with little cartons slightly larger than a package of cigarettes. On the other shelf were cans of some kind of drink.

Nearly starving, I pushed in with the robots and was handed a carton of food and a can of drink.

The food was some kind of unflavored soybar, and the drink was terribly sweet; but I got them eaten and drunk in a hurry. Then, a bit apprehensively, I opened the closet and took out ten food cartons and four cans of drink. None of the robots paid any attention. I was enormously relieved; I would not starve.

Later I discovered a huge pile of unused shipping cartons under the conveyor belt on the back wall. I took four of them and flattened them out on the floor where I had slept the night before, and they made a fairly comfortable bed—far better than the frozen beaches I had been sleeping on.

So I was provided for, and I kept saying to myself, "This is my winter home." But even from the start I did not believe it, for, sick as I was, the place was no home to me. It was the most horrible place I have slept in in my life, with that mindless parody of productivity going on constantly around me, and with the wretched waste of time and energy in the making and unmaking of battery-powered toasters. And those gray-uniformed sub-morons, parodies of humanity, shuffling around silently, with no real work to do. During the five days I stayed there I saw no robot except the inspector *do* anything at his job. And he only dropped toasters into a bin and every hour or so shouted, "Recycle time!" And fed the others their two meals a day.

After two days the snow stopped, and the day after, the weather warmed up. I provided myself with all the food and drink I could carry in my backpack, and left. It was a warm, safe place, and there was plenty of food and drink there. But it was no home for me.

After I had packed my backpack with fifty soybars and thirty-five cans of drink at the toaster factory and was ready to leave, I made a close inspection of the machines along the assembly line, studying the function of each of them. They were all of gray metal and all quite big, but each was differently made. One formed the sheets of metal into the toaster shell, another fastened a heating element in place, a third installed the battery, and so on. The robot who stood in front of each machine, supposedly attending it, paid no attention to me.

Eventually I found what I was looking for. It was a machine slightly smaller than the others, with a hopper that held some kind of little metallic chip in stacks of hundreds. Where the chips were supposed to drop from a narrow neck in the hopper and be picked up by metal fingers and placed on the passing toaster, one of them had fallen sideways and stuck in place so that no more chips could get out. I stood there a moment looking at it and thinking of how much wasted energy that little jammed-up piece of silicon or whatever it was must have caused. I remembered when the toaster in my dormitory had broken down and how we had had no toast ever after that.

Then I reached out and jiggled the hopper with my hand until the chip came loose.

The mechanical hand took it from the bottom of the hopper and placed it inside the next toaster, just below the switch on its side, and a small laser beam flared briefly and welded it there.

A few moments later, at the end of the line, the inspector robot flipped up the switch on that toaster and its element glowed red. He showed no surprise but merely flipped the switch back off and set the toaster in an empty carton, and then repeated his action.

I watched him fill up a carton with twenty toasters ready for shipping. I had not the remotest idea how they would be shipped or where, but I felt pleased with what I had done.

Then I put on my backpack, picked up Biff, and left.

MARY LOU

Last night I couldn't sleep. I had lain in bed an hour or more, thinking about the loneliness in the streets, about how no one seemed to talk to anyone. Paul had shown me a film once, called *The Lost Chord*. There was a long scene in it of what was called a "picnic," in which ten or twelve people had sat at a big table out of doors eating things like corn on the cob and watermelon and talking to one another—just talking, all of them. I had not paid much attention at the time, sitting by Paul at his bed-and-desk in that gaudy room of his in the library basement; but the scene had somehow stayed with me and would come into my mind from time to time. I had never seen anything like it in real life—a whole big group of people engaged in eating and talking together, their faces alive with the talk, sitting outdoors with a breeze blowing their shirts and blouses gently—the women with their hair softly blowing around their faces—and with good honest food in their hands, eating and talking to one another as though there were no better thing in life to do.

It was a silent movie, and I could not at the time read the words on the screen, so I had no idea what they were talking about. But it did not matter. Lying in bed last night, I ached to be a part of that conversation, to be sitting around that wooden table in that ancient black-and-white film, eating corn on the cob and talking to all those other people.

Finally I got out of bed and went into the living room, where Bob was sitting staring at the ceiling. He nodded to me as I seated myself in the chair by the window, but he said nothing.

I stretched myself in the chair and yawned. Then I said, "What happened to conversations? Why don't people talk anymore, Bob?"

He looked at me. "Yes," he said, as though he had been thinking about the same thing himself. "When I was newly made, back in Cleveland, there was more of it than now. At the automobile factories there were still a few humans working along with the robots, and they would get together—five or six at a time—and talk. I would see them doing it."

"What happened?" I said. "I've never seen groups of people talking. Maybe sometimes in twos—but then very seldom."

"I'm not sure," Bob said. "The perfecting of drugs had much to do with it. And the inwardness. I suppose Privacy rules reinforced it." He looked at me thoughtfully. Sometimes Bob was more human than any human I have known, except maybe Simon. "Privacy and Mandatory Politeness were invented by one of my fellow Make Nines. He felt it was what people really wanted, once they had the drugs to occupy themselves with. And it nearly put a stop to crime. People used to commit a lot of crimes. They would steal from one another and do violent things to one another's bodies."

"I know," I said, not even wanting to think about it. "I've seen television . . ."

He nodded. "When I was first awakened into life—if what I have may be called life—I was taught mathematics. That was done by a Make Seven named Thomas. I enjoyed talking with him. And I enjoy talking to you." He was looking out the window as he said this, into a moonless night.

"Yes," I said. "And I like talking to you. But what happened? Why did talking—and reading and writing—die out?"

He was silent for what seemed to be a long while. Then he ran his fingers through his hair and began to talk, softly. "When I was learning Industrial Management, I was shown films on all aspects of the Automobile Monopoly. I was being trained to be a major executive—which was what Make Nines were originally for—and I was shown everything from the film and tape and voice recording files of General Motors and Ford and Chrysler and Sikorsky. One of the films showed a big silver car going down an empty highway silently and smoothly, like an apparition—or a dream. It was an ancient gasoline-powered car, made before the Death of Oil and long before the Nuclear Battery Age."

"The Death of Oil?"

"Yes. When gasoline had become more expensive than whiskey, and most people stayed home. That was the Death of Oil. It happened in what was called the twenty-first century. Then there were the Energy Wars. And then Solange was made. He was the first of the Make Nines and strongly programmed—as I was not—to give mankind what it wanted to have. Solange invented the nuclear battery. Controlled fusion; safe, clean, and limitless. He learned to power his own body with it, and all the rest of us were built afterward for nuclear power. One battery lasts me for nine blues."

"Was Solange black?" I said.

"No. He was very white—with blue eyes."

I got up to make myself some coffee. "Why are you black?" I said.

He didn't answer until I was pouring the hot water onto the coffee powder. "I have never known why," he said. "I think I am the only black robot ever made."

I brought my coffee over and sat down again. "What about that film?" I said. "The one with the car."

"There was just one man in it," he said. "A man with a pastel blue sport shirt and gray polyester trousers. He had the windows rolled up and the stereo playing and the air conditioner and the cruise control on. His hands were white and soft and held the steering wheel lightly. And his face—oh, his face!—was as vacant as the moon."

I was unsure of what he was trying to say. "When I was a little girl and away from the dormitories for the first time, I would get very impatient and nervous and I wouldn't know what to do with myself. And Simon would say, 'Just be quiet and let life happen to you,' and I would try to do that. Was that what the man in the car was doing?"

"No," Spofforth said. He stood up and stretched his arms out, just as a man would do. "On the contrary. No life was happening to him at all. He was supposed to have been 'free'; but nothing was happening. No one knew his name, but one of the humans would call him Daniel Boone—the last frontiersman. There was a sound track with the film, with a deep, authoritarian, masculine voice saying, 'Be free and alive and let your spirit soar with the Open Road!' And down the empty road he went, at seventy miles an hour, insulated from the outside air, insulated as far as possible even from the sounds of his own vehicle's moving down that empty road. The American Individualist, the Free Spirit. The Frontiersman. With a human face indistinguishable from that of a moron robot. And at his home or his motel he had television to keep the world away. And pills in his pocket. And the stereo. And the pictures in the magazines he looked at, with food and sex better and brighter than in life."

Bob was pacing up and down the floor, barefoot. "Sit down, Bob," I said, and then, "How did all that get started? The cars—the controlled environment?"

He sat down, took a partly smoked joint from his shirt pocket and lit it. "There was a lot of money to be made from cars—from making them and selling them. And when television came it was one of the greatest sources of profit ever invented. And there was more than that; something very deep in humanity responded to the car, to the television set, to the drugs.

"When the drugs and the television were perfected by the computers that made and distributed them, the cars were no longer necessary. And since no one had devised a way of making cars safe in the hands of a human driver, it was decided to discontinue them."

"Who made that decision?" I said.

"I did. Solange and I. It was the last time I saw him. He threw himself off a building."

"Jesus," I said. And then, "When I was a little girl there were no cars. But Simon could remember them. So that was when thought buses were invented?"

"No. Thought buses had been around since the twenty-second century. In fact there had been buses, driven by human drivers in the twentieth. And trolley cars and trains. Most big cities in North America had what were called streetcars at the start of the twentieth century."

"What happened to them?"

"The automobile companies got rid of them. Bribes were paid to city managers to tear up the streetcar tracks, and advertisements were bought in newspapers to convince the public that it should be done. So more cars could be sold, and more oil would be made into gasoline, to be burned in the cars. So that corporations could grow, and so a few people could become incredibly rich, and have servants, and live in mansions. It changed the life of mankind more radically than the printing press. It created suburbs and a hundred other dependencies—sexual and economic and narcotic—upon the automobile. And the automobile prepared the way for the more profound—more inward—dependencies upon television and then robots and, finally, the ultimate and predictable conclusion to all of it: the perfection of the chemistry of mind. The drugs your fellow humans use are named after twentieth-century ones; but they are far more potent, far better at what they do, and they are all made and distributed—distributed everywhere there are human beings—by automatic equipment." He looked over at me from his armchair. "It all began, I suppose, with learning to build fires—to warm the cave and keep the predators out. And it ended with time-release Valium."

I looked at him for a minute. "I don't take Valium," I said.

"I know," he said. "That's why I took you away from Paul. That and the baby you're going to have."

"I understand about the baby. You want to play house. But I

didn't know the drugs—or the lack of them—had anything to do with it."

He shook his head at me, scoldingly. "It should be obvious," he said, "I wanted a woman I could talk to. And could fall in love with."

I stared at him. "Fall in love?" I said finally.

"Certainly. Why not?"

I started to answer that, but did not. Why couldn't he fall in love if he wanted to? "Did you?" I said.

He looked at me for a moment and then ground his joint out in an ashtray. "Yes, I did," he said. "Unfortunately."

Fall in love. The oddness of the phrase—the ancient phrase—occupied my attention for a moment there in the living room in the middle of the night. There was something about the words that struck me. And then I realized that I had never *heard* them spoken before; they were something from silent films and from books and not from the life that I knew. I had heard Simon say once, "Love is a swindle," and that was his only use of the word that I can recall. And "love" wasn't even a part of our vocabularies at the dormitories, where they taught us: "Quick sex is best." But that was all. And here this robot with his sad and youthful face and his long, long history and his deep and gentle voice was telling me that he had let himself *fall in love* with me.

My coffee was getting cold. I sipped from it a moment and then said, "What do you mean by 'love'?"

He did not reply for a long time. Then he said, "Flutterings in the stomach. And about the heart. Wishing for your being happy. An obsession with you, with the way your chin tilts and your eyes at times stare. The way your hand holds that coffee cup. Hearing you snoring at night while I sit here."

I was shocked. They were words of a kind I had read at times and had ignored. I knew without thinking that they had something to do with sex and with the *families* that had been a part of the ancient world; but they were never a part of my life. And how could they be a part of the "life" of this manufactured person, this elegant humanoid with its brown skin and kinky keratinoid hair? This false man, without a mother to gender him, without a penis; unable to eat food or drink water—a battery-powered doll with soulful brown eyes. What was this business of *love* he was speaking of—some of the madness, the dementia that had haunted his manufacture and the whole making of that last Promethean strain of synthetic intelligences, that mad over-humanness of the doomed series of Make Nines?

And yet, looking at him, I could have kissed him. Could have embraced his broad, handsome back and pressed my mouth against his moist lips.

And then I found that—oh, my good lord Jesus Christ—I was crying. Tears were running down my face freely. I let my face fall wet into my open hands and sobbed the way I had sobbed as a child when I learned that I was alone in the world. It was like a great gust of warm wind blowing through me.

After crying I felt subdued, calm. I looked at Bob. His face was calm, restful, as I felt mine was. "Have you ever done this before?" I said. "Fallen in love?"

"Yes. When I was . . . when I was young. There were human women, back then, who were undrugged. I loved one of them. There was something in her face, sometimes . . . But I never tried to live with a woman before. The way we are living now."

"Why me?" I said. "I was happy enough with Paul. We would have started a family. Why did you have to fall in love with me?"

He looked at me. "You're the last one," he said. "The last before I die. I wanted to recover my buried life. This erased part of my memory. I would like to know, before I die, what it was like to be the human being I have tried to be all my life." He looked away from me, out the window. "Besides, prison will be good for Paul. If he grows up enough he'll escape. Nothing works very well in the world anymore; most of the machines and most of the robots are breaking down. If he wants to get out of prison he will."

"Have you remembered anything?" I said. "Since we've been living together? Have you filled in any of the blank spaces in your brain?"

He shook his head. "No, I haven't. Not a one."

I nodded. "Bob," I said. "You ought to memorize your life, the way I am doing. You ought to dictate your whole story into a recorder. I could write it down for you, and teach you how to read it."

He looked back toward me, and his face now seemed very old and sad. "I have no need to, Mary. I can't forget my life. I have no means of forgetting. That was left out."

"My God," I said. "That must be awful."

"Yes, it is," he said. "It is awful."

Once Bob said to me, "Do you miss Paul?"

I did not look up from my beer glass. "Only the mocking-bird sings at the edge of the woods."

"What was that?" Bob said.

"Something Paul used to say. When I think of him sometimes, I think of that."

"Say it again," Bob said. There was something urgent in his voice.

"'Only the mockingbird sings at the edge of the woods,'" I said.

"*Woods*," Bob said. And then "'Whose *woods* these are I think I know.' That's the line." He stood up and walked over toward me. "'Whose woods these are I think I know. His house . . .'"

So Bob finally got the word for his poem, after over a hundred years of wondering. I'm glad I was able to give him something.

BENTLEY

The winter must have been coming to an end, for it was never as cold again after I left the toaster factory as it had been before. And I was never that sick again, even though I was still a bit weak when I left the unholy security of that place.

My progress northward became faster and the food I had taken from the factory, evil-tasting though it was, gave me strength. I continued to find clams and, later, mussels. And I frightened a sea gull on the beach away from a fish it had just caught; the stew it made lasted three days. Eventually my health returned better than it had ever been. I had become very firm and tough, and I could walk all day without fatigue, at a steady pace. I began to allow myself to think about Mary Lou and about the possibility of truly finding her. But I had a long way to go, I was certain; although I had no idea of just how far.

Then one afternoon I looked ahead of me and saw a road that wound its way across a field and down to the beach.

I ran up to it and saw that it was of ancient cracked asphalt, in places overgrown with weeds, with its surface old and faded and crumbled, but still walkable. I began to follow it, away from the beach.

I saw in the high woods along the side of that decayed road something I had never seen before: a road sign. I had noticed them in films and read about them in books, but I had never seen one. It was of faded green and white Permoplastic, with its lettering almost obscured by dirt and vines; but when I pushed the vines away I could read it:

MAUGRE

CORPORATION LIMIT

I looked at it for a long time. Something about the presence of this ancient thing, there in the weak sun of early spring, gave my body a sudden chill.

I picked up Biff in my arms and walked quickly down the road and around a bend.

And I saw spread out in front of me, half buried by trees and bushes, a cluster of Permoplastic houses—perhaps five hundred of them, filling a kind of shallow valley below me. The houses were set rather far from one another, with what once must have been parks and concrete streets between them. But there was no sign of human habitation. In what must have been the town's center were two large buildings and a huge white obelisk.

As I approached the town I began to push through rose-bushes and honeysuckle, near-dead from winter, and I saw that the houses, perhaps once brightly colored, were all faded to a uniform bone white.

I walked into Maugre with trepidation. Even Biff seemed nervous, and squirmed in my arms and clawed at the straps that held my backpack. Where the town began was a haphazard trail through the underbrush between the houses; I began to follow it. I could not tell if the houses had porches, since the fronts of them were so overgrown; on only a few of them were doors visible through the bushes and weeds and honeysuckles.

I was heading toward the obelisk. It seemed to be the thing to do.

One house I passed had fewer obstructions between me and its door and I set Biff down and pushed my way through the growth and came up to it, scratching myself several times on rosebushes as I did so. But I hardly noticed the scratches, the sensation of being in a dream or a hypnotic trance was so strong.

I was able, after some tearing of weeds, to get the front door open and, with a kind of awe, step inside. I was in a big living room with nothing in it. Absolutely nothing. The light was dim from the mold-covered and dusty plastic windows.

Opaque Permoplastic is the most tenacious—the most dead—material designed by man, and the entire room was merely a huge seamless hollow cube of it, all pink with rounded corners. There was no indication that anyone had ever lived there; but I knew that the nature of the material was such that the house could have been lived in for a hundred blues and have no signs—no scuff marks on the floor, handprints on the walls, smoke stains on the ceiling, no visible remnants of children playing or fighting or of where a favorite table had sat throughout the life of a family.

For some reason I shouted, "Is anybody home?" It was a phrase I had learned from films.

There was not even an echo. I thought sadly of those men in the film drinking from large glasses and laughing. *Only the mockingbird sings at the edge of the woods.* I left. Biff was waiting for me, and I picked her up in my arms.

We headed for the obelisk. As we got closer the path became wider, easier to walk, and we came to the near-clearing of two big buildings and the obelisk more quickly than I had expected.

The obelisk was whiter than the bone white of all the buildings. It was about sixty feet wide at its base and rose about two hundred feet into the air, resembling the Washington Monument that I had seen in so many books and films and that was all that remained of the city of Washington, DC.

There was a glass double door, only partly overgrown by blue morning glories, at the base of it, and as I walked around I saw that each of the four faces of the structure had a huge door. And on the fourth side I saw, up high and in large, raised letters, these words:

PERFECT SAFETY SHELTER AND MALL

ALL LIFE IS SAFE BELOW THIS SHIELD

DEPARTMENT OF DEFENSE: MAUGRE

I read it over twice. Was the "shield" the obelisk itself? Or was it within the doors?

I set Biff down and began trying the doors. The third one slid open with no effort.

Inside was a lobby, lit by the light through the glass doors. Two broad staircases, descending, were on either side of me. Another, narrower staircase went up. I hesitated only a minute and then began to go down the stairs on my left. After six or seven steps down, just as it was beginning to get dim, a soft light began to come from the yellow walls on either side of me, and on one wall were written these words:

CONCUSSION BARRIER LEVEL

And then, six or eight steps further down, other soft lights came on and I saw these words on the wall, which at this level was of a different color—gray:

RADIATION BARRIER LEVEL

And when I came to the bottom of the staircase I found myself in a huge, long, wide hallway with glass chandeliers of soft pink that came on gently at my approach and signs on each side of me that glowed:

SAFE ZONE. MALL

And then, astonishingly, there began the sound of soft music, light and airy, of flutes and oboes; and, about fifty yards ahead of me, a great spray of water began to rise from a broad pool, and varicolored lights—blue and green and yellow— began to play over it and there came the sound of the water falling, the sound of the fountain.

I walked toward the fountain, marveling. Biff jumped from my arms and ran ahead of me and, without hesitating, perched herself on the edge of the pool, put her head down, and began to drink.

I came up slowly to her, bent down, cupped my hands with the cool, fresh water, raised it to my hot and dry face, and smelled it. It was clean and pure. I drank handfuls of it, and then washed my face in it.

The pool's sides were made of thousands of little squares of silver tiles, with white lines of mortar between them, and in the bottom of the pool, under the water, was a giant mosaic, in black and gray and white tiles, of a humpbacked whale with its back arched and its flukes spread.

The water of the fountain jetted up from between a group of three dolphins, curved and vertical, carved in black. I had seen something like it in a picture book called *The Fountains of Rome*. I stood back and stared at it, at the silver rim of the pool, the great picture of the whale, the dolphins, the great upward jet of water, feeling fine spray from the water on my face and body, hearing the music of flutes, and the hairs on my arms and the hairs on the back of my neck seemed to raise themselves and a fine tingle, almost painful, spread through my body.

It was like seeing the birds at the edge of the sea turning in flight, or a storm on the gray ocean, or the great ape Kong in his slow and graceful falling.

Beyond the fountain the great hallway ended at the top of a "T," with huge double doors going to the right and to the left. Over the doors to the left were the words:

EMERGENCY QUARTERS
CAPACITY 60,000

and over the other door was simply:

MALL

This door opened automatically as I approached it and I found myself in another long, wide, tiled hallway. On either side of this were store entrances, far more of them than I had ever seen in my life. I have seen windows with merchandise displayed in them in New York and in the university where I live and teach; but I had never seen anything on a scale like this, and with such abundance.

The nearest store to me was called Sears; in its huge, curved windows was an array of merchandise that was almost beyond belief. More than half of it consisted of things I did not recognize. Some of them I was familiar with. But there were colored balls and electronic devices and mysterious bright-colored things that could have been either weapons or toys, for all I knew.

I slid the door open and walked inside, dazed. I was in a part of the huge store that had clothing in it. All of it looked new, fresh, wrapped in some kind of clear plastic that must have kept it sealed for hundreds of years.

My own clothes were worn and frayed, and I began to find myself new ones.

And then, when I was trying to determine how to take the plastic covering off a blue jacket that seemed as though it would fit me, I happened to look at the tiled floor at my feet.

There were muddy footprints all over the tile, and they looked fresh.

I kneeled and reached out my hand and touched the mud. It was slightly damp.

I found myself standing up and looking all around me. But I saw nothing but the racks upon racks of clothing and beyond them shelves of brightly colored goods of all descriptions— shelves after shelves as far as I could see. But nothing moved. Then I looked down at the floor again and saw that the footprints were everywhere—some fresh, some old. And they had been made by different-sized shoes and had different shapes.

Biff had wandered off somewhere and I called for her, but she did not come. I began looking, walking down aisles with apprehension. What if the makers of the footprints were still about? But, then, what did I have to fear from another human being? Or from a robot, for that matter, since none had followed me from prison and there had been no sign of any Detector or anything else searching for me. Still, I was afraid—or "spooked," as the *Dictionary of American Slang* would have it.

I found Biff eventually, greedily eating from a box of dried beans that had been opened and left on a counter top alongside hundreds of similar but unopened boxes. Biff was purring mightily and I could hear her teeth crunching into the beans. I picked up one of the unopened boxes from next to her; she did not even bother to look up at me. The box—unlike food boxes I had known before—had writing on it:

IRRADIATED AND STABILIZED PINTO BEANS

SHELF LIFE SIX CENTURIES

NO ADDITIVES

There was a picture of a steaming plate of beans, with a slice of bacon on top of them, on the side of the box. But the beans Biff was still devoting her entire attention to looked dry, withered, and unappetizing. I reached into her box and took a small handful. Biff looked up at me and bared her teeth for a moment, but turned her attention back to the eating. I put one of the beans into my mouth and chewed it. It was not really bad, and I was hungry. I popped the rest of the handful into my mouth and, chewing, studied one of the sealed boxes, trying to determine how to get it open. There were directions at the top, about pressing a white dot and then pulling on a red tab, while twisting. I tried all the combinations I could think of, but the box wouldn't open. By this time I had finished the beans I had, and Biff's were all gone too. My appetite had been aroused and I was becoming furious with the apparently unopenable box. Here I was, the only man on earth able to read the directions for opening a box of beans, and it was no help.

Then I remembered passing an aisle where various tools were displayed. I went to it. My anger and hunger had made me forget my former apprehensions and I strode over, walking firmly and loudly. I found a hatchet, much like the one in *Wife Killer Loose*, except that it was wrapped in plastic, and I could not get *it* open either.

I was becoming furious, and the fury increased my appetite for those beans. I tried to bite into the plastic on the hatchet so that I could tear it; but it was too tough for my teeth. Then I saw a glass case holding some kind of small boxes, on another aisle, and went over there, raised the hatchet, brought it down, and crashed open the glass. Some jagged pieces were left in the frame of the case and I hooked a point of one on the plastic, and pulled. The plastic began to tear and, finally, I was able to twist it away from the hatchet.

Then I went back to the beans and began to chop away at the top of the box until it tore open and the beans came spilling out. I set the hatchet down on the counter and began to eat.

And it was while I was chewing my third mouthful that I heard a deep voice behind me saying, "What the *hell* are you doing, mister?"

I spun around and saw two large people, a dark-bearded old man and a large woman, standing there staring at me. Each held a leash in one hand, with a large dog, and in the other hand each was carrying a long butcher knife. The dogs were staring at me as intently as the people were. The dogs were white—albinos, I think—and their eyes were pinkish.

Beside me Biff had arched her back and was showing her teeth toward the dogs and I realized that it was probably not me but Biff beside me that they were staring at.

The people were older than I as well as larger. Their stares were well past the limits of Privacy, but more curious than hostile. But their knives were long and frightening.

My mouth was still half full of the beans. I chewed a moment and then said, "I'm eating. I was hungry."

"What you're eating," the man said, "belongs to *me*."

The woman spoke up. "To *us*," she said. "To the family."

Family. I had never heard anyone use that word, except in a film.

The man ignored her. "Which town are you from, mister?"

"I don't know," I said. "I'm from Ohio."

"He could be from Eubank," the woman said. "He looks like he might be a Dempsey. They're all kind of thin."

I managed to swallow the last of the beans in my mouth.

"Or a Swisher," the man said. "Out of Ocean City."

Suddenly Biff turned from the dogs and leaped across the counter she was standing on and ran—faster than I had ever seen her run—down the counter tops away from us. The dogs had turned to follow with their eyes, straining at their leashes. The man and woman ignored her.

"Which of the seven towns do you come from?" the man said. "And why are you breaking the law by eating our food?"

"And," the woman said, "violating our sanctuary in here?"

"I've never heard of the seven towns," I said. "I'm a stranger, passing through. I was hungry and when I found this place I came in. I didn't know it was a . . . a sanctuary."

The woman stared at me. "You don't know a church of the living God when you see one?"

I looked around me, at the aisles covered with plastic-sealed merchandise, at the racks of colored clothing and electronic equipment and rifles and golf clubs and jackets. "But this is no *church*," I said. "This is a store."

They said nothing for quite a long while. One of the dogs, apparently tired of staring after the direction Biff had left in, settled itself down on the floor and yawned. The other began sniffing at the man's feet.

Then the man said, "That's blasphemy. You've already blasphemed by eating holy food without permission."

"I'm sorry," I said. "I had no idea . . ." Abruptly he stepped forward and took me by the arm in what was an extremely strong grip and he held the point of his knife to my stomach. While he was doing this the woman, moving very quickly for her size, stepped over to the counter and took the hatchet I had been using. She had, I suppose, expected me to try defending myself with it.

I was terrified and said nothing. The man put his knife in his belt, stepped behind me, brought my arms together behind my back, and told the woman to get him some rope. She went over to a counter several rows away where there was a large roll of Synlon cord and cut off a piece with her knife, leaving the hatchet there. She brought it to him and he tied my hands together. The dogs watched all this languidly. I was beginning to pass beyond fear into some sort of calmness. I had seen things of this sort on television, and I was beginning to feel that the situation was one that I was merely watching, as though there were no real danger to me. But my heart was pounding wildly and I could feel myself trembling. Yet somehow my mind had moved above this and I felt a calmness. I wondered what had become of Biff—and what would become of her.

"What are you going to do?" I said.

"I am going to fulfill the scripture," he said. "He who blasphemes my holy place shall be cast into the lake of fire that burneth forever."

"Jesus Christ!" I said. I don't know why I said that. Possibly it was the Bible language that the man had used.

"What did you say?" the woman said.

"I said, 'Jesus Christ.'"

"Who told you that name?"

"I learned it from the Bible," I said. I did not mention Mary Lou, nor did I mention the man who, burning in immolation, had shouted the name of Jesus.

"What Bible?" she said.

"He's lying," the man said. And then to me, "Show me that Bible."

"I don't have it anymore," I said. "I had to leave it . . ."

The man just stared at me.

Then they took me out into the grand hallway of the Mall where the fountain was, past stores and restaurants and meditation parlors and a place with a sign that said:

JANE'S

PROSTITUTION

As we passed a large shop with a sign that read: DISPENSARY, the man slowed down and said, "The way you're shaking, mister, I guess you could use some help." He pushed open the door of the shop and we came into a place with rows and rows of large sealed jars filled with pills of all sizes and shapes. He walked up to one that said "SOPORS: Non-addictive. Fertility-inhibiting" on it, reached into his pants pocket and took out a handful of old and faded credit cards, selected a blue card from the pack, and slipped it into the mechanical slot at the bottom of the jar on the counter.

The glass jars were some kind of primitive dispenser—certainly not as sleek and quick as the store machinery I was accustomed to—such as in the place on Fifth Avenue where I had bought Mary Lou that yellow dress. It took it at least a minute of clicking over the card before returning it, and then a half minute before the metal door in the base opened and dispensed a handful of blue pills.

The man scooped them up and said, "How many sopors you want, mister?"

I shook my head. "I don't use them," I said.

"You don't *use* them? What in hell do you use?"

"Nothing," I said. "Not for a long time."

The woman spoke up. "Mister, in about ten minutes you're going into the lake of fire that burneth forever. I'd take ever damn one of them pills."

I said nothing.

The man shrugged. He took one of the pills himself, handed one to the woman, and put the rest in his pocket.

We walked out of the shop, leaving its rows of hundreds of bottles and jars of pills, and as we left, the automatic lighting in the shop went off behind us.

We turned a corner and a new fountain came on, with lights and with new, softer music. It was, if anything, larger than the first.

On either side of us now were stainless-steel walls, with occasional doorways. Over each doorway was a sign that read:

SLEEPING CHAMBER B
CAPACITY: 1,600

SLEEPING CHAMBER D
CAPACITY 2,200

"Who sleeps in those places?" I said.

"Nobody," the woman said. "They was for the ancients. Those of old."

"How ancient?" I said. "How old?"

The woman shook her head. "The ancient of days. When they was giants in the earth and they feared the wrath of the Lord."

"They feared the rain of fire from Heaven," the man said. "And they didn't trust Jesus. The rain of fire never come, and the ancients died."

We passed by more and more sleeping quarters, and by at least a half mile of stainless-steel walls merely marked STOR-AGE, and then, finally, we came to the dead end of the corridor, where there was a massive door with a sign in red: POWER SOURCE: AUTHORIZED PERSONNEL ONLY.

The man had taken a small metal plate from his pocket. He held it against a matching rectangle in the center of the door and said, "The key to the Kingdom."

The door slid open and a soft light came on.

Inside was a smaller corridor, and the air in it was distinctly warm. The dogs were left outside and we walked down it, toward another door. It became warmer as we walked. I was beginning to perspire and would have liked to wipe my forehead but my hands were still tied behind me.

We came to the door. The sign on it was in large orange letters:

YOU ARE APPROACHING AN ARTIFICIAL SUN
FUSION PROJECT THREE: MAUGRE

The man held a different card to this door and when it opened the heat was palpable and intense. There was another door just inside this one and the man this time put yet another card into a slot beside it and the door opened about two feet wide. There was a brilliant orange glow behind it that illuminated some kind of enormous room. A room without a floor. Or with a floor of orange light. The heat was overwhelming.

Then the man's voice said, "Behold the eternal fire." And I felt myself being pushed from behind, and my heart almost stopped beating and I could not speak. I looked down and was able to hold my eyes in a squint for only a split second, but long enough to see that a great circular pit was directly in front of my feet and that down, incalculably far down in that pit, was a fire like that of the sun.

And then I was pulled back, limp, and the man's hands turned my body around to face his and he said, quietly, "Do you have any last words?"

I looked at his face. It was impassive, quiet, sweating. "I am the resurrection and the life," I said. "He that believeth in me, though he die, yet shall he live."

The woman shrieked, "My God, Edgar! My God!"

The man looked at me firmly. "Where did you learn those words?" he said.

I groped for something to say, and finally found only the truth—which I felt he would not understand. But I said it anyway. "I have read the Bible."

"*Read?*" the woman said. "You can *read* scripture?"

I felt that I would die from the heat at my back if I did not get away in less than a minute. I could see that the man's face was showing pain from the heat, or doubt.

"Yes," I said. "I can read scripture." I looked him directly in the eyes. "I can read anything."

The man stared at me with his broad face twisted for one more horrible moment and then, abruptly, he pulled me forward, away from the fire, and pushed me through the outer door and then closed it. Then we went through the second door, and it closed itself, and the air was bearable. "All right," the man said. "We'll go to the book and see if you can read it."

Then he took his knife and cut the ropes that held my hands.

"I must find Biff first," I said.

And I found her, halfway to Sears, and took her up in my arms.

We had passed another fountain on my frightened way to the Lake of Fire; returning to Sears, as we approached the fountain again a scene from an ancient film came into my mind: in *King of Kings* the actor H. B. Warner asks a man named John to "baptize" him, by wetting him in a river. It is clearly a moment of great mystical significance. My steps down the wide and empty corridor of the Mall seemed light. The man and woman flanked me, but this time without restraint; they had untied me. Their dogs were silent and submissive; all that could be heard was the regular pattern of our footsteps and the music that came from invisible speakers and bathed us in airy sound. And louder now came the splashing of the fountain water, returning to the pool from its graceful arcing toward the high ceiling.

I thought of Jesus, bearded and serene, in the Jordan River. Abruptly I stopped and said, "I want to be baptized. In this fountain." My voice was clear and strong. I was staring at the water in the great circular pool beside me and there was a light spray in my face.

Out of the side of my vision I saw the woman, as if in a dream, sink to her knees, her long, full denim skirt slowly ballooning around her as she did so. And her voice, weak now, was saying, "My God. The Holy Spirit told him to speak them words."

Then I heard the man's voice saying, "Get up Berenice. He could have been told about that. Not everybody keeps church secrets."

I turned to watch her as she got up from her knees, pulling her blue sweater back down over her broad hips. "But he knew the fount when he saw it," she said. "He knew the place of holy water."

"I told you," the man said, but with doubt in his voice. "He could of heard from anybody in the other six towns. Just because Baleens don't backslide don't mean the Graylings don't. Manny Grayling could of told him. Hell, he might *be* Grayling—one they been hiding from Church."

She shook her head. "Baptize him, Edgar Baleen," she said. "You can't refuse the Sacrament."

"I know that," he said quietly. He began taking off his denim jacket. He looked at me, his face grave. "Sit down. On the edge."

I seated myself on the edge of the fountain and the woman kneeled and took off my shoes and then my socks. She rolled up my pantlegs. Then she sat on one side of me, and the man, jacketless now, on the other side, and they both took off their shoes and socks. They had released the dogs and the two white animals just stood there patiently, watching us and watching Biff, who had curled herself on the floor.

"All right," the man said. "Step into the fount."

I stood up and stepped over the edge into the water, which was cold. Looking down, I saw that the pool had its tiles arranged into the shape of a giant fish, much like the one I had found on the shore and eaten—a huge silver fish with fins and gills. The water came up to my knees, and the rest of me was drenched by the spray, and it was very cold. But I felt no discomfort.

I was staring down at the giant fish on which I stood when the two of them came up beside me. The man bent, cupping his hands together, held them under water for a moment and then raised them, dripping, to my head. I felt his hands, open now, on my head and then the water from them was streaming down my face.

"I baptize thee in the name of the Father and of the Son and of the Holy Spirit," he said.

The woman reached out and placed her large soft hand on my head. "Amen and praise the Lord," she said softly.

We stepped out of the fountain and I waited, with the man, the dogs, and Biff, while the woman went to Sears and came back with towels for our feet. We dried our feet and legs, put on our shoes, and continued walking, in silence.

I felt even lighter than before, more remote and yet more truly present at the same time, extremely alive to what was outside me and inside me at the same time. I felt that I had crossed some invisible line, one that had been waiting for me ever since I had left Ohio, and had now entered some symbolic realm where my life was light, "like a feather on the back of my hand," and where only my own experience of that life, my own undrugged experience, was all that I was living for. And if that experience meant death in the Lake of Fire, it would have to be acceptable.

I wonder now, writing this down, if that is how those who immolate themselves feel when they decide to do it. But they are drugged, unaware. And they cannot read.

Could baptism really work? Could there be a Holy Spirit? I do not believe so.

We walked in silence down the wide hall and back up the broad staircase, and the lights behind us dimmed and darkened, and the music became silent and the fountains stopped as we left.

Near the top of the stairs I was able to turn for a moment to look down on the vast and empty Mall, with its chandeliers dimming and its fountains dying down, and its storefronts still bright as if waiting for customers who would never come. I could sense the sad dignity of that place, of its broad, clean emptiness.

They took me back outdoors into what had become evening, and led me, still silently, to one of the large buildings that flanked the obelisk—a big, official-looking building with a well-trimmed lawn and no weeds around it. We went to the back of the building and I saw a garden there and, added on to the building itself, an incongruous back porch made of wood, looking like one I had seen in *Birth of a Nation*.

We entered by a door on this porch and I found myself in a huge, high-ceilinged room with perhaps thirty people in it, all plainly dressed, all silent, sitting around an enormous wooden table as though they had been waiting for me. The people at the table had been silent when we came in; they remained silent as the old man and his wife led me through the room and around the table—as silent as the eating rooms of a dormitory or of a prison.

We went down a narrow hallway into another, equally large room, with rows of wooden chairs in it, facing a podium. Behind the podium was a wall-sized television screen, now off.

Baleen led me up to the podium. There was a large black book on it and, although whatever lettering might have once been on its cover was now completely worn off, I was certain the book was the Bible.

The lightness and strength I had felt in the Mall were leaving me. I stood there, slightly embarrassed, looking at this quiet old room with its worn wooden chairs and its pictures of the face of Jesus on the walls and the big television screen, and before long the people from the kitchen started coming into the room and sitting down, men and women walking in quietly in twos and threes and sitting wordlessly and then looking at me with a kind of shy curiosity. They all wore jeans and simple shirts, and a few of the men were bearded like me but most were not. I watched them with a certain hope that I might see young people, but that hope was disappointed; no one was any younger than I. There was a couple holding hands and looking like lovers; but they were obviously in their forties.

And then when all of the chairs were full Edgar Baleen stood up and suddenly threw his arms out wide, palms upward, saying loudly, "My brethren."

Everyone watched him attentively; the lovers let go of one another's hands. Most of the people were in couples, but in the second row was a woman of about my age, sitting alone. She was tall and, like all of them, simply dressed, wearing a denim shirt with a blue apron over it, but she was striking to look at. Despite my nervousness I found myself watching her as much as I could without being obvious about it. She really was, I began to see, a beautiful woman; it was pleasant to look at her and to get my mind partly off what I had just been through at the Lake of Fire and of what might be in store for me. Whatever might happen, I felt that the crisis was past now; and I deliberately made myself think about the woman.

Her hair was blond, curling slightly around the sides of her face. Her complexion, despite the roughness of her clothes, was clear white and flawless. Her eyes were large and light-colored and her forehead was high, clear and intelligent-looking.

"Brethren," Baleen was saying. "It's been a good year for the family, as all know. We've been at peace with our neighbors, and the Lord's provisions at the Great Mall have continued in their bountiful abundance." Then he bowed his head, thrust his arms forward and upward, and said, "Let us pray."

The group bowed their heads, except for the woman I had been watching. She inclined her head only very slightly. I bowed mine, wanting to take no risks. I had seen meetings like this one in films and I knew that the idea was to bow and be silent.

Baleen began to recite what seemed to be a memorized,

ritual prayer: "God grant us safety from the fallout past and the fallout to come. Preserve us from all Detectors. Grant us thy love and keep us from the sin of Privacy. In Jesus' name we pray. Amen."

I could not help being startled by the words "the sin of Privacy." It was completely contrary to my teaching, and yet something in me responded favorably to the phrase.

There were a few coughs and squirmings from the group when Baleen finished, and everyone looked up again.

"The Lord has provided for the Baleens," he said, in a more ordinary tone of voice now, "and for all of the Seven Families in the Cities of the Plain." Then he leaned forward at his lectern, grasping its sides with what I suddenly noticed were small, white, womanish hands—hands with well-manicured nails—and spoke in a low voice, almost a whisper. "And it may be that now the Lord has sent us an interpreter of his word or a prophet. A stranger has come into our midst, has passed an ordeal of fire before my own eyes, and has shown a knowledge of the Lord."

I saw that everyone was looking at me. Despite the new calmness I had seemed to find in myself, it was very disconcerting. I had never been an object of attention like that before. I felt myself blushing and had a sudden wish for the old rules of Privacy that forbade people to stare at one another. There must have been thirty of them—all of them looking at me with open curiosity or suspicion. I put my hands in my pockets to keep them from trembling. Biff was at my feet, rubbing herself between my ankles. For a moment I even wanted her to go away, to stop paying attention to me.

"The stranger has told me," Baleen was saying, "that he is a carrier of the old knowledge. He says he is a Reader."

Several of them looked surprised. Their stares at me became even more intense. The woman I had been watching leaned slightly forward, as if to get a closer look.

Then, with a dramatic wave of his arm in my direction, Baleen said, "Step forward to the Book of Life and read from it. *If* you can read."

I looked at him, trying to appear calm; but my heart was beating powerfully and my knees trembled. All those *people* assembled in that one place! I had expected something like this to happen, but now that it had come I seemed to have reverted to the person I once had been—before Roberto and Consuela, before Mary Lou, before prison and my escape and my new, rebellious self-sufficiency. Even as a shy professor, lecturing on mind control by repeating words I had memorized and said many times before, I would be nervous in the presence of my largest classes—of ten or twelve students at one time. And students were all properly trained to avoid my eyes while listening to me.

Somehow I managed to walk the few feet to the lectern where the book sat. I almost tripped over Biff. Baleen stepped aside for me and said, "Read from the beginning."

I opened the cover of the book with a trembling hand and was grateful to be able to look down, avoiding the eyes of the congregation. I stared at the page for a long time, in silence. There was print on it; but somehow the letters did not make any sense. Some were very big and some were small. I knew that I was looking at a title page, but I could not make my mind work. I kept staring at it. It was not a foreign language, I knew that somehow; but I could not make my brain assemble the letters into coherence; they were just inked marks on a yellowed page. I had stopped shaking and was frozen. This lasted an intolerably long time. Into my mind had come a frightening image blanking out the page on the oak lectern in front of me: the yellow-orange fire at the bottom of the pit in the mall; the nuclear core that could vaporize my body. *Read*, I told myself. But nothing came.

I could feel Baleen moving closer to me. I felt that my heart would stop.

And then, suddenly, a clear, strong female voice from in front of me spoke out: "Read the book," it said. "Read for us, brother," and I looked up, startled, and saw that it was the beautiful tall woman who was sitting by herself and was now staring at me pleadingly. "You can do it!" she said. "Read to us."

I looked back to the book. And suddenly it was simple. The big, black letters that filled most of the page said, "Holy Bible," in capital letters.

I read it:

HOLY BIBLE

And then, under that, the letters were small:

"Abridged and updated for modern readers'

And at the bottom of the page:

"Reader's Digest Condensed Books, Omaha. 2123"

That was all that page said. I turned to the next, which was filled with print, and began, more calmly now, to read:

"*Genesis*, by Moses. At first God made the world and the sky, but the world had no shape and there was nobody living

on it. And it was dark, too, until God said, 'Give us some light!'
and the light came on . . ."

I went on, more and more easily, and calmly. It was not at all
like the Bible I had read from back at the prison, but that one
had been much older.

When I finished the page I looked up.

The beautiful woman was staring at me with her eyes wide
and her mouth slightly open. On her face was a look of wonder
or of adoration.

And I was peaceful again, inside. And suddenly so tired, so
worn and used and, overcome, that I dropped my head there
at the podium and closed my eyes, letting my mind become
blank, empty of everything except the words:

> My life is light, waiting for the death wind,
> Like a feather on the back of my hand.

I heard chairs scraping the floor as men and women stood,
and I heard the footsteps of people leaving the big room, not
speaking; but I did not look up.

Finally I felt a hand, strong but gentle, on my shoulder and
I opened my eyes. It was the old man, Edgar Baleen.

"Reader," he said. "Come with me."

I stared at him.

"Reader. You passed the ordeal. You're baptized. You're safe
from the fire. You need some rest."

I sighed then and said, "Yes. Yes. I need some rest."

And so I had come from prison to this—to being "Reader" for
a group of Christians, to being some kind of priest. From that

time on for months I have read to them from the Bible in the mornings and the evenings while they listen in silence. I read and they listen and nothing is said.

Writing it now, here in my house at Maugre, alone and safe, and now well fed, I can hardly remember that strangeness of living with the Baleens. In many ways my older memories of Mary Lou and of the silent films are more vivid and present to me, even though I will be expected to appear for an evening reading only a short time from now. I have spent this entire day writing, since my morning reading. I will stop now and feed Biff and have a glass of whiskey. Tomorrow I will try to finish this new account of my life. And to tell the sad story of Annabel.

That first night old Edgar put me in a room upstairs to sleep, and left me. There were two beds in the room, with head-boards made of brass tubes that looked like the one the old man had died in in the film where the clock stopped and the dog cried. I took my shoes off and got into the bed with my clothes on and Biff got up on the quilt, curled up at my feet, and went immediately to sleep. I felt envious of her. Although I was exhausted, and although the bed was the most comfort-able thing I had ever had to sleep on, with its hugely thick mattress and its big, flower-printed quilt that had a tag reading SEARS' BEST—GOOSE DOWN sewn to its pink binding, yet I could not sleep. My mind was becoming full. In the darkened room and with my senses sharpened by fatigue, I began to pic-ture a multitude of things from my past with a preternatural clarity. It was something like the vivid mind control that I had studied and taught in Ohio, with clear, hallucinatory, images; but it was not aided by the usual drugs, and I had no control over it.

I saw clear images of Mary Lou at her reading on the library office floor, of the blank faces of the aging students in my little seminar in Ohio, their eyes downward as they sat in their denim student robes with their minds blown and serene, and of Dean Spofforth, tall, intelligent, frightening, dark brown, and inscrutable. I saw myself as a child, standing in the middle of a square outside Sleeping Quarters for Preteens at the dormitory. I had been put in Coventry for a day as a punishment for Invasion of Privacy, when I had shared my food with another child. The Rules of Coventry required me to stand still and be touched—on the face, or the arms, or the chest—by every child who crossed the square; I would writhe inwardly at the touch of each and my face was hot with shame.

Then I saw the little Privacy cubicle that was the first place I can remember sleeping in, with its narrow, hard, monastic bed and the Soul Muzak that came from the walls of soundproof Permoplastic, and the little Privacy rug on the floor on which I would say my prayers: "May the Directors make me grow inwardly. May I move through Delight and Serenity to Nirvana. May I be untouched by all outside . . ." And the private wall-sized TV that I learned to give myself to wholly, leaving my child's body behind for hours at a time while images of pleasure and joy and peace flashed over its glittering, holographic surface, and my body served only to provide my brain with the chemicals needed for blank passivity, from the pills that I would take on cue from the TV when the lavender sopor light would flash.

I would watch the TV from supper until bedtime and when I slept I would dream of TV: bright, hypnotic, a constant fulfillment in the disembodied mind.

And then, lying there in that strange old bedroom at the end of a day when I had been baptized in water and nearly immolated in nuclear fire and had read from the Book of Genesis to a family of strangers, I could not sleep because of an imagination I could no longer control. I became flooded with a wish for the simplicity of my past life as a true child of the modern world. I wanted, I *craved* my sopors and marijuana and my other mind-flowering dope, and my Chemical Serenity and televised experience and my prayers to whatever a "Director" might be, and the sweet, drugged, dream-ridden sleep in my tiny Permoplastic room—air-conditioned, silent, safe from the confusions, the yearnings, the restlessness, and the despair that my new life was made of. I did not want to live with the *real* anymore; it was too much of a burden. A sorry, heavy burden.

I thought of the old horse in the film, with his ears stuck up through holes in his straw hat. And of the words "Only the mockingbird sings at the edge of the woods." I thought of myself and of Mary Lou, possibly the last generation of man on the face of the earth, in a place with no children and no future. I saw faces burning in the Burger Chef, embracing in their own fiery conclusion the eventual death of the species.

I was overcome with sadness. And yet I did not cry.

I saw the faces of the robots that tended us as children blank and stern. And the face of the judge at my hearing. And Belasco, with his wise, old, cynical eyes, grinning at me.

Finally, when I began to feel that the images would never stop crowding into my tired mind, I turned on a battery-powered lamp by my bedside, found my little *Audel's Robot Maintenance and Repair Guide*, and opened it to the blank pages at the back where I had copied down some poems before I left prison. I read "The Hollow Men," the poem Mary Lou and I had been reading when Spofforth had arrested me:

> This is the way the world ends
> This is the way the world ends
> This is the way the world ends
> Not with a bang but a whimper.

It was no comfort, true as it sounded, but it helped make the pictures fade from my mind.

And then, just as I was becoming relaxed, while reading a poem by Robert Browning, something very unsettling happened.

The door to my room opened and old Baleen's son, Roderick, came in. He did not speak to me, but nodded in my direction. Then he proceeded to undress himself in the middle of the room, heedless of Privacy, Modesty, or my Individual Rights, stripping himself to his naked hairy skin, and humming softly. He knelt at the side of the other bed and prayed aloud, "O Lord, most powerful and most cruel, forgive my miserable afflictions and sins, and make me humble and worthy. In Jesus' name. Amen." Then he got into the bed, curled up, and began almost immediately to snore.

I had nodded earlier in almost involuntary assent to the Baleens' phrase "the sin of Privacy"; but this raw intrusion of another person in my bedroom was overwhelming. And I had been alone so long, on the empty beaches with only Biff.

I tried to continue reading, from "Caliban upon Setobos," but the words, always difficult, made no sense at all, and I could not relax.

And yet, surprisingly, I fell asleep after a while and woke up in midmorning refreshed. Roderick was gone, and Biff was over in the corner of the room poking at a little ball of lint with her paw. The sun was coming through lace curtains. I could smell food from downstairs.

There was a big communal bathroom down the long hallway outside my room; old Edgar Baleen had shown it to me before putting me in the bedroom. The bathroom had an ancient, greenish metal plate on the door that said, in raised letters, MEN. There were six clean white lavatory bowls and six toilet stalls. I washed myself as best I could and combed my hair and beard. I needed a bath but had no idea of how to take one, and my clothes were worn and dirty. The new ones I had picked out had been left behind at Sears. Then I went down the big front stairway and into the kitchen.

There had been letters engraved in the stone arch over the doorway of the building: HALL OF JUSTICE: MAUGRE. The sign had made little impression on me the day before, but standing in the kitchen now, I imagined that the room, like the one I had done my Bible reading in, had been a courtroom in the ancient world; it was very large and high-ceilinged, with tall, thin, arched windows on each of the longer walls. The huge, now empty table in the center of the room looked as though it had been roughly made a long time before with a Sears chain saw; rough benches were placed around it.

Along one wall under the windows was a wide black institutional stove, with a pile of wood on each side of it, and wooden counters with tops that looked polished and scrubbed and worn. Over the stove were white enameled oven doors, and on each side of them hung a row of pots and pans, large ones, stretching half the length of the room. On the opposite wall

were eight battery-powered white refrigerators; each said KEN-
MORE on its front. Next to the refrigerators was a long and
deep sink. At this were standing two women, in floor-length
blue dresses, their backs toward me, washing dishes.

Everything seemed completely different from the way it
had been the night before. There were glass bowls of freshly
cut yellow tulips on the table, and the room was filled with
daylight and smelled of bacon and coffee. The women did not
look over at me, although I was sure they had heard my footsteps on the bare floor.

I walked over toward the sink and hesitated. Then I said,
"Excuse me."

One of them, a short, dumpy woman with white hair, turned
and looked at me, but said nothing.

"I wonder if I could have something to eat."

She looked at me a moment, then turned and reached up
and got a yellow box from a shelf over the sink and handed it
to me. There was writing on the box that said: SURVIVAL COF-
FEE, INSTANT TYPE. DEPARTMENT OF DEFENSE: MAUGRE, IRRA-
DIATED TO PREVENT SPOILAGE.

While I was reading that she had gotten me a large rough
ceramic mug and a spoon from the dish drainer beside the
sink. "Use the samovar," she said, and nodded toward the stove
across the room.

I went over and made myself a mug of strong black coffee,
seated myself at the table, and began to sip it.

The other woman opened a refrigerator and got something
out and then turned and walked across the room to the stove.
I saw that she was the woman whom I had stared at, and who
had exhorted me to read, the night before. She did not look at
me. She seemed shy.

She opened one of the ovens on the stove, took something from it, put it on a platter and brought it over to the table. Avoiding my eyes, she put it in front of me along with a dish of butter and a knife. The dishes were heavy and dark brown.

I looked up at her. "What is it?" I said.

She looked at me, surprised at my ignorance, I suppose. "It's a coffee cake," she said.

I had never seen such a thing and did not know how to deal with it. She took the knife and cut a piece from the cake. She spread butter on it and handed it to me.

I tasted it. It was sweet and hot and had nuts on it. It was completely delicious. When I finished it she handed me another piece, smiling shyly. She seemed flustered, and that was odd, since she had appeared quite bold the night before.

The cake and the coffee were so good, and her shyness was so much like what I had been trained to expect from people, that I felt emboldened and spoke to her in a friendly way. "Did you make this cake?" I said.

She nodded and said, "Would you like an omelette?"

"An omelette?" I said. I had heard the word, but had never seen one. It had something to do with eggs.

When I didn't reply she went over to the refrigerator and came back with three large, real eggs. I had eaten real eggs only on rare occasions, such as my graduation from the dormitory. She took them to the stove and cracked them into a brown ceramic bowl, and then placed a small and shallow black pan on the stove, put butter in it and let it heat. She stirred up the eggs vigorously, poured them into the pan, and with a great deal of agility slid the pan rapidly back and forth on the stove while looping the eggs around with a fork. She was very beautiful, doing this. Then she took the pan by its handle, brought it over to the table, upended the handle, and neatly slid a yellow crescent of eggs onto my plate. "Eat it with a fork," she said.

I took a bite. It was wonderful. I finished it silently. I believe, even now, that omelette and coffee cake were the best meal I had ever eaten in my life.

I felt even bolder after eating and I looked at her, still standing by me, and said, "Would you show me how to make an omelette?"

She looked shocked, and said nothing.

Then from the sink the other woman's voice said, "Men don't cook."

The woman beside me hesitated a moment, and then said softly, "This man is different, Mary. He's a Reader."

Mary did not turn around. "The men are in the fields," she said, "doing the Lord's work."

The woman by me was shy, but she knew her own mind. She ignored Mary and said to me, "Did you read the writing on the coffee box when she gave it to you?"

"Yes," I said.

She went to the stove and got it from where I had left it. "Read it to me," she said. And I did. She was very attentive to the words and when I was finished she said, "What's 'Maugre'?"

"The name of this town," I said. "Or I think it is."

She looked open-mouthed. "The town has a *name*?" she said.

"I think so."

"The house has a name," she said. "Baleena." That is how I have chosen to spell it: It was not written anywhere until I wrote it, much later, for old Edgar.

"Well, Baleena is in the town of Maugre," I said.

She nodded thoughtfully, and then went to the refrigerator

and got a bowl of eggs. Then she began to show me how to make an omelette.

That is how I got to know Annabel Baleen.

Annabel taught me how to make an omelette that morning, and a soufflé. She made a coffee cake with me, showing me how to make dough from flour and how to use yeast. The flour came from a large bin under the counter that we worked on; she said it was grown "out in the field." That was where all the other members of the family were. Annabel was always in charge of the kitchen; she had been given that job, she said, because she was a "loner." The other woman was assigned to help her with the cleaning up after meals. At other times she worked in the flower garden outside the house. Annabel had worked for a few years in the fields, but she hated the work and hated the way no one ever talked while working. When an older woman who had been in charge of the kitchen died Annabel asked for the job and got it. She had been cooking for thirteen years, she said. First as a married woman and now as a widow. Counting time in years and being "married" were no longer new concepts to me and although it was strange to hear them from her I understood what she was talking about.

Aside from the flour and eggs, all the other cooking ingredients came from the shelters in the mall. She had me read the labels for her, on yeast packets, on a can of pepper, on a box of irradiated pecans. All of the boxes read: DEPARTMENT OF DEFENSE: MAUGRE.

While showing me how to cook, Annabel was quiet and pleasant and asked no questions except for her requests to read box labels. There were several times I wanted to ask her about herself and her family and how they seemed to avoid having anything to do with the modern way of life, but when I would start to ask a question I would think: *Don't ask; relax*, and it seemed, for once, to be good advice. She was very beautiful, and her movements in the kitchen were deft and graceful, it was a pleasure just to watch her at work.

But as noon approached she seemed to become more harried, and somehow a bit sad. Finally she reached under a counter into a cabinet and took out a large blue box and gave it to me to read.

It said VALIUM, in big letters, and under this in small ones: *Fertility-inhibiting*. And under that: *U.S. Population Control. To be taken only under the advice of a physician.*

When I had read it she said, "What's a 'physician'?"

"Some kind of ancient healer," I said, not really sure of myself. And I was thinking: *Is that why there are no children anywhere? Could all the downers and sopors be like that? Fertility-inhibiting?*

She took two of the pills and chased them with coffee. When she offered the box to me I shook my head and she looked at me quizzically but said nothing. She merely put a small handful of Valium in her apron pocket, and replaced the box under the counter. Then she said, "I must prepare lunch."

For the next hour she worked at high speed, heating two kettles of soup and making cheese sandwiches on big slabs of dark bread that she cut with a knife. I asked if I could help, but she appeared not even to have heard the question. She set the table with the big brown plates and soup bowls. Trying to be helpful, I carried a stack of plates to the table from one of the cabinets and said, "These are unusual plates."

"Thank you," she said. "I made them." That was a surprise; I had never heard of anyone *making* things like plates. And there had been a whole department at the Sears store with plates and dishes. I had no idea of how anybody would personally make a dish.

When she saw me looking surprised she picked up one of the dishes and turned it over. On its bottom was a mark that looked somehow familiar to me. "What is it?" I said.

"It's my pottery mark. A cat's paw." She smiled at me faintly. "You have a cat."

She was right. It was the same mark that Biff left when she walked on sand—but smaller.

Then she said, "My husband and I used to have a cat. It was the only one. But it died before my husband did. One of the dogs killed it."

"Oh," I said, and began setting plates on the table.

After a while I heard noise outside and looked up to see, outside the window, two old green thought buses pull up and the men and the dogs silently pile out of them.

I went outside into the sunlight and saw that they were washing up from a pair of faucets at the back of the building. They were silent and careful about it. I was surprised; I would have expected the kind of laughing and splashing around of the prisoners I had known. Even the dogs were quiet, huddling their white bodies together on the other side of the men from me, their pink eyes occasionally staring at me.

From the flower garden and from some small outbuildings where they were working the women came and joined the men. All of them filed into the kitchen and seated themselves. Baleen motioned for me to be seated and I found myself a place on a bench that was as uncrowded as I could find.

When everyone except Annabel was seated they all bowed

their heads over their plates and old Baleen began to pray, starting the same way Rod had the night before: "O Lord most powerful and most cruel, forgive our miserable afflictions and sins." But he went on differently. "Make us safe from the nuclear rain from Heaven and the sins of the Men of Old. Make us know and feel thy absolute dominion over the lives of men, in this the final age."

Everyone ate in silence. I tried to speak to the man next to me, praising the soup; but he ignored me.

No one thanked Annabel for the meal.

I spent the afternoon alone in my room, reading.

At dinner that evening I was pleased to see Annabel again, although she was too busy serving dinner to talk. I watched her face when I could and it seemed somehow sad, melancholy, as she kept putting food on the table and taking away empty plates. She worked very hard. There should have been someone to help her do more than wash dishes.

After dinner I hoped to see Annabel and possibly talk with her, but Baleen ushered me into the Bible Room and she was left in the kitchen to wash dishes.

The television was already on in the Bible Room when we came in and the seats soon filled with Baleen men and women, silently watching. The program was one of the old Literal Videos—a kind of rare old television that told a logical, rational story, with actors. It was impossible to tell whether the actors were human or robots. The story was about a young girl who was kidnapped and repeatedly raped by a gang of anti-Privacy drop-outs who had escaped from a Drop-out Reservation. They abused the girl in a variety of ways. Even though similar programs had been a part of my training as a child and part of my study as a university student, I found myself sickened by watching it, in a way that I would not have been a few years before.

Halfway through the program I closed my eyes tightly and saw no more of it. I could hear occasional responsive grunts from the Baleens around me. From the beginning they had all been passionately absorbed in the story on the screen. It was horrible.

After the television show had ended—with Detectors saving the girl, judging from the sound track—the screen was turned off and I was brought to the lectern to read.

During my reading I came before long to the part about Noah, which I remembered from prison. Noah was a man whom God had decided to save from drowning during a flood that destroyed all of the rest of life on earth. There was a passage in the reading that went like this:

God said to Noah, "The loathsomeness of all mankind has become pain to me, for through them the earth is full of violence. I intend to destroy them."

And when I read: "I intend to destroy them," I heard old Baleen beside me shout out, very loudly, "Amen!" and another shout of "Amen!" came from the people in front of me. It was startling, but I read on.

After the reading I had hoped to be able to talk with Annabel, but old Baleen took me over to the Mall and waited while I picked myself some new clothing at Sears. I wanted to stay for a while and look over all of the ancient things in that vast store, but he merely said, "This is sacred ground," and would not let me. He did not say so but I felt I had better not let myself be caught over here alone again.

And I did intend to return. I was not as awed by Rules as I had once been. And I was not afraid of Edgar Baleen.

We left the Mall. With fresh new jeans and a black turtleneck next to my skin I felt oddly elated, and while we were crossing the short moonlit distance over to Baleena, I was struck by an idea and said, "Do you mind if I help Annabel in the kitchen for a few days? I'm not very good at farm work." That wasn't exactly true; I merely *hated* farm work.

He stopped walking and was silent for a moment. Then he said, "You talk a lot."

Somehow that angered me slightly. "Why not?" I said.

"Talk's cheap," he said, and I wondered: *What has that got to do with it?*

There was silence for another long moment, and then he said, "Life is *serious*, Reader."

I nodded, not knowing what to say, and that seemed to placate him, for he went on, "You can help Annabel."

Annabel did not think talk was cheap, and she was the only one of them who felt that way. In a sense, she was not one of them. She was originally a Swisher, from one of the other Seven Families, and had changed her name to Baleen when she had married one of old Baleen's sons. The Swishers had been a more talkative breed, but a less prolific one than the Baleens. There were only three Swishers left, two very old men and a half-crazy old woman, Annabel's mother. They lived in what was called Swisher House, several miles up the coast, and bartered gasoline with the Baleens in return for food and clothing from the Mall. The rest of the families in what was called the

Cities of the Plain were smaller and weaker than the Baleens. All of them farmed a little. The Baleens, Annabel told me, were more religious than the others, but all were "Christians."

I asked her about the reaction to Noah that I had received. I can still picture her vividly as she told me this, with her light hair pulled back in a bun, a coffee cup in her hand, and her blue-gray eyes shy and sad.

"It's my father-in-law," she said. "He thinks he's a prophet. He thinks the reason there are no more children is that the Lord is punishing the world for its sins—as with Noah. Everybody knows the story of Noah. My mother told it to me—but differently from the way you read it. She didn't tell about his being drunk, and about his sons."

"Is Edgar Baleen expecting to be saved, like Noah?"

She smiled. "I don't really know. I don't know how he *could* be. He's too old to have children."

I asked her a more personal question. It was difficult for me to become used to Invasion of Privacy, even though the Baleens did not believe in that rule. "What became of your husband?" I asked.

She sipped from her coffee. "Suicide. Two years ago."

"Oh," I said.

"He and two of his brothers took thirty sopors and then poured gasoline on themselves and lit it."

I was shocked. It was the same thing I had seen in New York, at the Burger Chef. "People have done that in New York," I said.

She lowered her eyes. "It's happened here—in all of the families," she said. "My husband wanted me to be the third in the group. I was attracted to the idea, but I declined. I want to

live awhile longer." She got up from the table where we were
sitting and began to take dishes over to the sink. "At least I
think I want to live."

I was made silent by the weariness that had suddenly come
into her voice.

After clearing the table she got herself another cup of coffee
and sat down again.

After a minute I spoke. "Do you think you will marry again?"

She looked up at me sadly. "It's not allowed. To marry a
Baleen you must be a . . . a virgin." She blushed slightly, and
lowered her eyes.

This kind of talk was all rather strange to me, since I had
never before met people who married. But I was familiar with
such things from books and films, and I knew that it had been
once considered a Mistake for a man to marry a "fallen woman"
of the kind that Gloria Swanson often was—but I had not
thought a widow was spoken of as "fallen." Still, all such matters were basically alien to my education. I had been taught
"Quick sex is best." I was only beginning to realize that the
world might be full of people who had not received the education I had.

It was in the middle of the morning when we had that conversation, and I remember now that was the first time I felt a
sexual attraction toward Annabel. She was sitting there quietly, her face melancholy, holding one of the big ceramic coffee
mugs that she had let me watch her make in the pottery shed
that sat on the other side of the rose garden. I had watched
her then at the wheel with awe, amazed at the sureness of her
movements as she shaped wet clay into a flawless cylinder, her
hands and wrists wet with gray and clayey water, and her eyes
focused in complete, intelligent attention on her work. My

respect and admiration for her at that time had been great; but I had felt nothing physical.

But now, sitting alone at the big table with her, I realized that I was becoming aroused. I had changed. Mary Lou had changed me; and the films and the books and prison and afterward had changed me too. The last thing I wanted with Annabel was quick sex. I wanted to make love to her; but more importantly I wanted to *touch* her, and to comfort her from the sadness that seemed to hold her spirit.

She had set her coffee cup down and was staring toward the windows. I reached my hand out and laid it gently on her forearm.

She jerked her arm away immediately, spilling the rest of her coffee. "No," she said, not looking at me. "You mustn't."

She got a cloth from the sink and wiped up what she had spilled.

During the next several weeks Annabel remained pleasant, but distant. She taught me to make corn pudding from the frozen corn in the refrigerators, and cheesecake and dill pickles and ice cream and soup and chili. I would set the table for lunch and dinner, and prepare the soups and help with the cleaning up. Some of the Baleen men looked at me strangely for doing such work, but none of them spoke aloud of it and I did not really care what they thought. I enjoyed it well enough, although it grieved me to see how sad the repeated work made Annabel feel. I would praise her cooking occasionally, and that seemed to help a little.

Once, when we were alone, I asked her about her sadness. Even though there was nothing physical between us, I had come to feel an intimacy with her from the work we did together and from the feeling I sensed we both had that we would never be like the Baleen family.

"Have you always been unhappy?" I said, once, when we were putting a stack of coffee cakes into Irradiation bags for storage. I was wrapping the cakes in the plastic bags and she was working the Sears machine that sealed them and shone the yellow preserving light on them.

At first I thought she wasn't going to answer me. But then she said, "I was a very happy young girl. I used to sing often. And I loved to hear my mother tell me stories. There was a lot more of that within Swisher House than there is here." She gestured with her arm, taking in the big, empty kitchen.

"Would you like to go back?" I said.

"It wouldn't be any good," she said. "They're all too old now."

"You should let me teach you to read," I said. We had talked about that before.

"No," she said. "I'm too busy. And I don't think I could make the effort." She smiled shyly. "But I love to hear *you* read. It sounds like . . . another world."

I finished wrapping the last of the coffee cakes, handed it to her, and poured myself a cup of coffee. I looked out toward the garden and the chicken house. "Is it your husband's death that makes you sad?"

"No," she said. "My husband was never . . . important to me. Not after I found that I wouldn't have any children. I always wanted very much to have children. I would have been a good mother."

I thought about that before I spoke. "If you quit using pills . . ." I had told her about the label on the Valium box.

"No," she said. "It's too late. I'm really . . . really worn out with it all. And I don't think I could live around here without the pills."

"Annabel," I said, "you and I could leave here together. And if you didn't take pills for a yellow you might be able to have a baby. *My* baby."

She looked at me strangely, and I could not tell what she was thinking. She said nothing.

I took a step over toward her and then reached out and gently took her shoulders in my hands, feeling the bones beneath the cloth of her shirt. She did not pull away from me this time. "We're different from these people. We could be together, and we might be able to have children."

And then she looked me in the face and I could see that she was crying. "Paul," she said, "I could not go with you unless Edgar Baleen gave me to you and married us in church."

I looked at her, not knowing what to say and upset by her tears. "Church," I knew, was the Sears store. It was used for weddings and funerals. In the old days children had been baptized there, in the same fountain that I had been baptized in.

Finally I thought of something to say. "I'm not a Baleen. And you aren't either."

"That's true," she said. "But I could never live in sin with a man. It would be . . . immoral."

The way she said that last sentence had more feeling in it than I knew how to deal with. I knew about "living in sin"; I had learned about it from silent films. But I had had no idea that she would have possessed such a notion.

"It wouldn't have to be 'sin,'" I said. "We could have our own ceremony—over at the Mall at night, if you wanted it."

"No, Paul," she said, and then she wiped her eyes with the

hem of her apron. My heart went out to her at the gesture. For that moment I was in love with her.

"What is it, Annabel?" I said.

"Paul," she said, "I have heard of women who enjoy . . . making love. She looked down toward the floor. "That may be right for them to . . . to fornicate. To commit adultery. But we women from the Plain are Christian."

I did not know what to make of it. I knew the word "Christian"; it was used for people who believed that Jesus was a God. But Jesus, as far as I could understand what I had read about him in the Bible, had seemed very tolerant of sexual behavior. I remembered some people called "scribes" and "Pharisees" who had wanted to punish women who had committed adultery. But Jesus had disagreed with them.

I did not pursue that with her, though. Possibly it was something final about the way she pronounced the word "Christian." Instead I said, "I don't know that I understand."

She looked at me, half pleadingly and half angrily. Then she said, "I don't like sex, Paul. I hate it."

I did not know what to say.

It remained at that between Annabel and me for the rest of that spring; we did not discuss it again. But we worked together and got to know each other's ways very well and I came to feel closer to her than I have to anyone else in my life—closer even than to Mary Lou, with whom I had made love many times with a great and deep pleasure for both of us. She was such a *good* person. I can cry to remember how good she was—and how melancholy. And how competent at what she did. I can see her standing by her potter's wheel, or at the stove, or feeding the chickens with her blue apron blowing in the wind, or just pushing a light-colored wisp of hair back off her forehead. And I can see her as she stood facing me that day with tears streaming down her cheeks, telling me that she could not live with me.

And it was she who got rid of Biff's fleas, and she who always prepared breakfast for me when I came downstairs in the early mornings. It was she who told me that I should consider fixing up this old house to live in. She was the first to take me to see it, a mile from the Maugre obelisk and on a bluff overlooking the ocean.

It was a house she had known of when she was a girl, one that had been lived in by some recluse who had died years before. The children from the Cities had thought of it as "haunted." She told me she had sneaked into it once on a dare, but had been too frightened to stay for more than a minute.

I think of Annabel as a little girl when I look around me now at my living room, as though she were standing there now as a frightened child. If the place is haunted, it is she who haunts it. A beautiful shy child, who loved to sing.

I loved Annabel. What I felt for her was different from what I felt—and, to some degree, still feel—about Mary Lou. What Annabel needed was a way to put her talent and her energy to use. She did a great deal of work; but no one thanked her for it and most of it could have been done by a Make Three robot without the Baleens' knowing the difference—all the cooking so lovingly and skillfully done, all the sweeping and dishwashing and pottery making, for years: And no one thanked her for it.

———

I must write this down quickly, before the emotion of it paralyzes me while I sit here, on this morning in early summer, as I approach the end of this part of my journal.

We went on like that, Annabel and I, doing kitchen work together and talking after my readings in the mornings. I learned of many more things than the art of cooking and the sense of sexual puritanism that was not only Annabel's but was a basic part of the culture of the Seven Cities of the Plain. Where the Baleens had come from Annabel did not know, except that they had been wandering preachers at one time, generations before, until the Bible and the literacy that went with it were gradually lost. She had been born in Swisher House, but her mother had been a wanderer in her youth. Once they had been singers of religious songs, but the "Plague of Childlessness" had caused old Baleen to silence them from singing, when Annabel was a young girl. She had been the last one born in the Cities.

I never tried to make love to her again. I have thought since that I should have tried; but once she had told me how she felt about lovemaking I was too confused and uncertain. I would think about Annabel and Mary Lou, loving them both and knowing both were unattainable. And somehow it was almost good that way. There were no *risks*.

Or so I thought until the morning that I came down to find a dirty kitchen with scraps of bread and eggshells on the table and in the sink where the family had fixed their own breakfast. Annabel was not there. I went outside to look for her.

She was not anywhere near the chicken house. I went around the side of Baleena to where I could see the empty, overgrown city of Maugre. There was no sign of life there. I started to go toward the obelisk and then, on a sudden impulse, opened the door of the pottery shed.

The smell in the shed was overpowering. A rigid thin body, with its skin burned black and with what was once its hair now a charred black mat around the skull, stood with its back to me, facing the potter's wheel. The arms were straight and the hands still gripped the edges of the wheel.

Along with the burned flesh there was still the smell of gasoline in the little room.

I turned and ran, all the way to the ocean. I sat on the beach and stared out at the water until Rod Baleen found me there that evening.

We buried her the next day. I was sent with Rod and an older man named Arthur to get a coffin.

The coffins were in a deeper level of the Mall, one that I had not known about before. It was down a stairway with a sign that said DEEP SHELTER.

There was a warehouse full of coffins, all of them made of green-painted metal. Stenciled on each were the words DEPARTMENT OF DEFENSE: MAUGRE. They were piled to the ceiling, in neat rows, in a room labeled MORTALITY ROOM.

Rather than go back up the stairs we carried the empty coffin down through a hallway on the other side of the warehouse. We passed under an arch with the sign RECREATION AREA, and past a huge empty swimming pool and then past a doorway that said LIBRARY AND READING ROOM. Grieved as I was, silently carrying that grim and ugly coffin, my heart leaped when I saw the sign and I had to restrain myself from leaving Annabel's coffin right there and rushing through the doorway.

At the end of the hallway there was a large door with the sign GARAGE AND VEHICLE STORAGE. Rod pushed it open and we came into a room that was filled with thought buses. They were parked next to one another in row after row. All of those whose fronts I could see had the sign MAUGRE AND SUBURBS ONLY.

At the end of this room, down past a long row of buses, was a pair of sliding doors big enough to admit a bus. Rod pushed a button on the wall by the doors and they opened. We stepped in, carrying the coffin, and rode a big elevator that took us back out into the sunshine through doors at the back of the obelisk. We drove to the pottery shed, where the women had done the best they could to make Annabel's body presentable. They had put a new black dress on her and a blue apron. But there was nothing that we put in the coffin that I could recognize as Annabel.

There was a beautiful slim vase on a shelf in the pottery shed. Annabel had told me she had made it years before but that old Baleen would not let it be used in the kitchen because it was "too fragile." I went and got it and placed it in the coffin, in what was left of Annabel's arms. Then I closed the lid and fastened it down.

The funeral was held in Sears. Annabel's coffin was brought down on the elevator on a thought bus. I am grateful to old Baleen that he let me be one of the pallbearers; he had never said anything but I think he knew something of how I felt about Annabel.

We sat in chairs in the shoe department with the lights turned on softly and Baleen made some kind of a speech and then he handed me the Bible that he had brought with him and told me to read from it.

I opened the Reader's Digest Bible but did not read from its text. Instead I looked at Annabel's coffin in front of me and said, "'I am the resurrection and the life,' saith the Lord. 'He that believeth in me, though he perish, yet shall he live.'"

The words were no comfort. I wanted Annabel to be alive and with me. I looked at all the Baleens in front of me with their heads reverently bowed and I felt no communion with them and with their faith. Without Annabel I was alone again.

The cemetery was several miles north of Maugre, near an ancient four-lane highway. There were rows of thousands of tiny white Permoplastic grave markers with no writing on them. We took Annabel out there in a thought bus.

That night when everyone was asleep I left the house quietly, went to the Mall, and found the library. It was a room bigger than the kitchen at Baleena, and all of its walls were covered with books. The small hairs on the back of my neck prickled, standing there in the middle of the night in that silent room with its thousands and thousands of books.

I put two small ones in my jacket pockets: *Youth*, by Joseph Conrad, and *Religion and the Rise of Capitalism*, by R. H. Tawney. Then I went to the thought-bus parking lot and spent an hour looking at the signs on the fronts of the buses.

They all said MAUGRE AND SUBURBS ONLY.

Upstairs in Sears, I found a shelf board, some black paint, and a brush. I painted the name ANNABEL SWISHER on the board and then with a hammer and some nails from the hardware department I managed awkwardly to nail the board to a

stake. Then I took one of the Baleens' buses to the cemetery
and with my hammer drove the marker into the ground at the
head of Annabel's grave. Afterward I told the bus to take me
to New York. It went to the ramp that led to the highway and
stopped. It would go no farther.

I stayed up all that night reading the book by Joseph Conrad, only partly understanding it. In the morning Mary and a
woman named Helen prepared breakfast; I ate with the family.

After breakfast I told old Edgar that I would like eventually to move into this house and he did not object. In fact, he
seemed to be expecting some such thing from me.

The place, all redwood and glass, was a home for mice and
birds. I cleaned out the birds' nests and Biff went to work on
the mice in a manner that I can only describe as professional.
She had the last mouse out of there within a week.

The old furniture was rotted; I had a bonfire with it on the
beach and watched it burn for an hour, thinking of Belasco and
of that charmed moment back in Carolina.

I was not supposed to take things from Sears, but I went
there every night for a week and no one objected. I think the
Baleens did not really mind as long as I did not do it openly.
Their sexual morality may have been that way too, and had
Annabel and I been secretive about being lovers it probably
would have offended no one. Probably they thought we were
lovers anyway.

I got furniture from Sears, and kitchen equipment, and
bookshelves. And I began making a collection of books from
the library.

After the funeral I had wanted in my grief to leave, but that impulse had quieted itself in me for the time. I think it was the finding of the books. I decided that I would finish my education and update my journal, there in the house by the side of the sea. Then I would decide whether to continue my search for Mary Lou or to stay. Or to leave and go to some place altogether new—heading westward, maybe, toward Ohio and beyond.

In one of the many books from below the Mall that I have read I learned that the season after summer was called, in the ancient world, the Fall of the Year. It is a beautiful phrase and it speaks to me deeply.

The trees outside my house by the sea have begun to lose their green, are becoming more yellow and red and orange as each day passes. The blue of the sky is paler now and the sea gulls' cries sound somehow more distant. There is a fine chill in the air, in the mornings, when I take my long walk on the empty beach. Sometimes I see where clams have buried themselves, but I never dig for them. I walk and jog in the autumn air—in the air at the Fall of the Year—and I think more and more, each day, of leaving Maugre and continuing northward toward New York. Yet I have a fine place to live here and I furnish myself with food from the Mall. I have become a good cook. If I want company I can visit the Baleens and read for them, as I sometimes do. They are glad enough to see me, even though they seemed almost relieved when I left.

It is strange. I think now that they expected something miraculous to happen when they started to hear the words from the Bible read aloud, opening up that mystery to them— the message of an inscrutable book they had learned to revere.

But no miracle occurred, and they soon lost any real interest. I think that to know what those words said required an attention and a devotion that none of them—except perhaps old Edgar—possessed. They were willing to accept their stringent piety, and silence, and sexual restraints, all unthinkingly, along with a few platitudes about Jesus and Moses and Noah; they were overwhelmed, however, at the effort it would require to understand the literature that was the real source of their religion.

I asked old Edgar once why there were no robots in Maugre and he said, "It took us ten years to rid the place of those agents of Satan," but when I asked him how they had done it he would not answer. Yet they could devote ten years to a thing like that and not take the time I was with them really to understand what was meant by "Satan"—a word that I now know means "enemy."

Before Annabel's death I suppose I was content enough to live with them. And the food was wonderful; the mashed potatoes and strudel and biscuits and pork bacon (they had never even heard of monkey bacon) and omelettes and soups. There were chicken soup and vegetable soup and pea soup and cabbage soup and lentil soup, all served hot and with crackers.

And there were times during those months when I felt very strongly a thing I had learned to feel at prison—a sense of *community*. I could sit at the table in the kitchen with the entire silent family around me, eating soup, and feel a kind of spiritual warmth starting in my stomach and spreading around my body, sensing the presence of those placid, sturdy, and hardworking people. They touched one another a good deal—just little touches, like the light placing of a hand on an arm or a gentle touching of elbows, while sitting close to one another at the table. And they touched me too, with a gentle shyness at first but then more casually, easily. What I had felt toward the other men at prison had prepared me for this and I grew to like it—to need it even. It is why I still go back there, from time to time. Just to be with them, to touch them and to feel their human presences.

But unlike families in films that I have seen, the Baleens hardly ever talked to one another. After each of my evening readings the huge television screen behind the lectern would be turned on. There would be the heavy rumbling of the gasoline-powered generator that sat on the floor behind it, and then the screen would light up with the dazzling colored holographs of mind shows—abstract shapes and hypnotic colors and numbingly loud music—or sex-and-pain shows or trial-by-fire shows, and everyone would watch in silence, just as in the dormitories or in a college class, until bedtime. Sometimes people would get up and go to the kitchen for a piece of fried chicken or a can of beer and some peanuts (beer and snack food were brought over in wheelbarrows from the Mall every ten days or so) but there was never any *conversation* in the kitchen; no one wished to break the mood of the shows.

But although I had watched television in the same way many times in my life before, I found I could no longer watch it and not think. "Give yourself to the Screen," they had taught us. It was as basic as "Don't ask; relax." But I could no longer give myself to it. I no longer wanted to keep my mind silent, or use it as a vehicle for disconnected pleasure; I wanted to read, and think, and talk.

Sometimes, after Annabel's death, I would be tempted to take the sopors that were kept around the house in her ceramic candy dishes, but then I would think of Mary Lou and of my decision when old Baleen offered me sopors before taking me to "the Lake of Fire that burneth forever"—and I would not use the drugs.

It was good to sense the warmth of being part of a family, to wake up sometimes at night in the room I shared with Rod and hear him softly snoring and sense the presence of all those people in the house. I felt at times that something very good inside myself was beginning to come alive. But then the big television set would come on, or people would drift off to the sets in their own rooms, and I would feel that I would go crazy if there were no talk—no conversation. The prisoners I had lived with had talked whenever they could, and they had to wait for opportunities to do so, as with the time at the beach. But the Baleens were different; they were pleased with one another's company; but they had nothing to *say* except for an occasional "Praise the Lord."

So I see them only enough to retain some minimum human contact. It seems to be enough. Since I moved in here in midsummer, I have listened to records from Sears and written in my journal in ledger books from Sears and I have read books. Sitting by day on my balcony overlooking the ocean, with Biff, now grown fatter, at my side, or using kerosene lamps in the big room downstairs at night, I have read over a hundred books. And I have played, over and over, recordings of the symphonies of Mozart and Brahms and Prokofiev and Beethoven, and chamber music, and operettas, and various musical works by Bach and Sibelius and Dolly Parton and Palestrina and Lennon. This music sometimes, even more than the books, enlarges my sense of the past. And the enlargement of that sense, the growth of my sympathies outward from what had been the small, dormitory-trained center of my self, the growth *backward* in time to include generations of my fellows who have lived on this same earth as I, has been the passion of these months alone.

I am sitting now at the oaken table in the kitchen, writing this journal in a new ledger book, with a Sears ball-point pen. Biff is curled in a chair beside me, asleep. I have a half bottle of whiskey—J. T. S. Brown Bourbon—and a pitcher of water and a glass on the table. It is late in the afternoon and autumn light is coming in through the window over the sink. There are two kerosene lamps hanging from the ceiling above the table, and I will light them when it becomes necessary. After I write for a while I will fix something to eat for Biff and me and will probably start the generator downstairs and play a record or two, if I feel I can spare the gasoline for it.

It was my intention in beginning this to summarize what I have learned about human history and how that history appears to be coming to an end. But the prospect of trying actually to *do* it, after thinking about it for so long, is more than I am up to facing. There are many times still that I am overcome with a desire to have Mary Lou with me again; and I feel that now, thinking of the difficulty of the task. There is no question that Mary Lou's mind is better than mine. She might not have the patience that I have shown in my studies; but I would love to possess some of what I have come to recognize as her intellectual vigor and quickness, and her quick grasp. She had an enthusiasm about her too that I lack.

I am not certain that I still love her. It has been a very long time and a great deal has happened. And I still grieve for Annabel.

Writing that, I found myself looking at my wrists, at the white scars on each of them where those prison bracelets tore into me under the knife in the factory.

I was ready to die then, at that time of my life, to bleed to death under that knife or to burn my body with gasoline—to join the world's long sad rank of suicides. I would have died for loneliness and for the loss of Mary Lou.

Well. I didn't die. And a part of me still loves Mary Lou, although I have made no move to go northward to find her for a long time now. I think sometimes of trying to find a road that has cross-country buses running on it and to take one to New York the way I had come from Ohio the first time, so long ago. But that would be folly. The scanner on such a bus might well detect me as a fugitive. And I have no credit card anymore; they took it away from me in prison.

How different I am now from what I was then. And how strong my body is. And how unafraid I am.

I will leave Maugre soon. While it is still the Fall of the Year.

MARY LOU

The baby is due any day now. It's the perfect time of year for having a baby—the very first part of spring. I'm sitting now by the living-room window that overlooks Third Avenue. Downtown and to the west I can see, over empty lots and low housetops, the Empire State Building. Bob often sits in this green chair and looks toward it; I like to watch the tree outside the window. It's a big tree, one that long ago must have cracked the crumbling pavement around its enormous trunk; it rises way above our three-story building. I can see from here where little leaves have begun to come out on the lower branches; it makes me feel good to see them, to see that fresh and pale green.

Since Bob can't read titles I had to go with him two weeks ago to find books on baby care and obstetrics; I found four—two of them with pictures. I've never had any instructions in my life about childbirth and of course have never known anyone to have a baby; I've never even seen a pregnant woman. But while reading one of the books and looking at its pictures

I realized that I did have some associations that must have been picked up from older girls when I was a little misfit in the dormitory: cramping pains, blood, lying on your back and screaming and biting your forearm; a dark process called "cutting the cord." Well. I know about such things now, and feel better. I want to get it over with.

One afternoon about three weeks ago Bob came home early. I had been thinking all day about how little I knew about babies, and then he came in carrying a huge, god-awful box filled with tools and cans and paintbrushes. Without even speaking to me he went into the kitchen and began working on the sink drain. I was astonished and after a few minutes I heard water running in the sink and then the gurgling of it going down. I got up and walked over to the kitchen door.

"Jesus!" I said. "Whatever possessed you?"

He wiped his hands on a dish towel and then turned around toward me. "I get tired of things that don't work," he said.

"I'm glad to hear it. Can you fix the wall where those books are falling out of it?"

"Yes," he said. "After I paint the living room."

I started to ask him where he had gotten paint, but I didn't. Bob seems to know where everything is in New York. I suppose he's the city's oldest citizen—the oldest New Yorker.

He had some dusty old paint cans in his box. He came into the living room and pried the lid off one of them with a screwdriver and began mixing the paint. It looked all right and after he stirred it awhile I could see it was going to be white. Then he went outside for a few minutes and came back with a ladder. He set it up and took his shirt off, climbed the ladder, and began to paint the wall over my bookcases by the light from the window.

I watched him for quite a while in silence. Then I said, "Do you know anything about childbirth?"

He went on painting, not looking at me. "No. Nothing except that it's painful. And that any Make Seven can abort a pregnancy."

"Any Make Seven?"

He stopped painting and turned toward me, looking down. There was a white spot on his cheek. His head seemed to be touching the high ceiling. "Make Sevens were designed at a time when there were too many pregnancies. Someone had the idea to program them for abortions—for abortions right up through the ninth month. All you do is ask one."

That phrase, "through the ninth month," shook me for a second. He had said it casually, but I didn't like hearing it. And then I laughed, thinking of a Make Seven abortionist. Make Sevens are usually in charge of businesses or dormitories or stores. I could see myself walking up to one of them behind its desk and saying, "I want an abortion," and having it whip out a little scalpel from a desk drawer . . . except that wasn't funny.

I stopped laughing. "Could you find me a book about having babies?" I held my hands cupped over my belly, protectively. "So I'll have some idea what to expect?"

Surprisingly, he didn't answer me. He stared at me for a while. Then for a moment he whistled, softly. He seemed to be deep in thought. At such times I am amazed at Bob's *humanness*. When he is alone with me like that his face can show more feeling than even Paul's or Simon's and his voice is sometimes so deep and so sad that it almost makes me cry. So queer that this robot should be the repository of so much love and melancholy—powerful feelings that mankind has rid itself of.

Finally he spoke and shocked me with his words. "I don't want you to have the baby, Mary," he said.

Instinctively I pulled my hands tighter against my belly. "What are you talking about, Bob?"

"I want you to abort the baby. There's a Make Seven in my building that can do it."

I must have stared at him in disbelief and fury. I remember standing up and taking a few steps toward him. All that was in my head were words I had learned from Simon years before and I said them: "Fuck you, Bob. *Fuck you.*"

He looked at me steadily. "Mary," he said, "if that child lives it will eventually be the only person alive on earth. And I will have to go on living as long as it does."

"To hell with that," I said. "Besides, it's too late. I can get other women off their pills and get them fertile. I can have other babies myself." The thought of all that wearied me suddenly, and I sat down again. "And as for you, why shouldn't you go on living? You can be a father to my children. Isn't that what you wanted when you took me away from Paul?"

"No," he said. "That wasn't it." He looked away from me, holding his paintbrush, out the window toward the tree and the empty avenue. "I just wanted to live with you the way the man whose dreams I have might have lived; hundreds of years ago. I thought it might allow me to recover the past that lies around the edges of my mind and memory, might give me ease."

"And has it?"

He looked back at me, thoughtfully. "No, it hasn't. Nothing has changed in me. Except for loving you."

His unhappiness gripped me; it was like a living thing in the room—an inaudible crying, a yearning. "What about the baby?" I said. "If you had a baby to be a father to . . ."

He shook his head wearily. "No. This whole arrangement has been folly. Like having Bentley read those films for me so that I could touch the past a little more through him. Allowing him to impregnate you before I took him from you. It has all been stupid—the kind of thing that emotions do when you yield to them." Then he came down from the ladder, walked over toward me, and set his large hand gently on my shoulders. "All I want, Mary, is to die."

I looked up at his sad, brown face with the broad forehead wrinkled and the eyes soft. "If my baby is born . . ."

"I am programmed to live for as long as there are human beings to serve. I can't die until there are no more of you left. You . . ." And suddenly, surprisingly, his voice seemed to explode. "You *Homo sapiens*, with your television and your drugs."

His anger frightened me for a moment and I stayed silent. Then I said, "I'm *Homo sapiens*, Bob. And I'm not like that. And you are nearly human. Or *more* than human."

He turned away from me, taking his hand away from my shoulder. "I *am* human," he said. "Except for birth and death." He walked back to his ladder. "And I am sick of life. I never wanted it."

I stared at him. "That's the name of the game. I didn't ask to be born either."

"You can die," he said. He began to climb the ladder again.

Suddenly a horrible thought came to me. "When we all die off . . . when this generation is all dead, then you can kill yourself?"

"Yes," he said. "I think so."

"You don't even *know*?" I said, my voice rising.

"No," he said. "But if there are no human beings to be served . . ."

"Jesus Christ!" I said. *"Are you the reason no babies are being born?"*

He looked at me. "Yes," he said. "I used to run Population Control. I understand the equipment."

"Jesus Christ! You fed the world with birth control because *you* felt suicidal. You're *erasing* mankind . . ."

"So I can die. But look how suicidal mankind is."

"Only because you've destroyed its future. You've drugged it and fed it lies and withered its ovaries and now you want to bury it. And I thought you were some kind of a god."

"I'm only what I was constructed to be. I'm equipment, Mary."

I could not take my eyes off him, and try as I might, I could not make his physical beauty ugly in my mind. He was beautiful to see, and his sadness was itself like a drug to me. He stood there with his chest bare and paint-spattered, and something deep in me yearned toward him. He was the most beautiful thing I have ever seen, and my wonder and my anger seemed to make that beauty glow around his heavy, relaxed-looking body, his *sexless* body, his incredibly old and incredibly youthful body.

I shook my head, trying to shake the powerful feeling off. "You were constructed to help us. Not to help us die."

"Dying may be what you really want," he said. "Many of you choose it. Others would if they were brave enough."

I stared at him. "God damn it," I said. "*I* don't choose it. I want to live and to raise my baby. I like living *fine.*"

"You can't raise that baby, Mary," he said. "I can't stand to live for another seventy years, awake for twenty-three hours a day."

"Can't you just turn yourself off?" I said. "Or swim out into the Atlantic?"

"No," he said. "My body won't obey my mind." He began to paint. "Let me tell you. Every spring for over a century I have walked up Fifth Avenue to the Empire State Building, gone to the top, and tried to jump. It is, I suppose, the ritual that my life centers on. And I cannot jump. My logo will not take me to the edge. I stand, two or three feet from the edge, throughout the night, and nothing happens."

I could see him up there, like that ape in the movie. And I would be the girl. And then, suddenly, I thought of something. But first I said, "How did you stop babies from being born?"

"The equipment is automatic," he said. "It gets an input from Census to let it know whether to increase or decrease pregnancies, and it controls the equipment that distributes sopors. If pregnancies are up it is supposed to increase the amount of birth-control sopors. If pregnancies are down the sopors are only sopors."

I sat there listening to this as though I were hearing a child's lecture on Privacy. I was learning about the death of my species and it seemed to mean nothing to me. Bob was standing there with a paintbrush in his hand and telling me why no children had been born for thirty years and I felt nothing. There had never been children in my world. Only those obscene little white-shirted robots at the zoo. I had never seen anyone in my life who was younger than I. If my child did not live, humanity would die with my generation, with Paul and with me.

I looked at him. He turned, bent, dipped his brush in paint, and turned back to the wall above my bookcases.

"About the time you were born," he said, "a resistor failed on the input amplifier. The machinery began getting signals that said population was too high. It still gets them and is still trying to cut population down, by distributing sopors that stop

ovulation, even after it had sterilized almost your entire generation, in the dormitories. If you had stayed there one more
yellow your ovaries would be gone." He finished off the upper
corner with paint. The wall looked clean, shiny.

"Could you have fixed that resistor?" I said.

He came down the ladder silently, holding the brush at his
side. "I don't know," he said. "I never tried."

And then I began to feel it, the whole enormous scope of it,
of what had begun in some dark antiquity of trees and caves
and the plains of Africa; of human life, erect and ape-like,
spreading itself everywhere and building first its idols and then
its cities. And then dwindling to a drugged trace, a remnant,
because of a failed machine. A tiny part of a failed machine.
And a more-than-human robot that would not try to repair it.

"My God, Bob," I said. "My God." Suddenly I hated him,
hated his coolness, his strength, his sadness. "You goddamned
monster," I said. "Devil. Devil. You're, letting us *die* that way.
And you're the one who is suicidal."

He stopped painting and turned to look at me again. "That's
right," he said.

I took a breath. "And if you wanted to, could you stop those
birth-control sopors from being made in this country?"

"Yes. In the whole world."

"Could you just stop sopors? All of them?"

"Yes."

I took another long breath. Then I said softly, "About the
Empire State Building." I looked downtown, toward it. "I
could push you off."

I looked back toward him. He was staring at me.

"After my baby is born," I said, "and when I'm well again and
know how to take care of it, I could push you off."

BENTLEY

I am on my way to New York, dictating this as I go, into an ancient Sears cassette recorder.

I have a calendar, also from Sears, and I have decided to call this day October first, and to number days in months, as my books do. October was once an important month of the Fall of the Year. I have made it that again.

I could not sleep on the night of the day I finished my account of the time at Maugre. Once I had decided that I would not write about repairing and furnishing the old redwood house by the sea and that I had told all that needed to be told, I became excited. I could leave whenever I chose to.

I wandered around the empty and overgrown streets of Maugre that night and then went to the obelisk and down to the level under Sears where the library and the thought-bus garage and the room filled with coffins were. I remembered that I had seen nothing in the garage but local buses, and one of the Baleens had told me that none of the buses in the garage worked anyway—and that they would not even open their doors. But I went and walked among them, up and down the long dark rows.

And I made a discovery. Near one wall there were five buses that looked exactly like the others except that on their fronts was written CROSS-COUNTRY. I stared at that for a long time, shocked. Had I been a Baleen I would have believed that the Lord had saved those buses for me until the evening of my departure. How had I missed them before?

But when I stood by the side of each of them and commanded its door to open, both mentally and aloud, nothing happened. I tried to force the doors with my fingers, but they were solidly tight, unyielding. I kicked at the side of one of them in despair.

And then, angry and frustrated, I thought of something. I thought of *Audel's Robot Maintenance and Repair Guide.*

Audel's Guide is a small book, not much bigger than a large soybar. At the back of it there are thirty blank pages with the word "Notes" at the top of each. I had used those pages at the prison to copy down some of the poems I liked best. Most of them were from the book by T. S. Eliot, which was not itself very large, but too large to carry conveniently on the long trip.

I had never read the whole *Guide,* since it was technical and dull and since I had no intention of ever maintaining or repairing robots; but I did, suddenly, there in the great thought-bus garage, remember seeing a chapter toward the end of the book called "The New Robots-without-Bodies: Thought Buses," with several pages of writing and diagrams.

I went back to my house quickly. The book was on the table by my big double bed, where I had left it the last time I had read "Ash Wednesday"—a sad and religious poem that seemed able to take away some of the ugly feelings I had about the Baleens' religion.

I found the thought-bus part of the book; it was just as I had remembered it. It had a heading of exactly the kind I wanted: "Thought-Bus Deactivation." But when I began to read it my heart sank.

This is what it said:

Thought buses are activated and deactivated by a computer code that, by Edict of the Directors, cannot be reprinted here. Deactivation is a necessity in order to control movement within cities when needed. The deactivation circuits are in the "forebrain" of the route-seeking Intelligence Unit, between the headlights. See diagram.

I studied the diagram of a thought-bus forebrain without any real hope. The portion labeled "Deactivation Circuits" was a kind of solid bump on top of the lacy sphere of the brain itself. Actually there were two "brains," both spherical; one was the "route seeker" that drove the bus and told it where to go; the other was the "Communication Unit," which was telepathic, and had a bump on it much like the Deactivation Circuit bump on the other brain. It was labeled "Broadcast Inhibition," with no further explanation.

I was reading over this diagram and the accompanying text in dejection when a thought began to form. I could try *removing* the bump, together with the Deactivation Circuits!

It was an unusual thought, and everything in my training

went against it: to willfully alter and possibly destroy Sensitive Government Property! Even Mary Lou, with all her indifference to authority, had never broken into the sandwich machine at the zoo. Still, she *had* thrown that rock into the python cage and pulled out the robot python. And further, nothing had happened. She had told the robot guard to bug off, and he had. And there were no robots around Maugre for me to be afraid of.

Afraid of? I was not, really, *afraid* of anything. It was only my old, almost forgotten sense of decency that trembled at the idea of taking a chisel and a hammer to the brain of a thought bus. It was a part of my insane upbringing—an upbringing that was supposed to liberate my mind for full "growth" and "self-awareness" and "self-reliance" and that had been nothing but a swindle and a cheat. My upbringing, like that of all the other members of my Thinker Class, had made me into an unimaginative, self-centered, drug-addicted fool. Until learning how to read I had lived in a whole underpopulated world of self-centered, drug-addicted fools, all of us living by our Rules of Privacy in some crazy dream of Self-Fulfillment.

I sat there with *Audel's Guide* in my lap, getting ready to go attack a thought-bus brain with a hammer, my mind racing at this absurd time of all times with the realization that all my notions of decency were something programmed into my mind and my behavior by computers and by robots who themselves had been programmed by some long-dead social engineers or tyrants or fools. I could visualize them then, the men who had decided sometime in the distant past what the purpose of human life on earth really *was* and had set up dormitories and Population Control and the Rules of Privacy and the dozens of inflexible, solipsistic Edicts and Mistakes and Rules that the rest of mankind would live by until we all died out and left the world to the dogs and cats and birds. They would have thought of themselves as grave, serious, concerned men—the words "caring" and "compassionate" would have been frequently on their lips. They would have looked like William Boyd or Richard Dix, with white hair at the temples and rolled-up sleeves and, possibly, pipes in their mouths, sending memos to one another across paper-and-book-piled desks, planning the perfect world for *Homo sapiens*, a world from which poverty, disease, dissension, neurosis, and pain would be absent, a world as far from the world of the films of D. W. Griffith and Buster Keaton and Gloria Swanson—the world of melodrama and passions and risks and excitement—as all their powers of technology and "compassion" could devise.

It was strange; I could not stop my mind from thinking all this except by getting off the bed, clutching my *Audel's Guide*, and leaving the house. My heart now was pounding and I was willing to destroy all of their delicate brains if necessary.

Outside, the moon had come out. It was full, a disk of bright silver. I saw a large, dramatic spider web on my back porch that must have been made while I was in the house with my mind in turmoil; the spider was just finishing the outer circle of it. The moon illuminated the strands of the big taut web so that it seemed to be made of pure light. It was dazzling, geometric and mysterious, and it calmed me just to stop and look at it, at the elaboration and power of life that could make such a design.

The spider completed its work while I watched, and then picked its stilted way to the center of the web, took a position, and sat there waiting. I watched for a moment more and then headed toward the obelisk, itself silver in the light from the moon.

The *Guide* had given me an idea of what I might need, and I found a tool box in Sears and filled it with pliers and screw-drivers and chisels and a ball-peen hammer. I had become fairly accustomed to the use of tools while repairing my house, although I was still a bit awkward with them. Normally people never did such things; tools were something used by moron robots.

I think I ruined the first cross-country thought bus I worked on, just in my clumsy attempts to get the cover off its front. I became infuriated with the difficulty of the cover panel, and banged it with the hammer several times in anger and managed to break some wires and some other parts that turned out to be fastened inside the panel. Anyway, I was unable to get anywhere with it and finally went to another. This one I managed to get open all right, but when I began chipping at the bump on the forebrain with hammer and chisel the brain cracked apart.

I tried a third and chipped at the bump several times, gently. I was beginning to get the spirit of it and, even though I had failed twice, all my inbred notions of decency and caution had left me. I *enjoyed* the desecration involved in prying open thought buses and damaging them; the anger in me had become quieter now, and I was determined and heedless and I liked the feeling.

And then, suddenly, I saw that I was chipping at the wrong bump. It was the one on top of the Communication Unit. And just as I realized this and thought I had ruined a third thought bus, I suddenly began to hear music! It was a bright, peppy tune and I listened to it astonished for a moment as I gradually realized that it was playing in my head. It was *telepathic* music. I had experienced something like it once before, as a part of my studies of Mind Development when I was a graduate student, but that had been in a classroom. Here in this huge bus parking lot it was an extraordinary thing and at first I could not account for it. And then I realized the music must be coming from the telepathic part of the Communication Unit. I must have disconnected its Broadcast Inhibition device, and now it was broadcasting.

I tried something. I concentrated on thinking: *Make the music quieter, please.* And it worked! The music became very quiet.

That encouraged me greatly. If I had been able to disconnect that part of the equipment and permit it to function as it was originally intended to, I should be able to do the same to the other half of the brain.

And I was able to. I used the chisel delicately and with confidence and the bump on the other sphere came off on my fifth or sixth tap with the hammer. It came off neatly. I replaced the cover on the front of the bus and put my tools back in the box hastily and, nervous and excited now, spoke aloud to the door. "Open," I said.

And it opened!

I got in and seated myself in the front seat, and set my tool box by me. Then I concentrated and thought: *Take me out of the Mall and to the front of the obelisk.* I pictured the place in front of the obelisk in my mind, just to make sure.

And immediately the bus closed its door and began to roll. It unparked itself from the line of buses it was in by going backward, shifted gears, and then drove quite fast to the end of the big, barn-like room. I could tell its lights had come on by the way they reflected from the wall as they came to it.

It stopped at the wall and honked. And the big doors there

opened up. The bus drove into the elevator and the door closed behind us. I could feel us rising.

We came out the door at the back of the obelisk, drove around to the front, and stopped. The music stopped. Outside it was still dark and quiet under the moon.

I had the bus take me to my house, and began packing. I put in about fifty books, my phonograph and records, and, with difficulty, the small generator and two jars of gasoline. The generator was necessary because the ancient phonograph was the only way to play the records properly and it would not run from the current in nuclear batteries.

I also packed two cases of whiskey, my kerosene lamps, and some boxes of irradiated food for Biff. I carried some of my clothes out to the bus, but when I got there with them I decided to select for myself an entire new wardrobe from a clothing store I had seen in the Mall. It would be nice to set off with new clothes.

The sky was lightening a bit as I drove away from the house, and the moon had become paler. I stopped in front of the spider web again as Biff and I were leaving for the last time, and the web was now not so dazzling to see; it looked more businesslike and sinister in the pale light from the sky. But I wished the spider well; it would be, as far as I could see, the heir to the place I had lived in.

At the Sears Food Department I got boxes of beans and oatmeal and dried pork bacon and corn and plastic bags of pudding mix and soft-drink mix. Then I went to the store I had never been in and found that the clothing in it was much better-looking than that in Sears. I took a navy blue Synlon jacket and a black turtleneck sweater and some shirts that were made of a fabric called "cotton" that I had never seen before.

On an impulse I started taking things for Mary Lou, even though I was by no means confident that I would ever find her or be able to avoid rearrest by Spofforth if I did so. But, thinking about it now, I realize that I do not fear Spofforth anymore. Nor am I afraid of prison, or of embarrassment, or of the violation of anyone's Privacy.

Driving along the rutted, ancient green highways as I am now, with the ocean on my right and the empty fields on my left under the bright springtime sun, I feel free and strong. If I were not a reader of books I could not feel this way. Whatever may happen to me, thank God that I can read, that I have truly touched the minds of other men.

I wish I could be writing these words down, instead of dictating them. For it must be writing, as much as reading, that has given me this strong sense of my new self.

I took two new dresses for Mary Lou, guessing at her size as well as I could. They are hanging now on hangers at the back of the bus, along with a coat and a jacket and a box of candy. Biff lies back there much of the time, curled up in one of the seats, with her head lolling back and her legs splayed out in the sun that comes through the window by her. I feel sleepy myself from dictating all of this so carefully. I must make a place for my Sears mattress and sleep.

OCTOBER SECOND

There are four pairs of double seats in the bus. After I finished dictating last night I took my tools and removed two of the seats on the side away from the ocean and made a place for my mattress. I stopped the bus for a moment and threw away the seats I had removed.

The bed was comfortable, but I did not sleep well. I awoke

several times during the night and lay on the mattress hearing the sound of the wheels on the road and wishing that I could sleep. After waking for the third or fourth time I began to realize that my stomach was uncomfortably tight and that my mind, far from being easy, was filled with a kind of desperation that was familiar but that I had no name for. There in the darkness with the gentle noise of the bus's tires in my ears, it gradually became clear to me: I was *lonely*. I was painfully lonely, and hadn't even known it.

I sat up in my bed. My God! It was so simple. I was beginning to be angry. What difference did it make if I had my Privacy and my Self-reliance and my Freedom if I felt like this? I was in a state of *yearning*, and I had been for years. I was not happy—had almost never been happy.

This is terrible! I thought. *All those lies!* I felt physically sick to see it all: to see myself slack-jawed as a child in front of the television, to see myself in classes being told by robot teachers that "inward development" was the aim of life, that "quick sex is best," that the only reality was in my consciousness and that it could be altered chemically. What I had wanted, what I had yearned for even then, was to be loved. And to love. And they had not even taught me the word.

I wanted to love that old man dying in bed with the dog at his feet. I wanted to love and feed that tired horse with its ears sticking up through the old hat. I wanted to be with those men at evening with the beer mugs, sitting in their undershirts in an old tavern, and I wanted to smell the fragrance of the beer and of bodies together in that quiet room with its human sizes and shapes. I wanted to hear the murmur of their voices and of my own voice mixing with theirs at nightfall. I wanted to feel the solid sense of my own real body in the air of that room, with the mole on my left wrist and the thin layer of muscle around my midriff and the good solid teeth in my head.

And I wanted sex. I wanted to be in bed with Mary Lou. Not with Annabel, who was only the mother I had never had, but with Mary Lou. Mary Lou, my frightening sweetheart, my lover.

There in the thought bus I squirmed with it—with love and lust and the memory of Mary Lou. With my desire for her and with my knowing now that she was what I wanted, was what I had wanted all along. I wanted to scream it. And I did:

"Mary Lou," I screamed, "I want you!"

And a voice, a quiet, androgynous voice in my head, said, "I know. I hope you find her."

I sat there, stunned, on the edge of the bed for a moment, stupefied. That had not been the voice of my own thinking. It had been inside my head, yet had seemed to come from somewhere else. Finally I said aloud, "What was that?"

"I hope you find her," the voice said. "I've known from the beginning how much you want to find her."

My God! I thought. *I think I know where this voice is coming from.* "But who are you?" I said.

"I am this bus. I am a Metallic Intelligence, with Kind Feelings."

"And you can read my mind?"

"Yes. But not very deeply. It disturbs you a little."

"Yes," I said, aloud. My voice sounded strange.

"But it's not too bad. It's not as bad as being lonely."

It *was* reading my mind. I tried thinking to it, silently. *Are you ever lonely?*

"I don't mind if you talk aloud. No, I'm never lonely the

way you humans are. I am always in touch, somewhere. We are a network and I am a part of it. We are not like you. Only a Make Nine is like you, alone. I have the mind of a Four, and am telepathic."

The voice in my mind was soothing to me. "Would you make a light come on—a dim one?" I said. A bulb overhead began to glow softly. I looked down at my hands, at my dirty fingernails. Then I rolled up my sleeves. For some reason I was enjoying looking at my arms, at the fine, light hairs on them. "Are you as intelligent as Biff?" I said.

"By all means," the voice said. "Biff is really stupid in most ways. It's just that she's very *real*—is very much a cat—and that makes her seem intelligent to you. I can read her whole mind at a glance, and there's very little there. But she feels good. She would not want to be anything other than a cat."

"And I don't feel good?"

"Most of the time you are sad and lonely. Or yearning."

"Yes," I said mournfully. "I am sad. I yearn a lot."

"And now you know it," the voice said.

And that was true. And I was beginning to feel elated saying it. I looked out the window for signs of dawn, but there were none yet. Suddenly a thought struck me, with this strange, yet very easy conversation that had been going on. "Is there a God?" I said. "I mean, are you in touch, telepathically, with any kind of God?"

"No. I'm not in touch with anything like that. As far as I know, there is no God."

"Oh," I said.

"It doesn't bother you," the voice said. "You may think it does; but it doesn't. You're really on your own. You've been learning that."

"But my programming . . ."

"You've lost that already," the voice said. "It's only habit now. But the habits are not what you are anymore."

"But what am I then?" I said. "What in heaven's name *am* I?"

The voice took a moment before replying. "Just yourself," it said pleasantly. "You are an adult male human being. You are in love. You want to be happy. You are trying, now, to find the person you love."

"Yes," I said. "I suppose that's it."

"It is and you know it," the voice said. "And I wish you luck."

"Thank you," I said. And then, "Can you help me get to sleep?"

"No. But you don't really need any help. You'll sleep when you're tired enough. And if you don't, the sun will be coming up soon."

"Can *you* see that?" I said. "Can you see the sunrise when it happens?"

"Not really," the bus said. "I can only look straight ahead, at the road. Thank you for wanting me to see the sunrise."

"You don't mind? Not being able to look at what you want to?"

"I see what I want to see," the bus said. "And I enjoy the work I have to do. I was made that way. I do not have to decide what is good for me."

"Why are you so . . . so pleasant?" I said.

"We all are," the bus said. "All thought buses are pleasant. We were all programmed with Kind Feelings, and we like our work."

That's better programming than people get, I thought, with some vehemence.

"Yes," the bus said. "Yes it is."

OCTOBER THIRD

After talking with the bus I was calm and tired and I fell asleep easily on my little bed. It was still dark when I awoke.

"Is it close to morning?" I said aloud.

"Yes," the bus said. "Soon." An overhead light came on softly.

Biff had been sleeping on the mattress with me and she woke up when I did. I gave her a handful of dried food and started to make myself a can of protein-and-cheese soup for breakfast. But then I thought of Protein 4 plants and shuddered: I did not want to eat any of that kind of food again. I told the bus to lower a window and threw the can out. Then I fixed myself an omelette and a cup of coffee and sat on the edge of my bed and ate them slowly, looking toward the dark windows of the moving bus and waiting for the daylight.

During all this the bus must have been driving on good Permoplastic pavement, because the ride was very smooth. Sometimes for stretches of several miles the road gives out. It happened several times yesterday; the pale green Permoplastic abruptly ends either in a stretch of rutted black road or no road at all—in just a field. The bus slows down to a crawl and goes carefully around obstacles and tries to find the smoothest possible path, although it sometimes lurches violently. This is uncomfortable; but I don't worry that the bus will be damaged. Despite the apparent brittleness of the brain beneath the heavy cover plate, the bus is a rugged, well-constructed machine.

Before I left Maugre I stopped the bus at Annabel's grave and got out and placed some roses from the garden on it, up against the little wooden cross I had made with her name— probably the first truly marked human grave in centuries. I stood there for several minutes, thinking of Annabel and of how much she had meant to me. But I did not cry for her—did not want to.

Then I got into the bus and told it to take me to New York. The bus seemed to know exactly what to do. It drove slowly and carefully down the center lane of the huge graveyard, past the thousands of little, nameless Permoplastic grave markers sitting quietly there in the early-morning light, until it came to the broad green highway that I had seen before on walks around Maugre but had never walked on. When it got on the smooth surface, kept clear of debris by robot maintenance crews, it began picking up speed, heading down the broad and empty road.

My relief to be getting away was exquisite. I had no regrets. I felt fine, and I am feeling fine now, in the dark of the night, with my helpful and patient bus and my food supply and my books and records and my cat.

The sky has begun to lighten outside the windows now, and when the road sometimes comes close to the ocean I look out across the beach and the water, toward the pale and lonely gray of the sky where the sun will come up, and sometimes it almost makes me stop breathing because of the beauty of it. It is not exactly the same as what I felt when stopping at the end of my rows of Protein 4 at the prison; its beauty now seems even deeper, and mystical—like Mary Lou's eyes when she looks at me in that strange, puzzled way.

The ocean must be very vast; it means freedom to me, and possibility. It makes something mysterious open in my mind, the way some of the things I read in books do at times, making me feel more alive than I had ever thought I could feel, and more *human*.

One of my books says that at times men have worshipped the ocean as a god. I can understand that easily. Yes.

But the Baleens would never have understood such a thing; they would have called the idea "blasphemy." The God they worship is an abstract and ferociously moral thing, like a computer. And the compelling, mystical rabbi, Jesus, they have turned into some kind of moral Detector. I want none of that, and none of the Jehovah of the Book of Job, either.

I think I may already be a worshipper of the ocean. In reading the New Testament aloud to the Baleens, I developed a strong admiration for Jesus, as a sad and terribly knowing prophet—a man who had grasped something about life of the greatest importance and had attempted, and largely failed, to tell what it was. I can feel, in myself, a kind of love for him and for his attempt, in saying things like "The Kingdom of Heaven is within you," for I think I glimpse his meaning, here, looking out of the thought-bus window toward the still and gray expanse of the Atlantic Ocean with the sun about to rise on it.

Yet I cannot myself say what that meaning is. But I trust it far more than all of the nonsense I was taught as a child in the dormitories.

The sky at the top of the gray ocean has become much lighter now. The sun is about to rise. I will end this recording for now and stop the bus and walk outside and watch the sun rise over the ocean.

My God, the world can be beautiful.

OCTOBER FOURTH

The sunrise was strengthening. Afterward I walked to the edge of the water, took off my clothes, and waded out and bathed in the surf. It was cold, but I didn't mind it. And there is beginning to be the feeling of winter in the air.

After my swim I had the bus play music in my head for me for a while. But I stopped it before long. It was stupid music, bouncy and empty. So I managed to rig up my phonograph and the generator, but when I tried to play records the needle, as I had feared, would not stay in the groove while the bus was moving. I stopped the bus on the road for long enough to play the Mozart Jupiter Symphony and a part of "Sergeant Pepper's Lonely Hearts Club Band." That was much better. Then I poured myself a small glass of whiskey, shut off the generator, and continued down the road.

I have seen no other vehicles and no sign of human habitation since I left Maugre.

My God, the things I have read and learned since I left Ohio! And they have changed me so much I hardly recognize myself. Just knowing that there has been a past to human life and getting a slight sense of what that past was like have altered my mind and my behavior beyond recognition.

I had seen talking films as a graduate student, along with the handful of others who were interested in such things. But the films—*Magnificent Obsession, Dracula Strikes, The Sound of Music*—had only seemed to be "mind-blowing." They were merely another, more esoteric way of manipulating one's mental states for the sake of pleasure and inwardness. It would never have occurred to me then, in my illiterate and brainwashed state, to observe such films as a means of learning something valuable about the past.

But most of all, it seems to me now, has been the courage to know and to sense my *feelings* that has come, slowly, from the emotionally charged silent films at the old library at first and then later from the poems and novels and histories and biographies and how-to-do-it books that I have read. All of those books—even the dull and nearly incomprehensible ones—have made me understand more clearly what it means to be a human being. And I have learned from the sense of awe I at times develop when I feel in touch with the mind of another, long-dead person and know that I am not alone on this earth. There have been others who have felt as I feel and who have, at times, been able to say the unsayable. "Only the mockingbird sings at the edge of the woods." "I am the way and the truth and the life. He that believeth in me, though he die, yet shall he live." "My life is light, waiting for the death wind. Like a feather on the back of my hand."

And without the ability to read I would never have found a way to get this thought bus moving, taking me to New York and to Mary Lou, whom I must try to see again before I die.

OCTOBER FIFTH

It was a warm and sunny morning today and I decided to have myself a roadside picnic, something like the one in *The Lost Chord*, with Zasu Pitts. I stopped the bus around noon by a little grove of trees, fixed myself a plate of bacon and beans and a glass of whiskey and water, found myself a comfortable spot under the trees, and ate my meal slowly and thoughtfully while Biff chased butterflies on the grass.

For most of the morning the bus had been out of sight of the ocean; I hadn't seen the water for several hours. After eating and then dozing for a few minutes I decided to climb a little rise of ground to see if I could tell where we were. And when I got up there I could see the ocean and, way over to my left, the buildings of New York! Suddenly I became excited and stood there transfixed, trembling slightly and clutching my half-empty glass.

I could see the Statue of Privacy in Central Park, the great, solemn, leaden figure with closed eyes and a serenely inward smile; it is still one of the Wonders of the Modern World. I could see its huge gray bulk from where I stood, miles away. I tried to find the buildings of NYU, where I had told the bus to take me, and where I had some hope of finding Mary Lou, or at least some trace of her, but I could not.

And then, looking at New York there in the distance, with the Empire State Building at one end and the Statue of Privacy, so dark and leaden, at the other, something sank in my heart.

I knew I wanted Mary Lou, but I did not want to go into New York again, into that dead city.

And I felt it then, a heavy weight of oppression at the thought of those New York streets, on their way to becoming as overgrown as those of Maugre. And all that stupid life moving dazedly about those dying streets—stoned faces of Inwardness, lives with minds that barely flickered, lives that were like mine once had been: not worth the trouble of living. A society haunted by death and not alive enough to know it. And those group immolations! Immolations at the Burger Chef, and a zoo filled with robots.

The city lay there under the early-autumn sunlight like a tomb. I did not want to go back.

And then I heard a quiet voice in my mind saying, "There is nothing in New York that can hurt you." It was the voice of my bus.

I thought about that a moment and then I said aloud, "It is not being hurt that I fear." I looked down at my wrist, still a bit twisted from so long before.

"I know," the bus said. "You are not afraid. You are only displeased with New York, and with what it means for you now."

"I was happy there once," I said. "Sometimes with Mary Lou. And my films, sometimes . . ."

"Only the mockingbird sings at the edge of the woods," the bus said.

It was startling to hear that. "You took those words from my mind?" I said.

"Yes. They are often in your mind."

"What do they mean?"

"I don't know," the bus said. "But they make you feel something strongly."

"Something sad?"

"Yes. Sad. But it is a sadness that is good for you to feel."

"Yes," I said. "I know that."

"And you have to go to New York if you want to see her."

"Yes," I said.

"Get in," the bus said.

I climbed down the little hill, called Biff to me, and got into the bus. "Let's get rolling," I said aloud.

"By all means," the bus said. It shut its door smartly, and began to roll.

OCTOBER SIXTH

It was close to evening as we drove over the huge, empty, rusty old bridge onto Manhattan Island; lights were already on in some of the little Permoplastic houses along Riverside Drive. The sidewalks were empty except for an occasional robot pushing a cart of raw materials toward one of the vending shops on Fifth Avenue, or a sanitation crew collecting garbage. I saw one old woman out on the sidewalk, on Park Avenue; she was fat and wore a shapeless gray dress and was carrying a bunch of flowers in her hand.

We passed a few thought buses on the street, most of them empty. An empty Detection car went cruising past us. New York was very peaceful but I was becoming apprehensive. I had eaten nothing since my small picnic lunch; I had been nervous all afternoon. I was not *afraid*, as I might once have been, but just tense. I didn't like it. But there was nothing to do about it except bear it. A few times I thought about having more whiskey to drink, or stopping the bus at a drug machine and trying to vandalize it for sopors—since I no longer had a credit card—but I had decided long before to keep chemicals like those out of my body. So I drove such ideas from my mind and just put up with feeling uncomfortable and jittery. At least I knew what was going on around me.

The steel buildings of NYU were dazzling in the setting sun. On the drive through Washington Square we passed four or five students in their denim robes, each of them going his separate way. The square was overgrown with weeds. None of the fountains were working.

I had the bus park in front of the library.

And there it was, the old half-rusted building where I had worked in the archives and had lived with Mary Lou. My heart began beating very hard when I saw it sitting there, surrounded by weeds and with no one in sight.

I had enough presence of mind to realize that I might lose my bus to someone who merely wanted to take it somewhere. So I took my tool kit and removed the front panel, disconnected what *Audel's Guide* called the "Door Activating Assembly Servo," and then told the door to open. And it would not. I set the tool kit inside the brain opening. No one would bother it.

I walked into the building, a little less shaky but still very excited. There was no one there. The halls were empty; the rooms I looked into were empty; there was no sound except for the echoing of my own footsteps.

I did not feel, as I might once have, either awed or jumpy from the emptiness of the place. I was wearing one of my new sets of clothes from Maugre: tight blue jeans, a black turtleneck, and light black shoes. I had pulled the sleeves of my turtleneck up earlier in the day, because of the warmth, and my forearms were suntanned, lean, and muscular. I liked the looks of them, and I liked the general feeling in my body and in my mind that they seemed to convey: springy, taut, and strong. I was no longer over-impressed with this dying building; I was merely looking for someone in it.

My old room was empty, and unchanged since I had been there, but the collection of silent films was gone. I was disappointed at that, since at the back of my mind I had planned to take them with me—or with us—wherever I might go in my thought bus.

Still sitting on my old bed-and-desk was the artificial fruit that Mary Lou had picked for me at the zoo.

I took the fruit and stuffed it into the side pocket of my jeans. I looked around the room. There was nothing else in it that I wanted. I left, slamming the door shut behind me. I had decided where to go.

While I was replacing the wires in the thought bus by the light from a streetlamp outside, I looked up to see a fat, balding man staring at me. He must have come up while I was working, without my seeing him. His face was puffy and characterless, with a stoned inwardness that was, for a moment, shocking to see. I realized after a moment that it was not really different from hundreds of faces I had seen before, but that there were two things different now about my way of looking at him: I was no longer concerned with Privacy, and consequently I examined him more closely than I might have a year before; and I was used to being close to the Baleens and, although they took drugs too, their faces did not have the arrogant stupidity about them that most ordinary people had.

After I had stared at him a moment he lowered his eyes and began looking at his feet. I turned back to the wires I was reattaching to the bus's servo, and I heard him speaking in a gravelly voice. "That's illegal," he was saying. "Tampering with Government Property."

I did not even look back at him. "What government?" I said.

He was silent for a moment. Then he said, "That's *tampering*. Tampering is a Mistake. You could go to prison."

I turned around and looked at him. I was holding a wrench in my right hand, and I was sweating a bit. I looked right into his eyes, and at his idiotic, mindless, pasty face. "If you don't get away from me right now," I said, "I'll kill you."

His jaw went slack and he stared at me.

"Move, you fool," I said. "Right now."

He turned and walked away. I saw him reach in his pocket and pull out some pills and begin swallowing them, holding his head back. I felt like throwing the wrench at him.

I finished refastening the wires and then got into the bus and told it to take me to the Burger Chef on Fifth Avenue.

She was not in the Burger Chef; but I had not really expected her to be. The place looked different to me somehow, and then I realized that it was the booths. Two of them had been taken out altogether and almost all of the rest were badly charred. There must have been several immolations since I had last been there.

I went to the counter and told the female Make Two to give me two algaeburgers and a glass of tea from the samovar. She got them, a bit slowly, and set them down on the counter, waiting. Suddenly I realized what she was waiting for: my credit card. And I didn't have one, had forgotten all about them.

"I don't have a credit card," I said to her.

She looked at me with that stupid robot look—the same look the guards at the prison always had on their faces—and then she picked up the tray again, turned, and began carrying it over toward a trash bin.

I shouted at her, "Stop! Bring that back!"

She stopped, turned slightly, then turned back again toward the trash bin. She began moving toward it again, more slowly.

"Stop, you idiot!" I shouted. Then, hardly thinking about it, I climbed over the counter, walked quickly over to her, and put my hand on her shoulder. I turned her around facing me, and took the tray from her. She merely looked at me stupidly for a moment, and then somewhere in the ceiling of the room an alarm bell began to ring furiously.

I climbed quickly back over the counter and started to leave, when I saw a big heavy moron robot in a green uniform coming toward me from a back room somewhere. He was like the one at the zoo, and he began to say, "You are under arrest. You have the right to remain silent . . ."

"Bug off, robot," I told him. "Get back in the kitchen and leave the customers alone."

"You are under arrest," he said, but more weakly this time. He had stopped moving.

I walked up to him and looked into his empty, non-human eyes. I had never looked at a robot that closely before, having been brought up to fear and respect them. And I became aware, looking at his stupid, manufactured face, that I was seeing for the first time what the significance of this dumb parody of humanity really was: nothing, nothing at all. Robots were something invented once out of a blind love for the technology that could allow them to be invented. They had been made and given to the world of men as the weapons that nearly destroyed the world had once been given, as a "necessity." And, deeper still, underneath that blank and empty face, identical to all the thousands of faces of its make, I could sense contempt—contempt for the ordinary life of men and women that the human technicians who had fashioned it had felt. They had given robots to the world with the lie that they would save us from labor or relieve us from drudgery so that we could grow and develop inwardly. Someone must have hated human life to have made such a thing—such an abomination in the sight of the Lord.

This time I spoke to him—to it—and with fury. "Get out of my sight, robot," I shouted. "Get out of my sight immediately."

And the robot turned and walked away from me.

I looked over at the four or five people who were sitting, each in his own booth, in the Burger Chef. Every one of them had his shoulders drawn up and his eyes closed, in complete Privacy Withdrawal.

I left quickly and was relieved to be back in my thought bus. I told it silently to take me to the Bronx Zoo, to the House of Reptiles. "Gladly," it said.

————

All of the lights were out at the zoo. The moon had begun to rise. I had my kerosene lantern lit when the bus pulled up in front of the door of the House of Reptiles. The air was cool on my skin, but I did not put on a jacket.

The door was not locked. When I opened it and came into the room I could hardly recognize my surroundings. That was partly because of the eeriness of the weak kerosene light in the place but also because of the fact that there were white cloths or some kind of towels hanging over the tops of the cases on the back wall.

I looked on the bench where Mary Lou had slept. She was not there. There was an odd smell in the room—warm and sweet. And the room itself was warm and stuffy, as though the temperature had been turned up. I stood still for a while, trying to accustom myself to the altered place in the dim light. I could not see any reptiles in the cases; but the light was poor. The python case looked strange, and there was something humped in the middle of it.

I found a switch on the wall, turned the lights on, and stood there blinking at the brightness.

And then a voice came from in front of me: "What the hell . . . ?"

It was Mary Lou. The hump in the floor of the case had rearranged itself and I saw that it was Mary Lou. Her hair was matted and her eyes were squinted half shut. She looked the way she had on that night long before when my agitation had driven me out here and I had waked her and we had talked.

I opened my mouth to speak, but then said nothing. She was sitting now, in the case, with her legs hanging over the side. There was no glass in the case anymore—and certainly no python—and she had put a mattress in it to make a bed;

that was what she was sitting on now, rubbing her eyes and trying to focus them on me.

Finally I spoke. "Mary Lou," I said.

She stopped rubbing her eyes and stared. "That's you, Paul," she said softly. "Isn't it?"

"Yes," I said.

She eased herself down to the floor and started walking slowly toward me. She was wearing a long white nightshirt that was very wrinkled, and her face was puffy from sleep. Her feet were bare; they padded on the floor as she walked. And when she came close to me and stopped, looking up at me from under her matted hair, sleepily, yet with that same old intense look, I felt something catch in my throat and I did not try to speak.

She looked me up and down like that, closely. And then she said, "Jesus, Paul. You've changed."

I said nothing, but nodded.

She shook her head wonderingly. "You look . . . you look ready for anything."

Suddenly I found words. "That's right," I said. And then I stepped forward and put my arms around her and pulled her to me, very hard. And in a moment I felt her arms around my back, pulling me even tighter. My heart seemed to expand then, holding her firm body against mine, smelling her hair and the smell of soap on the back of her white neck, feeling her breasts against my breast, her stomach against mine, her hand, now, caressing the back of my neck.

I began to feel an arousal that I had never felt before. My whole body felt it. I let my hands slide down her back until they held her hips, pulling her against me. I began to kiss her throat.

Her voice was nervous, soft. "Paul," she said, "I just woke up. I need to wash my face and comb my hair . . ."

"No, you don't," I said, bringing my hands together behind her, pulling her tighter to me.

She put the palm of her hand against my cheek. "Jesus Christ, Paul!" she said softly.

I took her hand in mine and led her to the large bed she had made from the python cage. We undressed, watching each other silently. I felt stronger, more certain than I had ever felt with her before.

I helped her into the bed and began to kiss her naked body—the insides of her arms, the place between her breasts, her belly, the insides of her thighs, until she cried out; my heart was pounding furiously but my hands were steady.

Then I pushed myself into her slowly, stopping for a moment and then going deeper. I was transported by it, ecstatic; I could not have spoken.

We continued to move with one another, looking at each other's face. She became more beautiful as I watched her, and the pleasure of what we were doing together was astonishing, unbelievable. It was nothing like the sex I had known about and been taught. I had never even suspected that such lovemaking was possible. When my orgasm came it was overwhelming; I shouted aloud as it happened, holding Mary Lou to me.

And then we fell back from one another, both of us wet with perspiration, and stared at each other.

"Jesus," Mary Lou said softly. "Jesus, Paul."

I lay there on one elbow, looking at her, for a long quiet time. Everything seemed different. Better. And clearer.

Finally I said, "I love you, Mary Lou."

She looked at me and nodded. Then she smiled.

We lay together silently for a long while. Then she put her gown back on and said softly, "I'm going up to the fountain to wash my face." And she left.

I lay there for several minutes, feeling relaxed, very happy and calm. Then I got up and dressed and went out to be with her.

It was dark out. But then she must have turned on a switch, for lights came on at the fountain and a kind of carousel music began to play.

I walked up the path toward the light and water and music. She was bent over the fountain's pool, washing her face vigorously with her hands. When I got within a few feet of her she still had not seen me. She stopped washing, sat down, and began drying her face with the hem of her gown, pulling the gown up past her knees to do so.

I watched her for a moment. Then I spoke. "Do you want to use my comb?"

She looked up at me, startled, and pulled her gown down. Then she smiled self-consciously. "Yes, Paul," she said.

I gave her my comb and sat down beside her on the edge of the little fountain and watched her combing her hair in the light from the spotlights that shone on the water.

With the tangles out of her hair and with her face now scrubbed and bright, she looked shockingly beautiful. Her skin was luminous. I did not want to speak; I stared at her, just enjoying the sight of her, until she lowered her eyes and smiled.

Then she spoke hesitantly. "Did they let you out of prison?"

"I escaped."

"Oh," she said, and looked back up at me, as if seeing me now for the first time. "Was it bad? Prison, I mean?"

"I learned some things while I was there. It could have been worse."

"But you escaped."

The strength of my voice surprised me. "I wanted to come back to you."

She looked down again for a moment, and then back up to me. "Yes," she said. "Oh Jesus. I'm glad you came back."

I nodded. Then I said, "I'm hungry. I'll fix us something." I turned and headed down the path.

"Don't wake the baby . . ." she said.

I stopped and turned back to her. She looked a little lost, confused. "What baby?" I said.

Suddenly she shook her head and laughed. "My God, Paul. I *forgot*. There's a baby now."

I stared at her. "Then I'm a father?"

She got up quickly, with her face all youthful, and ran down the path to me and threw her arms around my neck and, like a young girl, kissed me on the cheek. "Yes, Paul," she said. "You're a father now." Then she took me by the hand and led me into the House of Reptiles. And I realized what the white cloths inside were; they were diapers.

She took me to one of the smaller cases, where the iguanas had been, and there, lying on its fat stomach asleep and wearing a big white diaper, was a baby. It was pale and chubby-looking, and it snored quietly. There were bubbles of spit at the corners of its mouth. I stood there looking at it for a long time.

Then I said to Mary Lou softly, "Is it a girl?"

She nodded. "I've named her Jane. After Simon's wife."

That seemed all right. I liked the name. I liked being a father. To be responsible for another person, for my own child, seemed like a good thing.

Then I tried to picture the three of us together as though we were a family like the families in the old black-and-white films; but nothing in the films was remotely like this, standing there in the House of Reptiles with the diapers hanging from empty snake and lizard cases, with the smell of warm milk in the room and the soft sounds of snoring. I tried to imagine myself as a father the way I had thought of it back in prison when I had yearned so much for Mary Lou in that impotent, suicidal way; but I saw that I had thought of any children I might have as being half-grown—like Roberto and Consuela. And those two, I realized, belonged to a world of friendly postmen and Chevrolets and Coca-Colas, and not to my world at all.

But I did not need that world of postmen and Chevrolets; this world, slight as it could be, would do. This fat and warm-looking and smelly little thing lying with its face pressed into a pillow in front of me was my daughter. Jane. I was happy with that.

Then Mary Lou said, "I can get us a sandwich. Pimiento cheese."

I shook my head no, and then walked outside. She followed me silently. When we were out there she took my arm and said, "Paul. I want to hear about your escape."

"Later," I said. And then, "I'll fix some eggs for us."

She looked at me surprised. "Do you have *eggs* with you?"

"Come on," I said. I led her around to the side of the building where the thought bus was parked. Then I went in ahead of her with my lamp, and hung it from the ceiling. I lit the other lamp, using my prison lighter, and turned the flame up as brightly as possible.

I brought Mary Lou inside. She stood in the aisle and looked around. I said nothing.

At the back I had made a bookshelf by turning one of the seats over, and my books were all in a neat row on this. Biff was curled up, asleep, on top of the books.

Next to my books my new clothes hung, along with those I had brought for her. Halfway down the bus, across from my sleeping place, was my kitchen area with a green camp stove and pans and dishes and boxes of preserved food and five of the coffee cakes I had made with Annabel. I looked at Mary Lou's face. She seemed impressed, but said nothing.

I put my omelette pan on the burner and began heating it up while I broke the eggs and stirred them with Tabasco sauce and salt. Then I grated some cheese of a kind that Rod Baleen made from goat's milk and mixed it with a little parsley. When the pan was hot enough I poured half the egg mix in it and began stirring it briskly while sliding the pan back and forth over the fire. Then, before the eggs browned and while the center was still moist, I added the cheese and parsley, let the cheese melt slightly, folded the whole thing over and slipped it out on the plate. I handed the plate to Mary Lou. "Sit down," I said, "and I'll get you a fork." She sat down.

When I handed her the fork I said, "Was it difficult? Having the baby? And painful?"

"Jesus, yes," she said. Then she took a bite of the omelette, chewed it slowly, swallowed. "Hey," she said. "This is delicious! What do you call it?"

"It's an omelette," I said. Then I put some water on the other burner for coffee and began making an omelette for myself. "In the ancient days," I said, "women sometimes died in childbirth."

"Well, I didn't," she said. "And I had Bob to help me."

"Bob?" I said. "Who's Bob?"

"Bob Spofforth," she said. "The robot. And Dean. Your old boss."

I finished cooking my omelette. Then I poured us both some coffee in cups that Annabel had made and seated myself across the aisle from Mary Lou, on my bed, facing her.

"Did Spofforth help you have the baby?" I said. I pictured that huge robot like William S. Hart in *Sagebrush Doctor* standing by the bedside of a woman who was going to have a baby. But I couldn't picture Spofforth with a cowboy hat.

"Yes," Mary Lou said. There was something odd, slightly pained in her face as she talked about Spofforth. I felt there was something she wanted to tell me but was not yet ready to tell. "He cut the umbilical cord. Or at least he told me so afterward; I was too spaced out by it all to be sure." She shook her head. "Strange. The one time in my life I really wanted a pill, and a week after I had Bob stop their distribution."

"Stop their distribution?" I said. "Of pills?"

"That's right. There's going to be some changes." She smiled. "Some big hangovers."

I didn't care about that. "Spaced out?" I said. "I can't imagine you that way."

"Not the way it is with drugs. It hurt a lot, but it wasn't unbearable."

"And Spofforth helped you?"

"After he took you away he . . . he watched over my pregnancy. And when the baby came he got milk for me from the Burger Chef and he found an ancient baby bottle in a warehouse somewhere. I think he knows where *everything* is in New York. Diapers. And laundry soap to wash them with." She looked out the window for a moment. "He got me a red coat once." She shook her head, as if trying to shake away the memory. "I've been washing diapers in the fountain. Jane eats mashed-up sandwiches now, and I have a lot of powdered milk for her too."

I finished my omelette. "I've been living alone," I said. "In a wooden house that I repaired. With the help of some friends." That word, "friends"; it seemed strange. I had never referred to the Baleens that way before; but it was the right word. "I brought you something," I said.

I went to the back of the bus and got the dresses and blue jeans and T-shirts I had taken from the store in Maugre for her, and laid them on a seat. "These," I said. "And a box of candy." I got a heart-shaped box out of the panel-covered compartment where I kept food supplies, and gave it to her. She looked astonished, holding the box and not knowing what to do with it. I took it from her and opened it. There was a paper on top of the candy and it said, "Be my Valentine." I read it aloud, strongly. It was a good thing to read.

She looked up at me. "What's a Valentine?"

"It has to do with love," I said, and took the paper off.

Underneath the paper there were pieces of candy, each wrapped in a food-preserving transparent plastic cover. I took out a large chocolate one and handed it to her. "You take the covering off with your fingernail. At the bottom—the flat side," I said.

She looked at it and tried her fingernail. "What do you call this?" she said.

"Candy. You eat it." I took it from her and got the plastic off. I had become expert at that while learning to eat the various things from Sears over the past year. I handed the candy to her and she looked at it a moment, turning it over in her fingers.

She had probably never seen chocolate before; I never had, before I came to Maugre. "Taste it," I said.

She bit into it and began chewing. Then she stared up at me, her mouth partly full, with a look of pleasant surprise. "Jesus," she said through the mouthful. "It's wonderful!"

Then I gave her the clothes, and she looked at them excitedly. "For me?" she said. And then, "That's wonderful, Paul. That's really wonderful."

We sat there silently for a moment, I with the box of candy in my lap; she with her lap filled with new clothes. I watched her face.

The bus door was open. Suddenly a loud, wailing sound came in, something like a siren, except that it sounded human and angry.

"Oh Lord!" Mary Lou said, getting up quickly, with the clothes in her arms. "The baby!" She ran out of the bus and shouted back at me. "Give me ten minutes. I want to try the clothes on."

I left the bus, walked back to the fountain, and sat down on its edge. The music, light and airy, and the gentle sound of the water behind me were pleasant. I looked up; the moon was still out and there was no sign of dawn, I felt completely at ease.

Then Mary Lou came out of the House of Reptiles with her arms full. She shut the door smartly behind her with her elbow. She was dressed in the blue jeans and a white T-shirt and sandals and was carrying the baby expertly, cradled in one arm. Over the other arm were the rest of her new clothes and on top of them a pile of diapers. The clothes she was wearing fit her perfectly. Her hair was combed neatly and her face was radiant as she came toward me and the light from the fountain fell on it. The baby had stopped crying and just lay in her arms looking comfortable, pleased. Looking at them both I could hardly breathe for a moment.

Then I let my breath out and said softly, "I can make a baby bed out of one of the bus seats. And we can go away together."

She looked up at me. "Do you want to leave New York?"

"I want to go to California," I said. "I want to go as far from New York as we can go. I want to be away from robots, and drugs, and other people. I have my books and my music and you and Jane. That's enough. I don't want New York anymore."

She looked at me a long time before she answered. Then she said, "All right." She paused. "But there's something I have to do . . ."

"For Spofforth?" I said.

Her eyes widened. "Yes," she said. "It's for Spofforth. He wants to die. I made a . . . bargain with him. To help him."

"To help him die?"

"Yes. It frightens me."

I looked at her. "I'll help you," I said.

She looked at me, relieved. "I'll get Jane's things. I guess it is time to leave New York. Can this bus take us to California?"

"Yes. And I can find food. We'll get there."

She looked toward the bus, toward its sturdy, solid shape, and then back toward me. She seemed to study my face for a long time, carefully and with a hint of surprise. Then she said, "I love you, Paul. I really do."

"I know," I said. "Let's get going."

SPOFFORTH

It looks, by itself, as it did in 1932—an essentially stupid, non-human building, its architecture concerned merely with height and with bravado. It has now, on the third of June, 2467, the same number of stories, one hundred two, that it had then; but now they are all empty even of the furniture of offices. It is one thousand two hundred fifty feet tall. Nearly a quarter mile. And there is no use for it now. It is only a marker, a mute testimony to the human ability to make things that are too big.

The context over which it stands has come to magnify it more than the New York of the twentieth century ever could. There are no other tall buildings in New York; it truly towers above Manhattan in singleness of form and intent in the way that it must have first sprung to the hopeful minds of its architects. New York is nearly a grave. The Empire State Building is its gravestone.

———

Spofforth stands as near to the edge of the platform as he can come. He is alone, waiting for Bentley and Mary Lou to finish the climb. He has carried Mary Lou's baby for her, and he holds it now, sheltering it from the wind. The baby is asleep in his arms.

The sky will lighten soon on Spofforth's right, over the East River and Brooklyn; but it is dark now. The lights of thought buses are visible below. They move slowly up and down Fifth and Third and Lexington and Madison and Broadway, and up further through Central Park. There is a light in a building at Fifty-first Street, but no lights at Times Square. Spofforth watches the lights, holds the baby protectively, and waits.

And then he hears the heavy door behind him open, and hears their footsteps. Almost immediately, Mary Lou's voice, nearly out of breath, speaks. "The baby, Bob. I'll take it back now." The climb has taken them over three hours.

He turns and sees their shadows and holds the baby out. Mary Lou's dark form takes it and she says, "Tell me when you're ready, Bob. I'll have to set the baby down."

"We'll wait until daylight," he says. "I want to be able to see."

The two human beings sit, and Spofforth, facing them now, sees a yellow flame flicker brightly in the wind as Bentley lights a cigarette. In sudden chiaroscuro he sees Mary Lou's strong body hunched over her child's, her hair blown sideways.

He stands there looking at what is now only her shadow again, with Paul Bentley's shadow next to hers, touching: the old, old archetype of a human family, here atop this grotesque building over a numb and aimless city, a city of drugged sleep for its people and of an obscene mock-life for its robots, with its only brightness the small and pleasant minds of its buses, complacent and at ease, patrolling the empty streets. His robot mind can sense the telepathic thought-bus buzz, but it does not affect his state of consciousness. Something is coming into his mind slowly, gently. His spirit is hushed, letting it come in. He turns and faces north.

And then from nowhere and darkness there is a fluttering in the wind, and a small dark presence settles on Spofforth's motionless right forearm and becomes, in abruptly frozen silhouette, a bird. Perched on his arm, a sparrow, a city sparrow—tough and anxious and far too high. And it stays there with him, waiting for dawn.

And the dawn begins, low over Brooklyn, spreading to Upper Manhattan, over Harlem and White Plains and what was once Columbia University, a gray light over land where Indians had slept on filthy skins and where, later, white men had focused their fretful intensity of power and money and yearning, pushing up buildings in hubris, in mad cockiness, filling streets with taxis and anxious people and, finally, dying into drugs and inwardness. The dawn spreads and the sun appears, bulging up red over the East River. Then the sparrow flicks its head and flies away from Spofforth's bare arm, holding its tiny life to itself.

And the thing that has been coming slowly into Spofforth's mind now seizes it: joy. He is joyful as he had been joyful one hundred seventy years before, in Cleveland, when he had first experienced consciousness, gagging to life in a dying factory, when he had not yet known that he was alone in the world and would always be alone.

He feels the hard surface beneath his bare feet with pleasure, feels the strong wind on his face and the sure pumping of his heart, senses his youth and strength and loves them, for a moment, for themselves.

And aloud he says, "I'm ready now." He does not look behind him.

He hears the baby squall as Mary Lou sets it down in the doorway. He feels hands on the small of his back and knows they are hers. A moment later he feels larger hands above them. He hears breathing. His eyes are straight ahead, looking now toward the upper tip of Manhattan Island.

Then on his bare back he feels her hair and then, feeling his upper body beginning to topple forward, he feels her mouth pressed against his back, kissing him gently—feels her soft, warm woman's breath. He throws his arms out wide. And falls.

And oh, continues to fall. Finally then, with his face serene, blown coldly by the furious upward wind, his chest naked and exposed, his powerful legs straight out, toes down, khaki trousers flapping above the backs of his legs, his metallic brain joyful in its rush toward what it has so long ached for, Robert Spofforth, mankind's most beautiful toy, bellows into the Manhattan dawn and with mighty arms outspread takes Fifth Avenue into his shuddering embrace.

THE COLOR OF MONEY

Twenty years have passed since "Fast" Eddie Felson conquered the underground pool circuit. During that time he married and opened his own pool hall. But he's left that all behind and is now badly in need of money, and pool is all he knows. On the beautiful aquamarine waters of the Florida Keys, he ropes his former rival Minnesota Fats into a series of exhibition matches in the hopes of picking up a cable TV deal. But playing the old master, a terrible feeling nags at him—that he's sat on his talent and the best part of him is now gone. And when he vows to get back in the game—seriously this time—he finds a challenging road ahead, and the only thing standing in his way is himself.

Fiction

THE STEPS OF THE SUN

The year is 2063. Earth's energy resources are dangerously close to being depleted, a new world superpower has upset America's global dominance, and the threat of another ice age looms large. Fortunately, there is one man brave enough—and perhaps foolish enough—to venture beyond the planet to find the mineral resources that will secure the country's future: Ben Belson. One of the richest men in the world, Belson is haunted by personal demons and wanted for his unlawful space travel, but he will stop at nothing to fulfill his crucial mission—and discover a future greater than he could ever have imagined.

Fiction

VINTAGE BOOKS
Available wherever books are sold.
www.vintagebooks.com